A
Horseman's
Mission

Books by Sandra Ardoin

<u>Contemporary Romance</u>
Hidden Veil Hometown Series
A Musician's Heart
A Horseman's Mission

Love at Christmas Inn Series
Love in Second Bloom
Leaving the Past Behind
Lost in Winter's Wonderland
Box Set: *Longing for Second Chances:*
Three Second Chance Romance Novellas

<u>Historical Romance</u>
Widow's Might Series
Unwrapping Hope
Enduring Dreams
Rekindling Trust

Barnes Brothers
The Yuletide Angel
A Reluctant Melody

A Love Most Worthy

A
HORSEMAN'S
Mission

HIDDEN VEIL HOMETOWN
BOOK TWO

SANDRA ARDOIN

CORNER ROOM BOOKS

ISBN: 978-1-7334630-8-9

Anxiety in a person's heart weighs it down,
but a good word cheers it up.
Proverbs 12:25

One

Lane Becker opened the cabin door and stepped into a scene straight out of *Goldilocks and the Three Bears*.

He planted his cowboy boots on the hardwood floor of the front room. One hand rested on his hip and the other held a paper cup with the dregs of an Americano from Jo E's Java. His gaze swept the first floor of the renovated cabin on his property. Everything looked in good condition. Better than he'd left it, actually.

Still . . .

Next to a closed laptop on the kitchen counter, he spotted an open food magazine. A woman's? Or was that a chauvinistic generalization?

A closed drawing pad was on the floor in front of the couch. Scattered colored pencils surrounded it. A child's belongings or those of an artistic, food-oriented adult?

Lane sniffed the air. Cinnamon? Sugar? Definitely coffee. Maybe a little vanilla from the semi-burned candle sitting on the mantle of the stone fireplace.

He'd come across a mystery for sure. When he left a week ago, this place was sparse of furniture and musty smelling. Today, it looked like a home and smelled like a bakery.

He entered the only bedroom on the ground floor. Boxes stacked two and three high along the inner wall had replaced the double bed. On the hunt for the piece, Lane climbed the narrow stairwell to the two bedrooms on the second floor. He peered into the first one and found the missing iron bed. Someone had covered it with a flowery pink and white spread.

A woman's silver wedding band and engagement ring rested on the chest of drawers. The oversized diamond winked at him. Behind the rings, a man Lane had never met stared at him from a framed photograph.

He opened the closet door and found skirts, pants, blouses, and women's shoes. No men's clothing, just an invisible trail of enticing scents, including an orange blossom perfume. Okay, a woman—a married woman?—slept in his supposed-to-be-vacant house. Who and why?

He peeked into the second bedroom. It contained a single bed with a navy-blue bedspread and a small chest. Normal looking, except for the boy's pajamas balled up on the bed, a cell phone thrown on the mattress, and an array of children's paperbacks on the nightstand. In one corner, a giant bean bag slumped like a deflated basketball. Two more boxes were beside it.

Exasperated by the invasion of his property, Lane jogged

down the stairs. In the kitchen, a pan of homemade cinnamon rolls, half of them missing, sat on the stove. The sight and smell intensified the gnawing ache in his empty stomach. Should he, or shouldn't he?

They were too tempting to ignore. Besides, he might as well collect a little rent from his unexpected "guests." He tore off a roll and bit into it. Still warm and with a texture that melted in his mouth. He shut his eyes and savored the spiciness of the cinnamon and the sweetness of the icing that dribbled to coat his fingers. Something a little different about the icing hit his tastebuds. Honey maybe? Whatever the flavor, either he was starving, or this tasted amazing.

His breakfast disappeared with four bites, and he stared at the pan. Should he eat another one? He resisted. No sense wearing out his welcome . . . on his own land.

After washing the stickiness from his hands, Lane opened the dishwasher. Inside, he found a large mug, a clear drinking glass, and two small plates. More evidence of only two people living here. He opened the back door. Someone had parked a silver, compact sedan behind the cabin.

Curiosity and irritation volleyed back and forth within him. Whoever trespassed had made themselves at home. Brazen, considering the main house was on the other side of a narrow strip of trees and less than five hundred feet away. The barn was a mere couple of hundred feet on the opposite side of the cabin.

He didn't need great deductive skills to guess who on the ranch knew Goldie squatted in his cabin. What he didn't know was why.

Lane dug the cell phone from his pocket and hit Monte's

number. Over the ringing of his great uncle's phone came the distinct sound of a creaking porch board. Ending the call, he crept to the front door. As he whipped it open, a high-pitched squeal lanced his eardrums.

A woman dashed across the porch and down the steps. After putting a safe distance between them, she swung around to face him, her fists clenched and held in front of her like an amateur boxer. Seriously? He outweighed her by a good sixty pounds, not to mention the muscle strength he'd built after years of working with horses.

Under other circumstances, he might have enjoyed how cute she looked in her attempt to appear threatening. Instead, he straightened to his full six-one height, reminding himself that this woman trespassed. She could even be a criminal. He studied her. Maybe a crazy one.

Not that she scared him. Clearly, though, he scared her.

She jabbed a finger at him. "What are you doing in my house?"

His lips crimped. She wanted to play it that way, huh? "*Your* house?"

"Yes. You have no business on this property." The soft, southern drawl contradicted the fierceness in her narrow-eyed expression, a look hard to pull off for someone as petite as this squatter.

"I hate to argue with you, ma'am, but I have all the business in the world." Lane stepped onto the porch but stopped when she backed up. "I own this property."

"No, you don't. Mr. Becker owns it. It's his land."

"That's right. *I* am Mr. Becker." A cloud of doubt crossed

her face. Without giving her time to recover, he said, "My name is Lane Becker. I own Crooked Creek Ranch."

Her squared shoulders sagged, but she didn't drop her fists. "You aren't the one who hired me and told me I could move in here."

She was an employee? Only one Becker could have hired someone while he was gone. "Would that person be a tough old man with a wiry, gray mustache?"

She stood like a wild-eyed mare looking for an excuse to spook. "He said his name was Monte Becker."

Lane sighed. What else had Uncle Monte done during his absence? "My uncle hired you? To do what?"

"He's your uncle? He doesn't own this place?"

"My great-uncle, and no, he doesn't."

"Oh." She unfurled her fingers, and her gaze dropped to the pair of flats she wore.

Lane propped his hands on his hips. Now what? He had promised the therapist a place to work while he helped oversee the upcoming programs for the equine center. How was Lane to fulfill that promise when this woman occupied the space?

She pointed to the coffee cup in his hand. "Jo at the coffee shop told me you were hiring." Blue-gray eyes stared up at him in innocence before they turned to unyielding resolve. "I'm Macie Newman, your new cook and housekeeper."

When he'd asked his friend, Jo, if she knew of anyone looking for a housekeeping job, he should have stressed that it wasn't a live-in position.

A waterfall of sun-streaked golden hair draped over Mrs. Newman's shoulders and framed the gorgeous face of a woman

11

he guessed was close to his own early thirties. Faded jeans and a short-sleeved knit shirt covered curves in all the right places. And those steely eyes told him she wasn't going anywhere. Not without a fight.

So, now he knew how Goldie found his horse farm. With that determination in her expression, he sensed something else brought her to his small hometown.

What, and how would he get rid of her?

Macie had no reason to doubt the claim of the cowboy standing before her. Then again, she hadn't doubted Monte Becker when he gave her the impression that he owned the place. He'd mentioned nothing about a man around her age, whose curious blue-eyed stare threatened to pierce her like a hook on her daddy's trotline.

In fairness, maybe the older gentleman hadn't said he owned the land. Maybe she assumed it, based on the fact he'd hired her and lived in the main house. Did he even possess the authority to give her a job? She should have asked more questions before accepting the position, but desperation could make one careless.

What if the man descending the porch steps in a slow and casual manner fired her? Returning to Charlotte was not an option. So what should she do?

Lane Becker approached her with caution, much as she imagined he might draw near a skittish horse. Did he expect her to turn tail and run? "Under the circumstances, I guess I should welcome you to Crooked Creek."

Welcome? He didn't intend to fire her? A flood of relief washed through her.

The valleys under his cheekbones deepened in color. "I've a confession. I've already sampled your cooking."

How could he . . .? *Ah.* "You ate the cinnamon rolls I left on the stove."

"Only one."

Macie tapped the corner of her mouth, hinting at the evidence of his breakfast—a dot of icing.

His brow crinkled in confusion at her gesture before wide-eyed understanding struck him. He swiped at his mouth with the sleeve of his plaid western shirt. "I hope you don't mind, because I don't regret it. Your rolls are better than the ones from the bakery in downtown Hidden Veil."

Obviously, he'd meant that as a compliment. After finding this job, she had avoided the town of Hidden Veil as much as possible and never stepped foot in the bakery, so she couldn't judge the depth of his praise.

Macie swallowed the inclination to inform this Mr. Becker of her stint as a sous chef in one of the finest restaurants in Charlotte—short as it was. There would be plenty of time to go over her resume later, and she guessed this man couldn't wait to do so. Why hadn't Monte told his nephew about her?

The conversation about the rolls brought another concern to her mind. "I don't want you to think I feed my son sweets daily, or that I'll prepare unhealthy meals for you. This was an exception, a treat for Alex."

"I'm not averse to a treat occasionally." His smile eased her concern.

"You're welcome to help yourself to another, Mr. Becker."

He held out a hand marred by a long, white scar running from under the sleeve of his western shirt to the knuckle of his middle finger. "Lane."

"Macie." She grasped his cool, callused palm. His firm, yet gentle grip reminded her of the Biblical idea of meekness: power under control. "It's nice to meet you."

Her gaze scanned him, from the immaculate cowboy hat covering short, brown hair to the pointed tips of his polished boots. Lane Becker's appearance shouted, "Cowboy on the loose!" in the Piedmont region of North Carolina. But if she had expected his speech to match Monte's country drawl and slap-dash grammar, she would have walked away disappointed.

Macie freed her hand from Lane's welcome and edged around him. "I should return to work. My son is waiting for me at the main house. I only came to pick up his phone and art supplies. We were in a hurry this morning and he left them." She'd prattled on with the explanation, not wanting her new boss to think she shirked her job.

Leaving the pad and colored pencils was unusual for her son. They often seemed an extension of his arm. The phone was another matter. While most parents found it hard to pry the devices from their children's hands, she often found it hard to get hers to carry it with him.

"I figured the drawing materials belonged to a child. How old is he?"

"Alex is nine."

His gaze slipped to her bare left hand. "Just the two of you?"

Ironically, Macie had not removed her wedding rings until after the move to Hidden Veil. Wearing them in Charlotte had provided an armor she felt she wouldn't need here, not while working for a man more than twice her age. She hadn't counted on working for a young, single man. But with his solid build and easy-going manner, she considered running upstairs to slide those rings back on her finger. "My husband, Derek, passed away two years ago."

"I'm sorry to hear it."

She was sorry to have lived it.

Time lessened the grief, but she missed her husband's laughter and carefree attitude. She reminded herself of how that same attitude left her a widow at twenty-nine. "Thank you."

Although she didn't want to talk about Derek, it didn't stop Lane from adding, "I saw the photo upstairs." He had prowled around her bedroom? She tried to hide her alarm, but the slight shake of his head said he noticed. "I thought we had trespassers and looked around. Don't worry, I didn't touch a thing."

"Except a cinnamon roll."

His lips spread to form a wide, friendly grin that projected a self-conscious and boyish expression. "There was that."

"*Was* being the key word." Macie returned the smile. He owned the home. How could she stop him from entering whenever he felt like it? "If possible, I'd appreciate a little notice before you enter the cabin next time."

That grin slid into a grimace. "Look, I don't know what my uncle told you, but—"

"Actually, Monte has told me little about anything but my duties. I misunderstood about his ownership of the place." And the age of the nephew. Monte had made it sound as though Lane was a younger man who came and went at will.

Lane opened his mouth and shut it again, as if weighing his words. "What did Monte tell you about your job?"

"Right now, it's keeping house and cooking for the two of you. He told me the property is being turned into some type of day camp that will open later this summer. Then, I'd be required to fix lunch for several people."

The idea of children and their parents near her home had sent Macie's comfort level plummeting, but she had no choice. Hidden Veil's rural location was perfect, the job opportunities less so. And this situation allowed her to remain with Alex. Besides, she'd always loved horses since having one of her own as a child.

"Monte tells me the property is almost three hundred acres. I suppose that gives the kids plenty of space to roam and not disturb anyone in the house." Like her son.

"Kids?" Lane massaged the back of his neck and muttered, "Why should it surprise me to learn Uncle Monte didn't explain everything?"

His words waved a red flag in front of her eyes. "Everything?"

"In three months, this place will become an equine therapy center helping military veterans and others suffering from PTSD."

Macie caught her jaw before it hit the dirt. She'd tried to save Alex from being forced to speak of the worst day of his life—over and over. Now, she realized there was no escape from do-gooders who claimed to know what was best for others . . . and her son.

Two

"You're a therapist?" Lane Becker didn't look like any therapist Macie ever imagined.

"No. My fancy title is Certified Equine Specialist. I'll act as a horse handler for a clinical psychologist responsible for the therapy portion. He's put together a program aimed at helping veterans and first responders learn to overcome their anxieties using horses."

Out of all the places in North Carolina to live and work, she chose a horse farm soon to be overrun with people suffering from traumatic anxiety like her son. How had that happened? Obviously, God's sense of humor could lean toward the bizarre. A voice inside countered with, *"Or clever."*

Even with the beauty of a clear blue sky, the meteorologist had predicted rain for later today. Since her arrival, she had hoped to keep Alex's problem from her employer—employers—

for as long as possible. Her son suffered enough from the trauma and embarrassment. As it was, Monte had already questioned whether there was something wrong with her child.

"Are you familiar with equine-assisted psychotherapy? It's referred to as EAP."

He lost Macie's sympathy at the mention of psychotherapy. To her, a head shrinker's ploys by any name would stink. "No."

"Our first scheduled session is September fifteenth. Our clients will interact with the horses to create new and better memories to replace the ones they brought home from combat or faced on the job."

Horse psychologists? That was even worse.

Her breath caught. From what she'd read about traumatized soldiers, some were violent or dulled their pain with substance abuse. "No one said anything about exposing my son to grown men—"

"And women."

"—to men and women with addiction problems." How would she protect Alex? His issue was not the same as theirs, not as volatile.

The easy-going demeanor disappeared, and a muscle jumped in Lane's clean-shaved jaw. "They're people who need help to deal with their experiences. If it makes you feel better, the therapist or I will be present." When she didn't respond, Lane frowned. "If you're bothered by the situation and not sure you can continue working here, I would like to know it now."

How she wanted to tell him of the problem. Her lips parted, then closed. She and Alex needed a place to stay. This job provided a living while allowing her to remain close to her son.

But she would look for other opportunities, something better. As much as she liked it on Crooked Creek, Hidden Veil wasn't the only small town in the Carolinas. "No, it's fine." *For now.*

Lane's stance relaxed, and he checked his watch. "I have chores in the barn before I head to my office."

"I'll get Alex's things and return to the house."

"We'll talk more later."

Right. His words reminded her that therapists earned their living by compelling patients to talk about things they would rather forget. Over her mother-in-law's objections, she had put a quick end to her son's troubling sessions with a psychologist.

Macie caught a whiff of spicy aftershave as Lane passed her on his way to the barn. What prompted the man to believe horses cured a person's anxieties?

After entering the cabin, she wrapped the cinnamon rolls in foil to carry to the house. If she and Alex hadn't run late this morning, she would have remembered to take them earlier.

She grabbed the pencils and drawing paper Alex carried with him everywhere. Upstairs, she retrieved the phone she'd given him after his first anxiety attack and slipped it into the pocket of her jeans.

The cabin sat closest to the business portion of the property, behind the men's two-story residence. The dirt and stone drive between the two homes resembled an old wagon trail. It crossed a short bridge in the middle of a narrow section of woods. With the trees in full leaf, drivers passing along the highway couldn't see the cabin built on partially wooded and rolling acreage. It made living here appealing—almost like a hideout.

Macie left a career she loved to move to a rural town with

little job opportunity. She chose this area for its familiarity, since her grandmother had grown up a few miles away. Macie had placed convenience and her career on the back burner for a chance to see a change for the better in Alex.

After learning of Lane's plans for his property, though, she doubted Crooked Creek was the right place for them. What if a veteran experienced a meltdown in front of Alex? Would it affect his chance to heal? How would the Beckers or their therapist react to seeing Alex undergo a panic attack? Would they insist she seek professional help for him? If they thought that would happen, they were wrong. *Way wrong.*

Macie marched outside and down to the main house. Her steps slowed on the wooden planks of the bridge that crossed a dribbling creek, and she peered over her shoulder at the man walking out of the large barn.

She had moved here believing she could help Alex more than the so-called expert who, in his zeal for treatment, ignored the pain it caused her son.

But what if she was the one in the wrong? What if, as her mother-in-law suggested, she'd made things worse for Alex?

She picked up the pace. Her son couldn't afford for her to be wrong. No, she hadn't erred in taking charge of Alex's healing. She simply chose the wrong place.

She had until September to rectify her mistake.

* * * *

Lane rubbed the ear that throbbed after he'd spent two hours on the phone, making one call after another. If only he could launch the center without paperwork and red tape.

Not that those headaches would change after the opening. There would always be paperwork, just like the pile that had sprouted on his desk while he'd been away.

Healing Springs Equine Therapy Center required money— an ongoing supply—to thrive and grow. Though the board of directors sought to lessen the financial burden for clients, they could use someone other than Lane to head up the fundraising effort. It wasn't his strength.

Dragging the therapist, Ron Gregory, along on his recent trip to meet with potential donors had proved fruitful. Although not everyone had agreed to support warriors and first responders with PTSD, they secured backing to get them through the first months. The commitments took a load off his mind, because Lane had sunk as much of his own savings into the center as he dared.

He spun around in the desk chair in his home office—his former bedroom—and stared through the glass of the second-story window. Raised in this house and invested in his business of breeding and selling quality Quarter horses, he'd never imagined branching out and using his property to provide services to help vets and others. Then he'd met Ron, who introduced him to the concept of Equine Assisted Psychotherapy. From that day, he'd dreamed of doing his part to ease another's burden . . . and maybe his own.

For his certification as a horse handler, Lane had taken part in sessions at various equine therapy centers over the past couple of years. His confidence in the value of the various programs rose with each experience. He believed God led him to put the ranch to good use by founding his own center. What better way to atone for his failing?

The chair creaked as Lane returned to the paperwork on his desk. Federal, state, and local forms, bills, correspondence, and grant applications covered the surface.

As he worked, the tempting smell of homemade bread and mayonnaise drew his attention. An hour ago, Macie brought the chicken salad sandwich to his office. Time had gotten away from him, and he left it unfinished on a tray.

He reached out and picked up half the sandwich, bit into it, then dropped it back onto the plate. Delicious, but it reminded him of another problem he faced. What should he do about his new housekeeper and cook?

The office door opened, and Monte rambled in on bowed legs. "Got your text. You wanted to talk to me?"

He waved his uncle into the room. "Have a seat. We need to discuss Mrs. Newman."

Monte stuffed his hands in his pockets and stared at his feet. "What about her?"

Gypsy trotted to Lane's side for a "welcome home" head rub. The Border Collie's tail slapped the side of the desk. "Hey, girl. I missed you." After stroking the dog's black and white coat, Lane motioned for her to lie down. He turned his attention back to his elderly uncle. "For starters, what do you know about Macie Newman?"

Monte's weak knee cracked as he eased into the upholstered chair on the other side of the desk. The sound was a gut-wrenching reminder that Lane would run this place without him one day. "Macie come from Charlotte ... said she was a chef at some fancy restaurant."

That explained the melt-in-his-mouth cinnamon rolls and flavorful chicken salad. "Why would a trained chef take a job at a place like this? Why move from a big city to a small town like Hidden Veil? Did you check her references?"

"She said she wanted her son to live in the country, and her grandma grew up near here. Jo Ledbetter told her we was looking for someone, so she come knocking on the door four days ago. I made sure she knew the job was more than fixing meals. She didn't mind. Before hiring her, I asked her to make my supper. Better than my cooking by far. Yours, too. My bet is she could run rings around the cooks at Rick Burns's restaurants. Didn't need more reference than that."

With the insufficient answer from Monte, Lane made a mental note to ask Macie why she quit a decent job in the city to move to Hidden Veil.

Monte's eyes narrowed at the tray holding Lane's lunch. "You didn't like the sandwich?"

"No, it's good." *Really good.* "The problem isn't her cooking, Uncle Monte. You know I had plans for the cabin. We agreed to hire a local woman who didn't need a place to live. Where am I supposed to put the counseling office? The cabin is the ideal location, and Ron expects to stay there if we set up multi-day workshops in the future. Where will the volunteers go for breaks? I'm guessing Macie won't share her home. She wasn't too pleased when she learned of my plans for the center." He took a breath. "Why didn't you tell her the truth?"

Monte rose from his seat and closed the office door, then returned and propped his hands on the edge of the desk. He leaned forward and lowered his voice. "I think they got problems."

"What problems?"

One bony shoulder jerked up and down. "I don't know, but have you met Alex?"

"The son? No. I came straight to the office without seeing either of them. Is there something wrong with him?"

"Ain't ever seen a kid so quiet and skittish."

"Some kids are quiet by nature. You say he's skittish. Of what?"

"Well, for one thing, Gypsy makes him uncomfortable."

Lane relaxed. "A lot of people shy away from a strange dog. He'll learn that the only thing to fear from Gypsy is a friendly tongue lashing." The dog's ears perked at the mention of her name, so he reached down and patted her back.

Monte shook his head. "I'm guessing it's more than that. You wait and see." He eased into the chair again, and his chewed-down fingernails drummed the padded arms. "From what I've seen, Macie don't often let Alex out of her sight. Her hovering tells me there's something going on. She's worse than a mama hen and always on guard."

On guard? "It sounds like you're suggesting she's trying to protect her son from something."

"When I asked about the boy's problem, her mouth locked tight as the adhesive on my dentures."

"They're in an unfamiliar environment. I'd wonder if she wasn't a little overprotective." And Monte likely offended her with the suggestion something was wrong with her son. His uncle was a fine man, but he could be tactless.

"I'm guessing there's something else going on."

"It's likely nothing more than the cautiousness of a timid kid and a caring mom's sensitivity." Lane stretched his tight neck muscles. Between the drive this morning and over two hours of office work, he'd sat too long without a break. "Let's go back to our housing situation. With the Newmans in the cabin, we need a place for Ron and the volunteers."

"*Humph.* No 'we' about it." Monte's mustache twitched, a sign of distress. "You got an empty room across the hall. Set him up there."

"An office in the house is inconvenient for him and us. It should be near the barn where the therapy takes place."

Monte squinted at Lane. "Well, I promised Macie the cabin and she's already living there. Wouldn't be right to tell her to move now, would it? Anyhow, I'm saving you money. Providing lodging means we ain't paying her as much."

Lane suppressed the urge to shake his head. His parents raised him to respect his elders, but sometimes his uncle made it difficult. Lane would never forget the blind date Monte set up for him in high school. His uncle didn't tell him about it until thirty minutes beforehand, leaving Lane little time to clean up and mentally prepare for a date with a stranger. The evening turned into a nightmare.

While he hated the idea of making Macie move, he didn't rule it out. She might understand if he explained his predicament and offered to help her find another suitable place to live. But what if she refused to vacate the cabin?

By hiring Macie Newman, his uncle had pinned him between two promises.

"We have three months until the first session. Anything can happen in that time." Such as Macie deciding Crooked Creek wasn't for her. "I guess we'll manage." Temporarily.

Monte's head bobbed. "Now you're talking."

With a knock on the door, Lane looked up. "Come in."

The subject of their conversation poked her head into the office. She glanced at the tray on the corner of the desk and frowned at the half-eaten sandwich. "I came for the tray, but I see you're not finished eating. If you don't like chicken salad . . ." Nothing in her manner suggested she had overheard their conversation.

"I do." He pointed to his desk. "I've been busy with this paperwork, then I need to update the website." He blew out a frustrated breath. "I know horses, not computers."

She nodded. "Websites can be tricky to update, but they're not too bad once you get the hang of it."

"You have experience?" Lane heard the hope in his voice.

"A little. Don't you have a web designer?"

He shook his head. "Budget won't allow it." He handed her the tray, but kept his hold on the desire to ask for her help with the website.

"Would you like me to put the sandwich in the refrigerator?"

"Sounds good. I'll eat it later." When she hiked an eyebrow, he added, "I promise."

Monte chuckled. "Don't fret none, Macie. He likes a mid-afternoon snack."

"At least you can eat a snack and it doesn't show." Her eyes widened and her porcelain cheeks turned as cherry as the tomato on the plate. "I meant it doesn't show on either of you." She spun and beat a hasty retreat into the hall, yanking the door closed behind her.

Monte's guffaw filled the office. "Yeah. Don't show on me neither."

Lane knew better than to smile. His never-married uncle pestered him at least once a month to settle down and start raising "them two-legged ranch babies." A smile would only encourage him.

Had Monte hired Macie because she was a knockout and available? It wouldn't surprise Lane to learn his uncle had more matchmaking in mind.

His gaze met the empty spot on his desk where Macie had removed the tray. Hopefully, her embarrassment meant the comment was off-the-cuff nonsense and not flirtation. The center's opening kept him too busy to date.

His chest heaved. Who was he kidding? He had no desire to pursue a romantic relationship with anyone. He didn't deserve that kind of happiness.

Monte pushed out of the chair, his knee cracking once more. "One of us best get some work done—namely, me. See you at supper."

Lane studied his uncle as the man hobbled to the door. "I wish you'd change your mind about the center. I could use your help with the horses."

Monte shook his head. "It's your mission. I got enough trouble with the cattle and whatever goes wrong with the equipment around here." His uncle paused with his hand on the doorknob and his back to Lane. "You know my heart ain't in this idea of yours."

Uncle Monte refused to understand Lane's commitment to open the ranch to veterans who needed help. As a soldier during the Vietnam War, his great uncle was as patriotic as they came, so Lane couldn't pinpoint the reason for his resistance.

"Why won't you support what I'm trying to do, Uncle Monte? If Matt had returned from Afghanistan with PTSD, wouldn't you want someone to help him?"

"Well, he didn't, did he?" Monte walked out the door and closed it behind him.

Lane's insides turned to ice. From her spot next to the desk, Gypsy whined, as though she sensed his shock. He reached down and stroked her back. The move brought as much comfort to himself as to the dog.

If he had done his job, Matt would be alive. He owed his brother and would satisfy that debt through the Healing Springs Equine Therapy Center.

Lane closed his eyes on the memory of Reagan Hartwell prostrate over Matt's flag-draped, closed coffin, weeping her heart out. If Matt had lived, he and Reagan would have married long ago. Lane would probably be an uncle now. That hadn't happened, and Reagan had never let him forget it.

Not even the success of the center could wipe out the debt he owed the couple for the future together that his bullying behavior cost them.

Three

Giggling, Alex squirmed away from Macie's tickles and ran across the expansive wooden deck off the back of the Becker's main house. Her son swung the back door open and walked into the den with its hardwood floor and stone fireplace. Although he barely showed the effects of their outdoor play, Macie breathed hard as she followed him inside, vowing to exercise more often.

Lane owned a beautiful home, not new or large, but livable and with an airy and open floor plan. Comfortable, like the image projected by its owner.

"Have fun?" The horseman stood at the refrigerator in his kitchen. Gypsy sat next to him, her thick tail sweeping the clean floor and leaving behind more dog hair that Macie would need to clean up.

Alex skidded to a halt with his wide-eyed gaze latched onto

her new employer.

As Lane stared at Macie, her skin grew hot. She hadn't seen him since retrieving the lunch tray. What if he had taken her stupid comment about his trim build wrong? The last thing she wanted was for him to think she sought more than a professional relationship between them. She didn't see herself as drop-dead gorgeous, but he hadn't turned up his nose after checking her out at the cabin that morning.

Macie studied him for a sign that he disapproved of her taking time out of her duties to play with her son. After seeing no hint of disapproval, an explanation tumbled from her, anyway. "Alex wanted a break from his schoolwork, so I suggested we play tag. I hope you don't mind."

"Nope. Boys need exercise. As long as the work gets done, I'm fine with it." A blissful smile crossed his face. "That roast in the oven drew me downstairs. Do I smell oregano and onion?" His brow crimped. "Something else I can't identify."

"It's my secret recipe." Macie grinned but declined to give up her ingredients.

"It smells good. We probably haven't eaten meat seasoned with anything more than salt, pepper, and barbecue sauce since my parents moved."

"Your parents lived here?" That explained the outdated flowery curtains and knick-knacks she dusted.

"I grew up in this house and later lived in the cabin until Mom and Dad retired to Wilmington a few years ago."

When Lane's focus shifted to Alex, she placed her hands on her son's shoulders and urged him toward the kitchen. "Alex, this is Mr. Lane. He's Mr. Monte's nephew."

Lane held out a hand. "Nice to have you and your mom with us, Alex."

His welcome warmed her. She'd gotten the idea when they first met that he wasn't pleased to have them on his property.

At first, Macie thought her shy son would refuse to shake Lane's hand, but Alex stepped forward and spoke a quiet hello. His gaze ran up and down Lane's jeans and boot-clad frame. As soon as the coffee shop owner mentioned to Macie that a position was available on a "ranch," Alex had shown an unusual interest in the setting. "Are you a cowboy like Mr. Monte?"

Lane grinned. "I raise and sell horses. He takes care of the cattle. Do you like to ride?"

"My son likes indoor pursuits." Macie ignored the query in Lane's penetrating scrutiny. She nudged Alex toward the dining room. "Why don't you finish your math?"

Alex dodged Gypsy, still uncomfortable with the dog after she jumped up on him at their first meeting. With Derek's allergies, Alex's contact with animals had been rare. His caution around the dog should answer Lane's question about riding, and make the cowboy think twice about offering to put Alex on a horse.

Once her child settled in a chair at the dining table in the adjoining room, Macie washed her hands and opened the oven to check the roast.

Lane followed her into the kitchen. "Math? I thought school was out by early June."

"I homeschool and believe in giving Alex a few lessons to keep his memory fresh over the summer."

"That makes sense." Lane pulled the lunch she'd saved him

from the refrigerator and removed the plastic wrap. He stood at the sink to eat the rest of the chicken salad sandwich while Gypsy stared up at him, running her tongue from one side of her mouth to the other.

"Are you sure you want to eat that? Supper's in an hour."

"I'm starving now. Don't worry, I'll be ready for that roast."

The quick disappearance of Lane's sandwich reminded Macie of how much a grown man could devour in a day. He swallowed the last bite. "How long have you homeschooled Alex?"

"Almost a year."

Her choice came after he suffered an intense anxiety attack at school. Though she didn't blame the other children for not understanding, it broke her heart to see her wounded son cry over the teasing of his classmates. The attack prompted the first of the decisions she'd made that went against her mother-in-law's wishes.

But she needn't go into her reason for homeschooling.

"Does he miss his friends in Charlotte?"

"A few."

"So, why not public school? It must be hard to teach while working a full-time job."

The dryer buzzed. Perfect timing. "I'd better remove the towels."

His lips pursed, but to his credit, he didn't push for an answer.

When she returned to the kitchen, Lane stood at the sink, rinsing the empty plate. She reached for it to add it to the dishwasher, and his arm brushed hers. An odd quiver shimmied through her, sending her sidestepping. What was wrong with her? First, she'd spouted something foolish in front of him. Next, she was as jumpy as a rabbit with its tail on fire. She shut the dishwasher and moved away. Only Derek's touch had caused her emotions to riot like that.

While washing the crumbs from his hands, Lane peered through the window above the sink. "Looks like the weatherman called it right this time. It's getting darker toward the west."

Macie glanced out the same window. In the distance, smoky-gray clouds tinged a deep blue hung in the sky. Maybe the thunderstorm would hold off until she got the men fed and the dishes done. If given the option, she favored sitting the storm out in the cabin, alone with Alex . . . just in case. Not that her son feared the sound of storms. His fear went far deeper than thunder and lightning.

Lane backed away from the window. "I'd better feed the horses before it rains."

In seconds, he'd walked out the back door and covered half the yard on his way to the dirt road that ran past her cabin and merged into the gravel drive at the barn. Gypsy trotted ahead of him.

Macie prepared the rest of their meal while thunder rumbled from a distance. Finished with his homework, Alex sat at the dining room table and drew in the sketch pad. Monte lounged in a recliner in the den and watched the local news.

Over thirty minutes went by. The trail from the barn remained empty. If Lane didn't return soon, she could kiss her perfectly cooked roast with its secret ingredients goodbye.

Worse, it might start raining. She wanted to return to the cabin before it did.

She waited a few more minutes, then walked into the great room. "Shouldn't he be back by now?" She winced as lightning streaked through the ever-darkening clouds. Raindrops peppered the window and dotted the deck. *Please either return soon or stay in the barn.* "Supper is ready."

Monte hit the off button on the remote, silencing the TV. "Lane's probably waiting out the storm. No sense letting the food get cold." He hobbled across the floor and poked his head into the dining room. "Come on, Alex. Let's eat."

As if his words conjured the rain, the sky opened and poured down buckets of water. Her heart thrummed in her ears. Alex could ignore the worst thunder and lightning, but the after-effects of a rainstorm could send him into an attack that froze his mind and body.

With a last look outside, Macie silently willed Lane to remain at the barn until the rain stopped. After dishing up the meal, she handed a bowl of peas to Alex to place on the table.

She heard the door leading into the laundry room from the garage open and close. A moment later, Lane padded around the corner into the kitchen—barefoot, clothes sopping, and water dripping from his hair and off his jaw.

"Alex—" Lightning crackled outside the window over the sink, and a deafening explosion of thunder shook the walls, cutting off Macie's warning.

Crash!

Macie stood open-mouthed as jagged pieces of the ceramic bowl littered the tile, and peas rolled like marbles across the kitchen floor.

At the croaky gasp from Alex, she ignored the spill and knelt next to her son. Broken pottery sliced her knee, but she overlooked the sharp pain. Massaging his upper arms, hoping to relax his heaving shoulders and trembling muscles, she focused on those terror-filled eyes.

Oh, no. Not again. Not now.

Not in front of the drenched horseman.

∗ ∗ ∗ ∗

Lane hadn't received a degree in psychology, but he had undergone enough training to recognize a boy in the throes of an anxiety attack.

Had the storm frightened Alex, or was Lane at fault because of his sudden entrance? Rushing over to help might make things worse. Besides, Macie appeared in control of the situation and able to calm her son.

"Breathe, buddy. That's it. You're all right." Macie maintained eye contact with Alex. She inhaled deep breaths and exhaled slowly in her attempt to coax the boy into doing the same. "Remember to focus on something pleasant, on good and worthwhile thoughts."

Lane backpedaled into the laundry room and listened to her gentle voice on the other side of the wall. Composed and reassuring, it contradicted the horrified look he'd seen on her face.

Macie's soft words brought to Lane's mind the verse in the fourth chapter of Philippians. The scripture urged Christians to focus on things of worth, wisdom he should pay more attention to daily. Time and again, he fell prey to demoralizing thoughts of the past.

When she appeared in the laundry room doorway, her hand quivered as she brushed a lock of hair from her eyes. Who calmed *her* in moments like this?

"He's fine now." Her gaze raked his wet state, then the floor. "Let me get you a towel to dry off before you come in."

Lane dried the worst of the rain from his skin and head and mopped up the floor with the towel. He tossed it on the washer in the laundry room, slicked back his hair, and crept into the kitchen. Monte sat at the breakfast room table next to Alex.

Thunder cracked again. Though not as intense, it rattled the window. Lane waited for another paralyzing event. Alex, his face as white-washed as the wall behind him and pinched with embarrassment, revealed no fear.

Now Lane knew. He triggered the attack. But why? "I didn't mean to scare you, Alex."

"It's okay." The little voice barely climbed above a whisper. "I'm sorry I broke the bowl."

Lane grinned to ease Alex's mind. "Accidents happen to all of us."

"Don't think nothing of it, Alex." Monte pointed to Lane. "That boy near drove his momma and daddy into poverty by breaking things when he was coming up, including a bone or two, if I remember correct. He was a daredevil, always doing risky things and getting himself and his little brother in trouble."

Monte's claim echoed through Lane. He'd always instigated trouble and often involved Matt. Was that the reason his uncle objected to the equine center? Deep down, he blamed Lane for Matt's death?

Get in line, Uncle Monte.

Growing up, Lane played sports and spent all his spare time outdoors, learning survival skills and becoming adept at tracking. He'd prowled every square yard of woods on and surrounding the property. Matt preferred video games and reading—indoor activities, like Alex. Lane chased the physical, while his brother pursued the intellectual.

It should have been Lane who enlisted in the Army. If only he'd kept his mouth shut and his opinions to himself, because Matt hadn't been prepared for such a life.

His uncle rose from his seat at the table. "You're still dripping, son. Let me get you some dry clothes." He ambled across Lane's path and their eyes met. His uncle stated in an undertone, "I told you something was wrong with the boy."

With a fierce fervor, Macie crawled on all fours and gathered the pieces of the broken bowl. Lane crouched next to her. "Don't worry about it, Macie. We'll get it later."

"No, I ..." Her hair hung down and covered her face. She swiped it behind her ears and returned to cleaning.

He placed a hand over hers. "Leave it."

"But—"

"It'll keep." He helped her up from the floor and noticed a cut on her leg below her knee and a smear of blood on the floor. "That cut needs to be cleaned."

She slipped her hand from his, tore a paper towel from the holder on the counter, and dabbed it against her skin. "It's nothing. I'll put some antiseptic on it when I get back to the cabin."

The cut didn't bleed excessively, so he let it go while she used a cleanser on the floor.

Monte returned with clean, dry clothes. He leaned toward Lane and lowered his voice. "The storm's passing, and they both look done in. Why don't you change out of them wet things and drive them home?"

"Alex might feel better if you take them. I'm thinking the sight of me set off his attack."

"I expect so. You burst in looking like some swamp creature. That thunder didn't help matters none. It near had me jumping outta my skin. But the boy's gotta get a hold on whatever frightens him."

Lane couldn't disagree with Monte's analysis, merely the simplicity of it. Sometimes, it wasn't easy to get over fear. Still, if the Newmans remained on the ranch, whether it rained or the sun beat down, he couldn't avoid Alex.

He held up the clothes and said to Macie, "I'll change. Why don't you prepare some of that food to-go? When I'm done, I'll drive you and Alex home."

Before she could argue, he retreated to the half-bath off the laundry room to become less like a swamp creature.

Four

By the time they reached the cabin, the rain had subsided and the rubber on the truck's windshield wipers scraped dry glass, so Lane shut them off.

The short drive had been silent apart from the hum of the engine, a splash whenever the tires rolled through a puddle, and the *thunk-thunk* of the truck passing over the bridge.

He stopped in front of the cabin. Alex hopped out of the rear seat, rushed to the porch, and disappeared inside.

Lane opened the driver's door, but Macie laid a hand on his arm, stopping him from walking her to the cabin. "Give me time to take our food inside and settle Alex. Afterward, I'll come out and explain."

He bobbed his head and shut the door. For several minutes, he waited behind the steering wheel, eager to hear the reason for Alex's attack.

Once she reappeared, she paused on the porch, inhaled a clear breath of courage, then climbed into his truck. "I didn't want Alex to overhear. He's embarrassed enough."

"There's no need for anyone's embarrassment."

Macie sighed. As though she hadn't heard him, she said, "After what happened tonight, if you would like to hire someone else, I'll understand."

Hire someone else? Lane gripped the steering wheel. She'd given him the perfect solution to his problem and the opportunity to satisfy his obligation to the center and Ron.

Monte's instincts about Alex were spot-on. No wonder he hired Macie. Despite the gruff exterior, no one's heart beat with more compassion for those who hurt than his uncle's. That fact underscored the mystery surrounding Monte's refusal to assist troubled veterans.

Macie stared straight through the windshield, as feminine and fragile as the image on the cameo pin his grandmother used to wear.

Beautiful.

Lane shook off the thought. He was not a teenager on a date.

He had no right to pry, but if the Newmans remained on Crooked Creek, he wanted to help. That meant he needed to know more about the boy's issue. "How long has Alex suffered from anxiety attacks?"

"The first one happened a few months after Derek died." Her hands entwined in her lap. "The two of them were close ..." Her voice cracked, and she cleared her throat. "My son took his father's death hard."

A knot formed in Lane's stomach. Clearly, she still carried a hefty amount of grief as well. He reached out, then withdrew his hand before touching her arm. "Will you tell me what happened to your husband?"

She stiffened against the seat back. "He drowned."

Lane waited for her to reveal more . . . if she would.

"Derek took Alex to the mountains for a rafting trip. The raft hit rapids and, somehow, it tipped over." She turned toward Lane, her eyes waterlogged with unshed tears. At the same time, they reflected suppressed anger more than grief. "My son watched his father die, and I wasn't there to prevent it."

Lane struggled against the impulse to wipe away the tears that now streamed down her face. He doubted she would appreciate that kind of comfort from a stranger. Nothing kept him from listening, from trying to understand her and her son better.

"My husband thrived on thrill-seeking experiences—skydiving, rock climbing. That sort of thing. He wanted Alex to take part in life rather than sit back and watch it pass by as his own father had done. Derek's thirst for adventure cost him his life, Lane, and he almost took Alex with him."

Lane's fingers strangled the steering wheel. He and Derek Newman had a lot in common. The difference being, so far, Lane had survived. Although she knew little about him, the thread of iron in her voice said she made the comparison between them. Probably because of Uncle Monte's comment earlier.

Macie swiped at the tears and climbed out of the truck. She turned and hung on to the door like only it held her up. "I'm sorry for the trouble we caused tonight. Thanks for the ride."

She shut the door softly behind her and hurried into the cabin.

He sat in the truck and tried to wrap his mind around what she'd told him. Alex's reaction made perfect sense. According to Ron, certain triggers could spark people's anxieties. He'd stood in front of the boy, dripping wet and looking like a swamp creature, as Monte described him. It must have set off a flashback to the time Alex saw his father's drenched body.

Lane had let hunger drive him to rush to the house in the rain, forcing both mother and son to relive the past. He lowered his chin and pinched the bridge of his nose while praying for them both and asking God to keep him sensitive to Alex's feelings.

Macie carried a load of anger, fear, and grief. "*I wasn't there to prevent it.*" And guilt. How well he knew those emotions.

While Lane better understood her situation, it didn't explain her reaction this morning when he described his plan for the ranch. Logic told him she should want to learn more about a program able to help people like her son. Instead, she acted as if equine therapy was a scam.

How could Lane call himself a man—a Christian—who cared for the well-being of others while making Macie move out, forcing additional stress on her and her son?

Letting her remain, though, left him with a dilemma. Where would he put Ron and the volunteers?

* * * *

Macie grabbed her coffee cup and carried it outside. Morning sunbeams fought to break through a rare but light summer fog that hovered over the dips in the rolling landscape. A fitting symbol of the fog that hung over her future.

Lane hadn't fired her last night, but it could still happen, and bringing Alex here hadn't eliminated his problem with anxiety. Yet.

She shouldn't expect a five-day miracle.

Each evening, sitting on this porch brought back memories of growing up on her parents' farm. After years of living in the city, she had forgotten the tranquility of a rural night—the inky blackness, especially when giant trees blocked the moon. Some might consider the clicks and calls of insects and night-prowling animals disturbing. She found them melodic and comforting. Since coming to Crooked Creek, she had slept better than she had in two years. Last night being the exception.

She leaned against a porch post, sipping the hot drink and letting it warm her. Within minutes, the rising temperature made quick work of the fog. A heightened freshness filled the air, the clean scent of pine trees and country living. It hinted at the horses grazing in the green pasture across the dirt drive from her cabin.

Alex remained upstairs in bed. Thankfully, he'd slept through the night, undisturbed by nightmares. Macie had convinced herself he only needed a quiet, relaxed environment like this ranch to gain control of his fear. Even with last night's setback, she wasn't ready to admit failure. Alex's healing belonged in her hands.

No one knew him better. Not even his grandmother.

She pushed away from the post, ready for the possibility of a last day at Crooked Creek. As she turned to go inside, Lane broke from behind the copse of trees hiding the main house from the cabin. Her grip tightened on the cup as he hiked toward her. She hadn't expected to see him so early. Had he come to give her notice to clear out?

He crossed the damp grass and stopped at the bottom of the porch steps. "Good morning, Macie."

She nodded her greeting. "Have you had coffee yet?" The question came out of nowhere, probably prodded by a case of nerves. Why should she be nervous? She'd planned to look for another job, anyway. Maybe it was a blessing, if she believed in those anymore. Maybe—

She could "maybe" all day, but she wouldn't know the truth until he told her.

"I never turn down a cup. Black."

Rather than invite him into the cabin, she brought the coffee to him on the porch. While she was inside, he'd made himself at home in one of the Adirondack chairs, lounging as though nothing bothered him. A good sign? He didn't strike her as the type to let much unsettle him. If so, he hid it well.

She handed him the coffee mug and sat in the adjacent chair. "You're out early."

"I'm an early riser."

"I've known my daddy to get up at four o'clock and leave the house before five. Of course, he practically goes to bed when the stars come out."

Lane swallowed a swig of coffee. "What does he do?"

"He's a farmer."

"Then you're used to country life."

"It's been a long time since I've lived on the farm."

Marriage. Culinary arts training. A move to Charlotte. As a family, the Newmans had returned to her childhood home only for occasional short and hectic visits. So many relatives and old friends to visit left them little time to soak up that slower pace and carry it back to their busy lives.

When she decided to leave Charlotte, she considered a move to her hometown, but rejected it. As with Derek's mother, her family's well-meaning interference wasn't in Alex's best interest. So, she chose the place she remembered passing through as a child.

"Hidden Veil has changed since I was here last," she said. "It's grown from a farming town to one that attracts people looking for a quaint character and a slower pace. It's become a smaller version of Southern Pines or Blowing Rock."

Businesses like Jo E's Java, an antique store, candle and soap shop, and an old-fashioned soda fountain and ice cream parlor contributed to the allure. They appeared to thrive.

What if she opened a restaurant here, something more refined than the Red Dog Diner? She rejected the idea immediately. That took resources she didn't have right now.

"Mayor Hildenburg says towns die through lack of change and has worked hard to draw younger residents to Hidden Veil." Lane sipped the coffee, then propped the cup on the wide arm of the chair. "It's working."

Selfishly, Macie hoped the town wouldn't change and grow too much. At least, not while she was here. "You told me your parents retired to Wilmington. It seems an unusual move for small-town, country folks." Did that sound snobbish?

"They've always loved the beach." Steam rose from Lane's cup as he turned it in his hands, round and round, his thoughts seeming far flung. "Dad suffered a heart attack ten years ago. He raised those black baldies you've probably seen in the pastures on the other side of the creek."

She'd certainly noticed the black cattle with the white faces and the pride Monte took in caring for them.

"Seven years ago, Mom persuaded my dad to quit ranching and do some of the fun things they'd talked about for years. Uncle Monte took over running the cattle business, but Dad still keeps his hand in with an occasional visit."

"Then you've handled the equine end for a long time."

"I got my degree in animal science." He kicked out a leg to show off a well-worn, brown western boot. "I belong here, wearing these, not wearing a suit and sitting in some cubicle."

"Why work with vets?"

Had she imagined a wince? Hard to tell, since he seemed good at catching and hiding his emotions. "Some of them need the help." The quiet moments that followed appeared to bring an end to any enlightenment on his part.

To lift the silence, broken only by occasional whinnies from the horses in the pasture, she added a teasing note to her voice. "No interest in raising cattle? And you claim to be a cowboy."

He matched her smile with his own. "I prefer to think of myself as a horseman. But I did my share of steer wrestling and bull riding in high school before a shoulder injury sidelined me. I still team rope in an event now and again with my friend Sutton Vance."

A shoulder injury. That scar on his hand. Bull riding. *Here's another man who thrives on dangerous activities.*

She pointed to the hand wrapped around his coffee cup. "Is that how you got the scar?"

Lane examined the old injury as though he'd never noticed the white line that ran across his skin. "A skiing accident." He glanced around him. "Did Monte tell you this cabin belonged to my grandparents?"

Macie's lips flattened at the abrupt change in the subject. Last night, Monte mentioned Lane's brother. She considered asking about him, too, but figured she'd meddled enough for today. Their roles were as employer and employee, not friends and confidants, so she accepted his wish to withhold certain information from his past.

What did it matter, anyway, when she would probably be gone soon? Even if he let her stay in her job, it was in Alex's best interest to keep a proper distance from the Beckers, especially this man at her side. He'd probably like nothing more than to suggest someone root around in her son's head—someone like his therapist friend.

"From the wood frame and simple arrangement inside, I figured the cabin was old. You've done a lot to update the interior."

"I lived in it until Mom and Dad moved. Recently, some friends helped me clean it up and add a few touches."

"I appreciate the thoughtfulness. It was perfect when we moved in." She waited for him to say more about the cabin, but he simply stared at his cup.

He gulped the rest of his coffee. "Nothing beats a good cup of morning coffee. Monte's is like sludge and mine is always too weak. Thanks, Goldie."

"Goldie?"

He laughed. "Sorry. It's the first thing I thought of when I found the cabin occupied. Goldilocks."

"A strange woman who invaded your property." She stared into her own half-empty mug, not sure how she felt about him giving her a pet name. The reason was logical and cute, if too informal and a little flirty. It reminded her of the need to keep things professional between them. It was nice, though, to share a time of frivolous banter with a male again—someone much older than Alex.

"I'd better get moving." He handed her his cup.

Before he left, she needed to know if the incident last night affected her job and ability to remain here, even if temporarily. "Lane, about what happened . . ."

"There's nothing to worry about, Macie."

Her gaze locked on his, drinking in the warmth and concern she observed. "Then it's all right with you if we stay?"

For the slightest instant, his brow creased, then smoothed out again. "Of course you can stay."

After learning about Lane's plans yesterday, she had decided to look for another job. Now, a flood of thankfulness swept through her. Something she couldn't explain. Maybe it was a relief that came from knowing the Becker men had witnessed Alex's problem and accepted her son despite it. Maybe it was because Lane didn't base their stay on the condition that she allow a therapist to treat Alex, a subject he hadn't even brought up.

He graced her with that boyish grin that gave her heart a

whirl. "You've probably found a church … if you attend, I mean."

Church? At one time, their small family attended regularly. Since Derek's death and her son's attacks, Macie and Alex's presence inside a church had been sporadic. She often missed it. Other times, she used her anger with God as a good excuse to sleep in on Sunday mornings.

Lane watched her, so she said, "No, I'm not familiar with the churches here."

"You could try ours on Sunday."

What if she said no? Would he change his mind about letting her stay? "What time is the service?"

"Eleven. You're welcome to ride with Uncle Monte and me."

How would Alex feel about being in a church sanctuary—a large room—with strangers? "I'd like to talk to my son first."

"Sure. No pressure, but if you want to go, we can pick you up about ten-thirty Sunday morning." He rose from the chair. "Work calls."

The words hardly left his mouth when a horse whinnied, high and demanding, from somewhere inside the barn.

She laughed at the exaggerated glower on his face. "You should hurry."

Macie remained on the porch as Lane strode to the barn. Rather than the Stetson of the day before, he wore a misty blue ball cap like the one her father had worn for years. Lane's sported "Healing Springs Equine Therapy Center" in white letters on the front. Shoulders squared and back straight, Lane's posture revealed the strength and confidence of a man prepared to take on any task.

A steer wrestler? Skier? Monte had called his nephew a daredevil. If she focused on that aspect of Lane's character, instead of the kindness he seemed determined to show her, she could maintain a distance between them. She could ignore his gentle voice, intelligence, and compassion toward her and her son. She could resist the temptation of a horseman whose jeans and t-shirt fit like they were custom made.

Macie carried the coffee cups into the cabin. Pressed by friends to date, she'd given in a few times. But since Derek's death, she hadn't experienced this strong of an attraction to another man.

She shook her head. A romantic relationship held no interest for her. Not when her focus must remain on Alex and his healing.

Besides, Lane had one thick, bold strike against him. She'd fallen for someone with a thrill-seeking spirit once already, and it devastated her family. She owed it to herself and her son not to let it happen a second time.

Five

"Why are we going to church?" Alex set his half-empty milk glass on the table and stared at Macie.

"I told you, we don't have to, but Mr. Lane invited us. It would have been rude to say no." Macie tried to read Alex's face and fathom his thoughts with little success. Had agreeing to attend the service today been a mistake? Her fork clattered on her breakfast plate. "Look, it isn't too late to cancel if you're uncomfortable with the idea." Part of her wished he'd rather stay home.

Alex picked at the scrambled eggs, his favorite breakfast. "I guess it's okay. I kind of miss going to church."

He missed it? "You never said so."

"I didn't think you wanted to go, since you're mad at God and all."

He sensed that? "It's more like disappointment."

"Because Daddy died or because I'm sick?"

Macie gaped at her son. "Who said you were sick?"

"Grandma Eva. She said the doctor would help me get well."

"That doctor—" Macie drew in a deep breath. Losing her temper wasn't the way to handle this situation. "Grandma Eva has good intentions, but she doesn't know you like I do." She reached across the table and squeezed his hand, confused over which of them needed the most reassurance. "Finish eating and get dressed."

Forty-five minutes later, Macie and Alex followed Monte down the aisle of The Rock Community Church with Lane trailing behind. The congregation held the service in an old Quonset hut on the outskirts of downtown. A wing built on each side of the arched metal building added to the oddity.

Like Alex, she missed the organized worship and gathering with other believers, but her son was right. Her trust in God's care had taken a hit with Derek's accident. It took another hit the day of Alex's first attack. What did that say about her faith?

Too much, and none of it good.

Dates with her husband revolved around exciting activities. Backpacking in remote areas, snow skiing, motorcycles. They had shared a love of adventure. He'd even proposed in a balloon as it carried them over the countryside. Since his death, she hadn't taken part in anything riskier than driving.

She should have insisted Derek not take Alex to the river when she couldn't go. If she had gone with them, she might have saved her husband's life and her son's emotional well-being.

Monte hobbled across the fourth row from the front, saving

empty seats for Alex, Macie, and Lane. Based on a quick observation, the congregation numbered under seventy-five, and she'd guess Monte was the oldest. Feeling curious eyes crawling over her and Alex, she regretted not asking to sit in the back of the sanctuary where they wouldn't draw as much attention.

Lane leaned sideways, his shoulder brushing hers. "Relax."

She was certain he meant that whispered word as encouragement, but he could say that, couldn't he? He appeared the epitome of contentment and peace, dressed in his best pair of jeans and the crisp, white dress shirt Macie had ironed on Friday. She practiced subtle, but deep, inhales and exhales, doing her best to loosen up. Unlike her, Alex seemed fine.

From the corner of her eye, Macie caught a flash of dark hair. She turned her head. A woman in her early twenties stood in the aisle at the end of the row. Her bright smile and impish face showed no sign of having seen the worst in life. "Good morning, Lane."

The muscles in the arm pressed against hers tightened, but Lane smiled. He rose from his seat and introduced Brianna Hartwell to Macie and Alex. "Macie is our new housekeeper."

The young woman's eyebrows arched. "Housekeeper? Oh, I thought . . ."

Because of Macie's physical closeness to Lane, she could guess what Brianna Hartwell thought. With a shift in the chair, she put a couple more inches between herself and her boss.

"It's nice to meet you, Macie."

"You, too."

Brianna focused on Lane. "Are you finding sponsors for the center?"

Macie considered that akin to asking Lane how much money he made, but the horseman seemed to brush it off. "People want to see results first, so funding is slow. But we'll never know the end of needing financial support."

The young woman laid a hand on Lane's arm. "I can't help in that way, but if you're still looking for volunteers, I'll devote some hours when I'm not in school. If that's okay with you."

Over the past couple of days, Macie had overheard phone conversations that told her Lane sought volunteers. Why would Brianna think he wouldn't want her help? Maybe they had dated, and it didn't end well. No. Macie couldn't picture the steady, mature horseman dating a bouncy, college-aged woman.

Lane hesitated, then nodded his response. "I'd welcome the help if you don't think it will cause trouble."

So, there was an interesting story to their relationship, a story Macie had no right to ferret out.

"It's my life. Maybe we can talk it over soon?"

"Sure."

An older, grumpier version of Brianna Hartwell stopped at the girl's side and grabbed her arm. In a firm voice, she said, "It's time to sit down."

Brianna yanked free. "I'm talking, Reagan."

"You can talk another time." Reagan cast a frosty glance at Lane.

The poor man looked as if his favorite horse had thrown him. Macie turned her head and stared at the pulpit. She didn't want them thinking she latched on to every twitchy undercurrent in the quiet, but heated, discussion.

Brianna's voice rose. "You're my sister, not my boss."

"This isn't the time, ladies." Lane's normally placid voice held its own trace of impatience.

Reagan stalked off, and Brianna excused herself. Lane retook his seat.

Macie couldn't help herself. She whispered, "Is everything all right?"

"Sure."

Sure. Clearly, she'd erred. Brianna hadn't shared an unhappy past with Lane. It was Reagan. Brianna was collateral damage.

As a small band began a praise song, Lane's arm pressed against Macie's and he leaned sideways. "The Hartwells are old friends."

She squelched the impulse to laugh. *Could have fooled me.*

His relationships—past or present—were his concern, not hers. "Brianna seemed nice."

"Yeah, she is."

The tickle of his breath at her ear and the ruffle of her hair sent a pleasant warmth through her. A warmth she rejected. Not only did the man pay her salary, but his questionable hobbies were reason enough to crush this odd attraction she felt toward him. Add in Alex's problem, and anything romantic happening between them was out of the question.

Dressed in jeans and an open-collared shirt, the young pastor made announcements from the podium. Rather than listen, Macie's mind replayed the sponsorship discussion between Lane and Brianna. A pushover for charitable causes, her mother-in-law had the money to donate. Eva Newman also had wealthy connections. One call from Macie might provide Lane with ample funds to operate the center. One telephone call Macie wouldn't make, not with the current strain in the in-law relationship. Besides, how could Macie ask Eva to invest money in something without endorsing it herself?

After forcing her focus back to the service, she enjoyed the contemporary worship. A man named Kyle Callahan played guitar and led the small band. He performed a solo of "Reckless Love," his voice giving the song a definite country music style that didn't diminish the heartfelt quality of the lyrics.

At one time, she had been certain God loved her . . . loved her whole family as she loved and served Him. Then, on that fateful day, He removed his protection from both her husband and her son. Unable to understand why, it felt like a betrayal. Yet, it was amazing how one hour of encouraging word and song could ignite a desire in her for more.

At the end of the benediction, Lane led them out of the sanctuary. Macie kept Alex close to her side as they stepped into the glare of the noon sun.

"Macie."

She glanced behind her at the woman who owned the coffee shop in town. "It's nice to see you again."

"You, too." Jo Ledbetter gestured to the man beside her, who shook hands with Lane. "I wanted to introduce Kyle."

She nodded to the musician. "I enjoyed your solo."

"Thanks. We're glad you came this morning."

"Kyle is a professional songwriter. We stole him from Nashville." Lane laughed. "I should say, Jo bought him at an auction."

"God stole me, and Jo reaped the reward." Kyle grunted when the coffee shop owner elbowed him in the ribs.

Lane eyed Macie's curious glance. "I'll tell you about it another time. Monte's already in the truck, so we'd better go."

After their goodbyes, Lane pressed a hand to Macie's back and guided her toward the parking lot. From her left, she heard her name spoken and looked over her shoulder. Brianna stood next to a woman about her age, both of them watching her.

Brianna's gaze dropped to Lane's hand on Macie's back, speculation clear in her expression. For the second time that morning, Macie eased away from her employer. She urged Alex toward the truck at a speed she hoped outpaced any talk.

When Lane stopped at the cabin, she thanked him for the invitation and the ride, then hopped out of the pickup. Without a backward glance, she followed Alex into the house, trying to block out the sound of Lane's truck as it thumped across the bridge on the drive back to the main house.

Macie climbed the stairs to change clothes before fixing lunch for her and Alex. As she placed her earrings inside the small jewelry box in a drawer of the chest, her fingers brushed the rings she had stopped wearing days ago. She picked up the wedding band and eyed it, rolling it between her thumb and index finger. With a bare ring finger and Lane sitting beside her in church, people naturally might misunderstand their relationship. No doubt Brianna Hartwell had. How many others had done the same?

Macie shoved the gold band on her finger where it belonged—where Derek placed it years ago.

Wearing it would dispel rumors. It had nothing to do with

Lane reviving a desire for his company the moment his hand pressed against the curve of her back.

* * * *

Lane entered the tack room. The taste of Macie's streusel and coffee lingered on his tongue. Another weekday at the crack of dawn had drawn him to the cabin before going to the barn.

Not that he planned each visit. To put it simply, he and Macie adhered to the same morning schedule. The stop was a pause before the hectic activity of the day. Nothing more than a few minutes of conversation between two people awake with the sun.

Keep telling yourself that, Becker. Macie might buy it. But you? Not a chance.

He pulled two halters from pegs on the wall and attached lead lines to each. Carrying one set, he draped the other over his shoulder. Macie infiltrated his thoughts countless times each day. Even now, the memory of her voice, low and roughened by the early hour, whispered in his ears. Kindhearted and a loving mother, he tried to understand her headstrong doubt about his plans for the center, especially when it might help Alex.

But the image that played in his mind most often was of her barefoot and relaxed in the Adirondack chair. This morning, she'd caught her hair in a messy blonde pile on her head as though she'd been running late. The notion popped into his mind that she hadn't wanted to miss seeing him today ... the notion of a man with no business hoping it was true.

Yesterday, while completing another grant form, he'd smiled as he listened to Macie belt out the words to a country tune playing on the radio. She had a voice that was neither hard on the ears nor angelic. He pictured her dancing from room to room as she cleaned and sang.

Once Macie reached his office, she jerked to a stop and almost dropped the dusting rag and can of furniture polish. "I thought Alex and I were alone in the house."

Lane balanced a teasing remark on the tip of his tongue. He swallowed it and pointed at the stack of papers on his desk. "Always something."

"I'll come back later." She took a step.

"Wait." The word exploded from his mouth like a firecracker from a tube. "You're doing a great job and the meals are great."

Dimples bracketed each side of her mouth. "Great."

Never a man with a silver tongue, that level of conversational ineptness was a first for him. "I only wanted to say it's a pleasure having you here."

And like that, wariness encircled Macie like the loop of a rope. She hiked a thumb over her shoulder and backed into the hall. "I should see how Alex is coming with his reading assignment. Let me know when you're finished and I'll come back."

They hadn't spoken again until he stopped at the cabin this morning.

Sure, he'd crushed on females in the past, even considered himself serious about one or two women. That was before he saw how Matt's death broke Reagan's heart. Why should he expect happiness with one woman when he'd caused another enormous pain?

Lane shook the grim thoughts away, slipped the first halter on Selena, and led the mare and her foal from the stall. He regretted placing his hand on Macie's back after church ... of allowing the hunger for something deeper than friendship to gain a foothold in his heart.

He barely knew her, and if she mistook his interest for something unprincipled, it would reflect poorly on the center.

This fascination with Macie must stop, especially since she now wore her wedding band. She twisted it around her finger in his presence. To ensure he noticed and recognized the hint to keep his distance?

After he haltered Selena's stablemate, Coco, he led both horses, along with the prancing filly, to the pasture across the drive and turned them loose.

He was headed back to the barn when gravel crunched under the tires of Sutton Vance's ancient, beat-up Ford. The truck rolled up the drive, a gooseneck trailer hitched to it. His best friend braked in front of the barn, opened the driver's door, and planted his long legs on the ground.

The halters Lane had removed from the horses jangled on his shoulder as he ambled over to meet his friend. "I didn't know you woke up this early."

Sutton grinned at the jab. "Who said I'm awake?"

Lane pointed to the trailer. "Thanks for picking him up."

"Jasper may not have the same pedigrees as your pretty Quarter horses, but he's as good-natured as they come. He'll work well for you."

"I'll need a couple more therapy horses, but the current four should get us started."

"I'll keep an eye out." Sutton grew pensive. "I believe in what you're doing, Lane. Matt would be proud."

Lane spoke past the choking tightness in his throat and the guilt that sat like a draft horse on his chest. "I hope so."

The hinges squealed as he opened the trailer's door for Sutton to lead the newly purchased Appaloosa gelding onto the drive. Spotted head held high and ears perked, the small gelding sniffed the air, then let out a loud and gut-shaking whinny answered from various locations around the barn.

The heaviness of a moment ago dissolved, and Lane laughed. "He knows how to make an entrance."

"Can't call him shy. That's for sure." Sutton patted Jasper's thick neck, then handed the lead line over to Lane. His brow crinkled under the cap he wore. "I thought you said your new therapist was a guy."

Lane followed Sutton's gaze. Macie tugged Alex onto the cabin's porch and shut the door behind them. She had brushed her hair into a bouncing ponytail and wore sandals that smacked the wood as she trotted down the steps. "That's not Ron."

"You don't say."

Lane grimaced at the sarcasm. "I forgot to tell you. Monte hired a housekeeper while I was gone."

"I should let Monte hire a housekeeper for me."

Sutton's quiet whistle scraped Lane's nerves, and his fingers curled around the lead rope, threatening to burn indentations into the nylon. "Don't you have work to do?"

His burly friend eyed him. "Touchy."

"Busy."

"Right."

After a morning of mucking stalls and exercising horses, Lane hiked back to the house at noon. Macie had left a note saying she and Alex were running errands and his lunch was in the refrigerator.

He grabbed the plate and wandered through the den. His foot kicked Alex's sketch pad on the floor. Had Monte tripped over it, he might have fallen and broken something.

When Lane tossed the pad onto the sofa, it fell open to a page in the middle of the book. Curious, he set the plate on the coffee table and flipped through the drawings. Cars. Skateboarders. Basketball players. Macie. All subjects typical of a boy his age. But, man, the kid had a promising future in the art world.

The last several pages depicted horses, many of them Lane recognized by the build and color—Selena, Coco, Dandy, Smokey. Alex had included himself in the drawings. He fed the horses, cleaned the stalls, led them to and from the pasture. He'd recorded Lane's work, but inserted himself into the scene.

For a boy whose mother claimed he preferred indoor pursuits, Alex's drawings displayed the opposite.

Six

Macie had to get away from Crooked Creek and the way the cowboy's—the horseman's—morning visits affected her emotions. Thankfully, the pantry at the main house needed restocking.

Before driving through town to the local food mart for groceries, she pulled into a parking space on Main Street. Red brick buildings with the stylish design of early twentieth-century architecture made up the bulk of the structures, though a few were newer—1950s to the 1980s. The mix of styles gave the town both a charming and outdated appearance.

But for Macie, the cherished places were the colorful Victorian homes that remained standing—like jewels in a tarnished crown. Twenty-first century owners had lovingly given most of them new life.

"What are we doing, Mom?"

"I thought we could use some exercise." As well as a more in-depth exploration of their new town. "Come on. Let's take a walk."

Alex climbed out of the car, and the two of them strolled along the sidewalk.

Gas lamps flickered with small flames, even on this sunny day. Planters overflowed with colorful summer foliage and blooms. Purple petunias, black-eyed Susans, yellow dahlias, vibrant coleus. Although they drooped in the midday heat, their presence added to the town's appeal. Oh, how she would enjoy planting flowers in her own garden again.

They passed an insurance company, a florist, a realtor, and a barber, the latter reminding Macie that Alex needed a haircut soon, and she should look for a stylist for her hair.

She assumed most of the people who entered and exited the service businesses were locals. They nodded or smiled a silent greeting. Now she was a local ... for however long her stay lasted.

They crossed an alley, and Macie stopped to peer through the window of Yesteryear Antiques and Collectibles. She pointed to a utensil with a round, flat bottom laced with holes. "Grandma Jessie had one of those. I think she still does."

"What's it for?"

"It's a potato masher." She clasped her hands together and pumped them up and down in a show of smashing cooked potatoes.

"You use the mixer."

Macie laughed. "And glad I am to do so."

They moved down the sidewalk, reaching Locke's Old-Fashioned Drug Store and Soda Fountain on the corner of

Main Street and Jacobson.

"They have ice cream, Mom. Can we get some?"

"Let's save that for another day. Okay? I thought we'd go to the coffee shop and get a smoothie."

The day she and Alex visited the town, preparing for a move here, she had stopped in at Jo E's Java to inquire about a job. It was from Jo Ledbetter that she first learned of the position at Crooked Creek. The woman had shown her nothing but a friendly welcome. Today, Macie could use a few minutes of listening to a soprano voice after days of hearing nothing but tenors.

"You liked the smoothie you had before, right?"

"It was good." He shrugged. "Okay."

On their way toward the one stoplight in downtown, Macie noticed the "Soda Fountain Manager Wanted" sign in the window of the ice cream and soda shop. Her footsteps slowed, but instead of going inside to see about the position, she kept walking.

So far, things were pleasant at Crooked Creek, and she couldn't imagine she'd make any more money dishing out ice cream than her present salary provided. Besides, her current job came with housing.

While waiting at the stoplight to cross the street, she glanced back at the business. She would keep the position in mind if things became more uncomfortable with Lane or his new mission to help those with PTSD.

As they passed the front of In Harmoni, Macie breathed in a mix of various floral and herbal scents coming from products sitting on an outside table. The front window displayed bars of soap, along with bottles of lotions and shampoos, all wrapped with an In Harmoni label. A sign in the window said everything was locally made. Macie promised herself to return another day to shop.

She slipped into Jo E's behind Alex. The coffee aroma reminded her of sitting in the comfortable chairs on the porch of the cabin, talking with Lane—the exact thoughts she'd left the ranch to escape. Maybe this was a mistake.

Despite her worry over growing too fond of the horseman, he had a way of putting her at ease while they chatted. They discussed various subjects, skirting the heavier conversations. After he left each morning, she fought a desire to follow him around all day, just to talk to him.

"Hey, welcome back." Jo crossed the room to greet Macie and Alex. "How are things going with the job at Crooked Creek?"

"Fine, so far. Thank you for telling me about it."

"I'm glad it's worked out for you and Lane."

Macie lost her smile, and she stiffened. Were rumors going around about them? Her gaze bounced over the room, hitting on each of the four customers sitting at tables scattered around the space. She shouldn't have agreed to go to church with Lane. At the least, she and Alex should have arrived separately and sat in a different row.

"He's been so busy lately. You've taken a load off both his shoulders and Monte's."

Oh. Macie relaxed.

Jo's attention shifted. "I bet you're here for another orange cream smoothie, Alex."

The woman's memory of her son's drink order amazed Macie. "We'll take two."

While Jo prepared the smoothies, she jerked her head toward Kyle, who talked to an older woman across the room. "As Lane said, Kyle recently moved to Hidden Veil, too."

Based on the look that passed between the couple, it hadn't taken him long to feel at home. "I remember. I enjoyed meeting him on Sunday."

"Lane has an amazing place, doesn't he?"

"Yes."

Kyle stepped up to them. "I hope the ceiling fan works in that cabin."

She cocked her head in confusion. "It does."

He laughed. "I helped Lane get the cabin ready and installed the fan."

"Ah. You're the one I have to thank for the comfort."

"No thanks needed. Lane is a good friend." Kyle's eyebrows dipped. "I thought he planned to—" With one look from Jo, he broke off his statement. Why?

"I don't believe I know you, young man."

Macie's focus snapped to the woman in her late fifties or early sixties who had addressed her son. She laid a protective hand on Alex's shoulder. "We just moved to Hidden Veil."

"I'm Gloria Hildenburg." She smiled at Macie.

Hildenburg? Where had she heard the name? Then it hit her. "It's nice to meet you. Is your husband the mayor?"

The woman's eyes bounced wide. "*I* am the mayor."

Oops. Macie hadn't done her homework. She sought to make amends. "I understand you're doing a great job attracting new residents."

The woman's demeanor changed with her smile. "Well, aren't you sweet to say so? Nothing would work without businesses like this one. I also teach at the elementary school and enjoy getting to know my students." She eyed Alex. "Judging by your age, I'm guessing you will be in my class come August."

Before the gregarious woman could overwhelm Alex, Macie said, "He's homeschooled."

Again, the mayor addressed Alex. "I'm sure your mother is a fine teacher, but our students will give you a warm welcome should you decide to join us."

"He won't."

Mayor Hildenburg frowned, and her lips parted as though she longed to argue with Macie over the statement.

Kyle angled closer to Jo. "I'd better get back to work." He kissed the coffee shop owner, a quick but sweet peck on the lips that said more than goodbye. It said he couldn't wait to see her again. Macie missed receiving that type of kiss.

The teacher-mayor watched him leave. "Ah, such a talent." She turned to Jo. "I wish you'd use your influence to convince him to perform at the Fall Festival, Jo Ella. He keeps dodging my invitation."

"I'll do what I can, Mayor." Jo winked at Macie.

Macie wracked her brain, trying to remember if she'd ever heard Kyle Callahan's name before last Sunday. She came up with nothing. Was he supposed to be a famous musician?

As though she'd read Macie's mind, Jo explained. "Kyle used to be part of a Nashville country band. He's a Christian songwriter now and saves his performances for special events."

"Like the Fall Festival." Mayor Hildenburg's thin eyebrows arched with her pointed gaze at Jo.

"I'll talk to him." Jo placed the smoothies on the counter. "No promises."

"Thank you, Jo Ella. How is Vera?"

Jo's lips turned down. "Better. The doctor seems pleased with her progress." She turned to Macie. "Gran had a heart attack a few weeks ago."

"I'm sorry." Macie knew well the pain associated with losing someone special and caught herself voicing a silent prayer for the woman's healing.

"As she keeps reminding me, she's a 'tough old bird.'" Jo smiled, though it appeared half-hearted. "Are you planning to attend the July Fourth fireworks at the lake?"

At the lake? *No way.* Macie hedged, not wanting to respond too quickly with a refusal. "I hadn't heard about any celebration."

"They begin at sundown." Gloria Hildenburg put on her mayor's hat and spent a few minutes extolling the virtues of a Hidden Veil Independence Day celebration.

"If you decide to attend," said Jo, "several of us get together to eat a potluck supper and watch the show. You're welcome to join us."

A pang in Macie's chest almost had her saying yes.

Jo grabbed a pencil and notepad from the counter. "Let me give you my number. You can let me know."

The two women exchanged cell phone numbers. While Macie didn't plan to attend the fireworks, it would be nice to think she'd made a female friend here—friend enough to call or text.

Macie retrieved the smoothies from the counter, ready to hand Alex his. She looked down. He was gone. Her panicked glance darted around the coffee shop. "Alex? Alex!"

For the first time in two years, he'd slipped away from her. How could she have missed his absence? She always made it a point to know where he was at all times. Maybe not when he was at school, but at least she knew where to find him. What if someone abducted him?

Jo stepped from around the counter, a worried expression on her face. "He's probably at the table around the corner where I keep some games."

She led Macie to the other side of the room and stopped at a large table that seated six. No Alex.

Macie's heart accelerated, and her chest heaved with the effort to breathe. "Call the police. We need to find my son."

A door at the back opened, and Alex walked into the room.

She rushed to him. "Honey, are you all right?"

He stopped, and his eyes narrowed. "I only went to the bathroom."

"Please don't disappear without telling me." Especially into a bathroom that a stranger might also occupy. Had she known, Macie would have waited for him outside the door.

She handed him his smoothie. "Let's go."

As they walked outside, heat filled her face. Not from the oppressive temperature, but from knowing multiple people had watched her in full panic mode. Her reaction to Alex's disappearance had probably convinced them there was something wrong with her.

But they knew nothing about her circumstances.

＊　＊　＊　＊

Macie lounged in the Adirondack chair with Alex sprawled across the porch floor at her feet, a green colored pencil in hand.

Releasing a quiet sigh into the still-bright evening, her glance drifted to the empty road. Tonight, she'd found herself unable to focus on much more than a certain horseman's nightly appearance.

Leaning forward, she determined to put Lane from her mind. "What are you drawing, honey?"

Alex's arm fenced in the picture. "Nothing."

For the past few days, he'd begun keeping his artwork from her. Why wouldn't he let her see?

Macie opened her mouth to insist he show her when Lane passed the wall of trees and brush. Ahead of him, Gypsy trotted to the porch. The dog waited at the bottom of the steps until Alex closed his sketch pad and tapped his leg. She trotted up the stairs and stretched out alongside Macie's son. Given the intellect of a Border Collie, Macie attributed Gypsy's restraint to respect for Alex rather than a fear of him.

The two shared a delicate truce these days, much like she and Alex. His truce and her embarrassment over her behavior at the coffee shop yesterday.

Macie shelved her disappointment over the drawings, dodged around Alex and the dog, then bent over the porch rail. "Where are you off to?" As if she didn't know.

Lane leaned a shoulder against the rail. "I'm off to see the wizard, Goldie."

"Don't you have your stories mixed up, cowboy?" His laughter wheedled a smile from her—another one. Her face had received quite a workout since coming to Crooked Creek. "You're late tonight."

He stepped closer, his voice husky. "Keeping track of me?"

Her amusement withered. Her teasing had ventured into dangerous—okay, flirtatious—territory, so she couldn't blame him for responding in kind. "Only for the sake of the poor hungry horses."

Lane stuffed his hands in the front pockets of his jeans and peered around her to her son. "Hey, Alex, if it's all right with your mom, how would you like to come with me and meet Jasper?"

Macie braced herself as her son's gaze shifted between the adults. She looked at her watch. "Remember that TV show you wanted to watch? It's about time for it to start."

Alex stared at her with a look of confusion, no doubt recalling that she'd told him earlier he couldn't watch television tonight. He gathered the pencils and slapped the sketch pad closed. "No thanks, Mr. Lane."

The tension in her body eased. How could she feel both relief and frustration? Though they lived in the country now, it didn't mean she wanted Alex to follow in the footsteps of Lane and Monte. Not when the two of them worked with large and unpredictable animals. In that case, she might as well have returned to her hometown. Her dad would introduce Alex to every piece of equipment he owned—hazardous farm equipment capable of taking a limb or worse.

Ironically, she had enjoyed the outdoors while growing up,

doing the things she now considered risky for her son. Had her parents worried whether she and her brothers would survive to see adulthood? If so, they never showed it. They never curbed their children's sense of adventure.

But Alex was different. He wasn't like her or her brothers. He needed—

Coddling?

No, that wasn't it. Of course, it wasn't. But some children required more security than others. She glanced at Alex. Even if they resented it.

Once her son closed the door, Macie descended the steps and stood toe-to-toe with Lane. "Please don't pressure him to become involved with the horses."

With his hands still stuffed in the pockets of his jeans, Lane rocked back and forth on the heels of his boots. "You think I put pressure on Alex by asking if he wanted to meet Jasper?"

"My son doesn't deal well with new situations."

"Are you sure it's Alex who doesn't deal well?" Lane heaved a weighty sigh. "One day, you won't be around to cushion life for him, Macie. You'll have to trust in his ability to cope."

Cushion Alex's life? "Is that how you think I see my role as his mother? Because I'm trying to keep him from harm, I'm cushioning his life? You think I don't trust him?"

His gaze flashed to the door, then back to her. "Walk with me?" When she looked over her shoulder at the cabin, he held out his hand. "He'll be fine for a few minutes."

She couldn't help but worry about her son. She had almost lost him once and had lost his father.

From a nearby tree, an owl hooted as if, in its proverbial

wisdom, it agreed with Lane and urged her to accompany him. She ignored his hand but followed her boss across the yard.

Since when did she act based on the opinion of an owl?

Seven

Lane walked alongside Macie down the drive leading to the barn. A slow pace. A calm evening. Perfect summer temperature. Macie's sweet perfume competing with the clean crispness of nature.

Like a magnet to steel, her hand drew his. He flexed his fingers and slipped them into the front pockets of his jeans. Again. It was becoming a necessary habit around her, and she'd already rejected his hold once tonight.

The abrupt chill in her attitude reminded him that too much stood between them. The biggest obstacle was the gold band that wrapped her finger like prison wire.

"It's clear what you're trying to do."

"Macie—"

"I don't want Alex coerced into participating in your therapy experiment."

"You got that idea from a simple invitation?"

Inside the barn, Lane flipped a switch that lit the interior, even though the sun wouldn't set for another couple of hours. He entered the feed room, scooped pelleted feed into a multi-gallon bucket, and left the room. "You're right. I'd like to see Alex do more than live life through his drawings. But I'd never coerce him into doing something that makes him uncomfortable."

The last thing he wanted was to pressure anyone to do something they feared. Not again. He'd skied that mountain years ago, and it led to disaster.

The scar on his hand throbbed, but it was all in his mind. Just as it was whenever he recalled the day he received the injury.

Stalls constructed of wood and iron bars lined each side of the lengthy barn. Five equine heads with ears perked popped through the space in the metal yokes of the doors. At each stall, Lane poured feed into individual buckets and made sure the animal had fresh water.

Macie trailed him down the aisle as he worked. "You believe my son isn't free to do the things he wants to do? He likes to draw, and he's good at it."

"It was an invitation, not a command. If you'll recall, I told him he needed your permission."

"It was an invitation you should have run by me first. As it was, you put me on the spot."

Lane froze at her criticism. She had a point. It was unfair to her and Alex. "You're right. I'll remember next time."

From a stall at the far end of the barn, Jasper called to them. Dozens of rust-colored spots stuck out like large freckles on an otherwise white face. Lane approached the stall and rubbed those freckles. "How's it going, boy? Looks like you feel at home here."

The horse had shown no sign of distress or nervousness over being in a new place. His calm personality would fit in well with what Lane had in mind for him.

"Why did you really ask Alex along tonight?"

Apparently, Macie objected to letting the discussion go. *Fine.* He entered the stall, shut the door, and poured the last of the feed into Jasper's bucket. How did he approach what he wanted to say without upsetting her further?

Rather than eat, Jasper pressed his chest against the door. He stretched his neck until his muzzle touched the side of Macie's face. Lane expected her to jerk away from the horse. Instead, she ran the flat of her hand along the smooth curve running between Jasper's nostrils, an absent-minded motion. Jasper sniffed her palm and blew out a snort.

"You haven't answered my question."

"I've seen Alex's drawings."

Her caress of the gelding halted. "He showed you?"

"He left his sketch pad on the floor the other day. I flipped through it. I'm no expert, but I think he's a talented artist."

She returned to mollycoddling his horse with strokes that were more mechanical than aware. "What did you see?"

Lane tapped Jasper's left front knee. The gelding hiked his leg and allowed an examination of the hoof. It gave Lane something to do while he pondered a response. "Among other things, I saw drawings of horses."

"Horses?"

"Crooked Creek horses."

"In the past, Alex has shown me his artwork." Hurt laced her quiet voice. "Lately, he's been secretive about it."

Lane examined each hoof as he tried to think of something to soothe her wounded feelings. "Maybe Alex thinks you would disapprove of the subjects."

"I've never disapproved of anything he's drawn, except—"

Bent over the final hoof, Lane turned his head toward her. "Except what?"

Macie's lips, pressed together in a tight line, looked as if someone glued them together. She ran her hand down Jasper's face. "What difference does it make if my son draws horses? It doesn't mean he's interested in being around them."

Lane released his hold on Jasper's leg and straightened. "Alex put himself in those drawings."

"You're implying he's a candidate for your equine therapy?"

How did she get that from what he said? He hushed an inner growl over the woman's one-track mind. "That's not my decision to make."

"But it's your therapist's?" She shook her head. "If Alex has an interest in horses, it makes sense he would have accepted your invitation tonight, right?"

"Not if you intervened, which you did." Lane grabbed the bucket, walked out of the stall, and slid the latch on the door. "Why won't you let Alex out of your sight?"

"It's not a matter of letting him out of my sight. It's a matter of keeping him from making a poor choice and paying the consequences."

"Like Derek?" Inwardly, he cringed at the question that leapt from his mouth. He sighed. "I didn't bring you here to quarrel, Macie. I only wanted to let you know—"

"Mom." Alex stood outside the barn with the golden light of the sun beaming on the back of his head.

How much of their conversation had he overheard?

Macie shot a glance at Lane before gracing her son with a tight smile. "I thought you were in the house, buddy."

"I changed my mind. I want to see Mr. Lane's new horse." Alex's attention swiveled from one side of the barn to the other. "Can I come in, Mom?"

The lines between her eyes showcased her indecision. "Are you sure?" The boy nodded. After a moment, she did too.

Lane stepped to the center of the concrete aisle. "Walk down the middle if that's where you're most comfortable."

Alex crept toward them, past the feed room on the right and the tack room on the left. The horses poked their heads through the stall yokes. He eyed each inquisitive animal as he passed stall after stall, yet his steps never faltered. Lane studied him, alert for trembling or fear. The straight shoulders and curious gaze revealed an unwavering determination. Lane hoped Macie recognized her son's courage.

Alex stopped in front of them, his attention on Jasper. "Is that him?"

"Yes."

"He looks like one of those dalmatian dogs, but his spots are brown."

Lane's breath whooshed out in a laugh.

*　*　*　*

Lane...

The warning stuck in Macie's head, and her brain screamed to march Alex to the cabin. But her legs refused to move. She had to trust Lane to watch over him, right? And she was right here to back him up.

After placing a hand on Alex's shoulder, Lane fixed his gaze on her, the silent question obvious in the grooves running across his brow. He had assured her he would do nothing to cause Alex discomfort and her son appeared relaxed.

With her neck as stiff as if she'd starched it, she managed a slight bob of her head. Using the gentlest of pressure, Lane urged Alex closer to the stall, but kept him outside the horse's reach.

"He's a leopard Appaloosa. If you come closer, you'll see he has spots all over his body."

Alex's arms hung at his sides as if he were boxed into a small space. "He's smaller than the others."

"Almost fourteen hands to the top of his shoulder."

Just the right size for a child Alex's age.

What was she thinking?

Alex cocked his head, and Lane explained that a hand represented four inches. He turned his hand sideways to demonstrate. "It's a way to measure a horse's height. No matter the size, though, horses are powerful creatures. Each one deserves respect and proper treatment."

Alex raised his arm, then lowered it, evidently thinking twice about touching Jasper.

"If you're upset, Alex, he'll sense it and react to it. If you're relaxed, he'll sense that too."

Macie had wrestled her craving for adventure into submission after becoming pregnant. Now, contrary to a moment ago, she wanted to urge Alex to loosen up and reach out. But what if the horse reacted to her son's apprehension and scared him?

The animals and their earthy smells reminded her of being eleven and flying around barrels on the aging horse her father had purchased. She'd taken her share of tumbles off the gelding. But in all her precarious past behaviors, she had never experienced Alex's close call with tragedy.

Her son wasn't her. He wasn't his father or Lane Becker.

Lane scratched under Jasper's rust-colored mane. The gelding leaned into the touch, expressing his pleasure in a throaty whicker. "This one talks a lot."

A hint of a grin tipped one side of Alex's mouth. That grin said he wasn't sure if he should find that interesting or weird.

Lane patted the gelding once more. "He's ready to call it a night."

Macie wrapped her arm around Alex. "And it's time for your bath."

"Aw, Mom."

Lane shut the rear door, cut off the light, and slid the front door of the barn closed. Macie lagged behind Alex, who skipped carefree toward the cabin with Gypsy at his side. She required a few moments to adjust to what had happened inside.

Alex climbed the porch steps. "Thanks for showing me Jasper, Mr. Lane."

"Any time."

Macie didn't give in to her inclination to shoot a frown at

Lane. "I'll be in soon, Alex. Go get your bath, please."

"Okay."

Alex disappeared inside. Shadows from the surrounding trees immersed the cabin in the hint of dusk. She faced her boss. "Thank you for not pushing him to touch the horse. He's not ready for that."

"He's braver than you let him be, Macie. He proved that tonight."

He blamed her for Alex's fear? "You don't know what life has been like the past two years."

Lane clasped her arm in a gentle grip and led her to the porch steps, where they both sat on the smooth wood. "No, I don't, and I'm sorry you've had a rough time. But I've seen people control their anxiety when they learn to handle their fears the right way."

"The right way means time and a tranquil, non-threatening environment."

"What if he needs more?"

He sounded like Eva. It was Derek's mother who had pushed her into contacting the psychologist. "You're talking about therapy."

Lane's features softened. "It's clear that's not an option for you. Why not?"

Macie rubbed her arms to chase away the cold that rose from the memories. "Alex saw a man in Charlotte. Once he found out my son enjoyed drawing, he gave him a pencil and paper so he could draw detailed images of what happened the day of his father's death. Can you imagine how Alex reacted to being asked to draw Derek floating face down in the w-water?" Her fingers shook as she tucked a piece of hair behind her ear. Seeing Alex's drawings had horrified her and still did. "Alex left the office in tears and begged me to not take him there."

"So you stopped all sessions?"

"What was I supposed to do? I depended on an expert to help my son, not push him to reenact what happened through a bunch of drawings."

"I get it, Macie. Maybe that psychologist was the wrong fit for Alex. But don't enable your son's fears by letting your own hold him back." Lane's quiet voice enfolded her in a verbal hug as if he believed its gentleness removed the sting from his words.

"Don't you dare think I'll risk Alex's safety—emotionally or physically—because you believe a horse can change him into someone who takes chances."

"I would never want him to take dangerous chances." Lane's voice grew hard. "But he needs to learn to handle the memories and adversities in life or his future will hold endless panic attacks."

They stared at one another in wordless disagreement until Lane rose from the step and tapped the brim of his cap. "Goodnight, Macie."

She stood on the porch long after he crossed the bridge and disappeared. Who did he think he was to say her fear stopped Alex from healing?

Macie entered the cabin and fired up her laptop. Lane Becker was nothing more than a . . . a horse wrangler. Because he had hired some shrink to work with hurting veterans, it didn't mean he could analyze her or her son.

Two weeks wasted when she should have spent it searching

for another job.

No sense in putting it off any longer. It was time.

Eight

As he rounded the tree line, Lane's cheery whistle faded with a lengthy exhale. No one waited for him on the cabin's porch this morning. No coffee cups sat on the small, rustic table between the chairs. No clouds of steam swirled in the morning air.

He checked his watch. Not early. Not late. For the past week, he had shared a hot cup of coffee and a few minutes of conversation with Macie while Alex slept. He deemed it a standing appointment. Today, he stood alone.

Goldie had skipped out on him.

Lane crossed the grass to the porch. Maybe she'd popped into the house for a minute or overslept and needed a wake-up call. Perched at the door with his hand raised, ready to knock, her angry words from the night before echoed in his ears. *"Don't you dare think I'll risk Alex's safety once more— emotionally or physically—because you want to change him into someone who takes chances."*

It wasn't a fair accusation. He wanted to help her bring Alex out of his shell, sure. But change him into a chance-taker? No way. Apparently, though, she considered those goals the same.

Macie had convinced herself her way was best for Alex. Seeing the kid in the barn last night, determined to approach Jasper, encouraged Lane to open his mouth. He should have kept it closed.

He'd hoped to show her she smothered her child's natural curiosity and interest in a world beyond his drawings. But in doing so, he'd alienated her. As Monte would say, he'd jumped from preachin' into meddlin'.

Lane refused to push anyone else into participating in uncomfortable activities. He hadn't pushed Alex, though, had he? Not in the same way he'd pushed Matt in the past. Never that way again. He'd learned his lesson.

At the same time, his nature bucked at sitting by while Macie set her son up to be powerless in handling the difficulties of life. If Alex was willing, why not let him explore his courage?

Lane retreated down the porch steps. Even though Alex's timid manner reminded him too much of Matt's, Alex was Macie's son—her responsibility and not Lane's.

As he lumbered toward the barn, he thought he heard the screen door open behind him. His footsteps slowed, but after a moment of indecision, he picked up the pace.

She was smart to put distance between them, because he couldn't take a front-row seat to watch what she was doing to Alex. Even worse, he couldn't risk turning the boy into another Matt Becker.

He fed the horses and led Jasper to the portable pen behind the barn. The gelding trotted the interior of the steel panels and called to the horses in the adjoining pasture. He'd give his newest therapy horse a couple of days to get acquainted with the others before he set Jasper loose to join them. It might save the Appaloosa some scars as he found his place in the hierarchy.

Lane folded his arms over the top rail and watched Jasper. Instead of the horse, he saw Macie and Alex.

Lord, maybe Crooked Creek can be their place of safety while they explore the world again.

The strains of Chris Young's "The Man I Want to Be" played from the holster on Lane's belt. He pulled the phone out. "Becker."

"Hey, Lane, it's Brianna."

"Hi."

He liked the Hartwell family and, years ago, looked forward to calling Reagan his sister-in-law. Because of him, though, Matt and Reagan never got the chance to unite the Hartwell and Becker families.

"When can we meet to discuss what you're expecting from your volunteers?"

He should turn Brianna down before he caused more conflict between the sisters. Seeing Reagan's anger in the sanctuary slit his conscience, and Macie had witnessed him bleed all over the church's padded chair.

Despite Reagan's feelings about him, he couldn't afford to turn away anyone's help. "How about tomorrow? I'll take you to lunch."

"I'm booked for lunch. How about breakfast on Saturday?

I'll stop by your place. We can head to town from there."

He glanced over his shoulder at the cabin. Saturday was Macie's day off and not a morning he expected to share with her. After her no-show today, what difference did it make, anyway? "I'll meet you at the barn around seven."

"See you then."

With the rest of his early chores complete, around noon, he tightened the cinch around Smoky's mouse-colored belly. A short time later, he led the grulla paint to the arena, stepped into the stirrup, and swung his leg over the saddle. The eagerness for exercise built in the gelding, an eagerness he shared.

After a period of warming up Smoky's muscles, Lane loped the horse inside the oval arena. He lost count of the cracked boards they passed. Two loose posts leaned outward, and the whole arena hollered for a fresh coat of white paint. The tasks already occupied a line on his to-do list—several lines—so he may as well buy the lumber and paint and get started. He'd stow the supplies in the large shed at the side of the barn until he found time to tackle the job.

Lane frowned when he saw he wasn't alone. Alex watched him through the top and middle boards of the arena. "Hey, Alex."

"What are you doing?"

He reined in Smoky near the gate. "Getting ready to practice for a team roping event."

"Can I watch?"

He struggled to answer the question, his mind stuttering. Only hours ago, he'd chewed himself out for getting in between Macie and her son. So, what now? "Does your mom know you're here?"

"No, sir." The boy's shoulders slumped. "Does that mean I can't stay?"

Lane studied Alex. No noticeable unease. A good sign. Still, he ought to send the kid back before Macie went crazy with worry … or went ballistic over Lane's interference. Let her decide if Alex should be here. "You should ask your mom—"

"She fixed your lunch, but she got a phone call, so I brought it to you." Alex ran to a covered rain barrel at a corner of the barn and grabbed the cooler bag he'd set on the top. Rather than bring the lunch to the arena, he leaned over and studied the ground around the barrel. "Are these cougar tracks, Mr. Lane?"

Cougar? Not this side of the mountains.

Lane dismounted, leaving the horse standing ground-tied as taught. He walked to the barn and crouched, examining the faint paw prints left in the dirt from the last rain. Alex hung back, so Lane waved him closer.

The boy crept to Lane's side and bent forward, hands on his knees. "It is from a cougar, isn't it?"

"Good guess. Do you see these lobes?" Lane pointed out the two rounded indentions at the heel. "A cougar's pad has three. Look at these claw marks." He gestured to the tiny pricks at the top of the toes. "Normally, a cat doesn't leave those. Also, a cougar's print would be wider." And larger.

"Then what is it?"

"I'd say it belongs to a wild," Lane fought a grin, "Gypsy."

Alex straightened and scowled. "The dog?"

Lane washed his hands at the outside faucet, then took the bag and led Alex to the arena. "When I was a kid, I found tracks

I insisted belonged to a doe and her fawn. Turned out to be from one of my dad's cows and her calf." He left off that he'd been half Alex's age.

"At least they weren't from a dog."

When they were in their teens, Lane had taught Matt to track. It was one of the few outdoor activities both Becker boys enjoyed.

Lane opened the cooler bag, pulled out the homemade potato chips, and shared them with Alex. "If you're interested, I'll teach you how to identify animal tracks." The rash statement rekindled the memory of Macie asking him to consult her first before issuing the boy an invitation. "I'll need to ask your mom's permission first."

The scowl made an encore visit. "She won't let me do it. She won't let me do anything."

A potato chip hung from Lane's fingers halfway to his mouth. How could he encourage Alex without belittling the concerns of his mother? "She loves you and wants to keep you safe."

"I know, but she doesn't believe I'm brave like you told her." Alex's chin fell. "At least, I wish I was."

How did he know what Lane had said? "You heard our conversation last night?"

"The bedroom window was open."

Lane sealed the empty chip bag and stuffed it in the cooler. He searched for an appropriate response to Alex's resentment, a feat as challenging as walking a tightrope over Niagara Falls.

Nibbling at the turkey sandwich Macie had made, he asked himself if he really believed in Alex's courage. Or had he merely tried to get Macie to loosen her hold on the kid? Both, really. "Some people look at bravery as undertaking a dangerous action without fear. In reality, Alex, heroes do what's necessary, even when they're afraid."

"Is that why you want to help soldiers? Because they're scared sometimes? Like me?"

He hadn't discussed his true motivation for establishing the center with anyone but Sutton, and he didn't intend to share it with a child. "Everyone gets scared sometimes. The important thing is to learn to deal with fear in the right way. You showed courage in coming to the barn last night rather than staying inside the cabin."

The boy's brown eyes sparkled with the praise. "Yeah."

Lane re-wrapped the sandwich and stuffed it in the cooler to finish later. "I have work to do. You should go back to the house."

Lane ambled to the header's box at the north end of the sandy arena and dragged a bale of straw stuck with a plastic steer's head toward the center. With the practice dummy in place, he grabbed his rope from where it hung looped over the saddle horn.

He and Sutton had set aside this afternoon to prepare for the roping competition. Once his teammate arrived, they would practice with the horses and a real steer. For now, he would use the dummy to loosen up his shoulder.

With the rope coiled in his left hand and the loop in his right, Lane stood several feet behind and to the left of the straw bale. He twisted his wrist, feeding more rope into the ever-growing loop that swirled over his head, then released the loop to float over the plastic horns. When it caught, he pulled it tight, then loosened it.

"Will you show me how to throw the rope?"

Alex was still here?

Lane peered over his shoulder. Sure enough, the boy stood on the bottom board of the fence, watching him. Would Macie object to her son tossing a loop over a piece of molded plastic? Lane's mind rushed to think of ways Alex could hurt himself, finding nothing more dangerous than the boy tripping over the rope. But he had gone one round with her over the past twenty-four hours. He should put off round two as long as possible. "Not today."

"Can I ride your horse sometime?"

Whoa! Time to slow things down. "Your mom would put us both in time out for life if she caught you on a horse." Lane hooked a thumb over his shoulder, pointed toward Smoky. "And it takes experience to handle that guy."

A moving shadow in his peripheral vision alerted him to someone coming. Macie rounded the corner of the barn, closing the distance between them at a pace shy of a jog. Every limb, every stride, mimicked the tightness in her expression. "Alex, I've been looking for you."

"You found me." The mumbled comment reached Lane's ears, but he doubted Macie had heard. "I'm okay, Mom."

"I can see that." Her strained voice contradicted her words.

"Alex brought me lunch."

She placed a hand on her son's head. "A nice gesture, buddy. Let's go back to the house. It's time for *your* lunch."

"But Mr. Lane's going to teach me about animal tracks and

roping."

"I said with your mom's okay." He was in enough trouble with Macie.

She squeezed her eyes shut and probably counted to ten, or maybe twenty, because it took time for her to reopen them. Once she did, she held out her hand for her son to take. "Maybe another time. Mr. Lane is busy."

"If you don't object, Macie, he can drop the mister." Lane handed her the cooler, his appetite gone. "It sounds stuffy and not something I'm used to hearing."

She hesitated. "I suppose that would be all right."

But not the tracking and roping.

As they walked away, Lane leaned against the arena rails and shook his head. Macie kept Alex on a tight rein with the tenacity of a green rider on a gentle horse. If she wasn't careful, the boy would bolt one day and leave her sitting alone in the dust.

Smoky nudged Lane's back as if to remind him of his presence. Lane pulled a mint from his pocket, unwrapped it, and held it out it to the gelding. As the horse crunched the candy, he said, "I'm wondering who needs the most help, Smoke—Alex or his mother."

Or me.

The boy's insight about soldiers had hit Lane like a lightning bolt. From the moment he'd learned Matt had enlisted in the Army, Lane never considered his brother's courage, only his lack of preparedness.

What did it matter? In the end, because of Lane's bullying, all Matt received for his service was a sniper's bullet and a grave at Hidden Veil Hills Cemetery.

Nine

Macie rose early on Saturday to catch Lane and apologize for losing her temper and ditching their morning chats. She slouched in the porch chair, embarrassed by the childishness that prevented her from sharing coffee with him.

Where was the horseman? For the past twenty minutes, she had waited on the porch, expecting him to round the tree line. Even if they usually didn't meet on Saturday, the horses expected to eat and be turned out to pasture, so he would pass by.

He would.

She eyed the half-full coffeepot on the small table, then rose from her seat. As she leaned over the railing to peer toward the main house, the wooden bridge spanning the creek convulsed with a *thunk-thunk, thunk-thunk.* She hurried to the chair, plopped into it, and crossed her legs as if she had nothing in mind but taking in the fresh morning air.

The nose of Lane's truck cleared the trees. He slowed the vehicle in front of the cabin, poked his hand out the window in a stiff-armed imitation of a wave. "Morning, Macie."

Her lips parted, but he drove on before giving her a chance to respond. The plan to redeem herself sank into a quagmire of uncertainty. Should she go to him or wait to see if he returned?

He parked in front of the storage building near the barn, climbed out of the truck, and disappeared inside, shutting the door behind him.

She lingered on the porch, hoping he'd double back to talk to her. When waiting proved futile, she eyed the coffee growing cold in the glass pot on the table. She checked her watch and glanced at the building again. The door remained closed.

Yesterday's phone call from Mr. Locke interrupted her intention to take Lane his lunch and set things right between them. Seeing Alex at the arena brought back her concern over Lane's interference in their lives, and the intention to apologize had flown from her mind.

Excuses.

She deserved to be snubbed and didn't blame Lane for not stopping to talk to her.

Macie twisted the wedding band on her finger. Time spooled in reverse, bringing into the present the emotions that sidelined her after her husband's death.

Blame. Loneliness. Abandonment. Disappointment. Hurt.

Each emotion cramped her stomach with the new worry over her current state. Somehow, Lane had wheedled his way to the top of her list of friends as surely as he'd wheedled his way into Alex's problem. How had she had let that happen after such a short time?

She started down the porch steps. If he wouldn't come to her, she would go to him.

Lane exited the building and approached the front of the barn at the same moment a silver Honda rolled down the drive. Macie recognized Reagan Hartwell behind the wheel.

The woman parked near the barn and climbed out of the car dressed in snug jeans. Her red tunic top complemented hair as dark as the coffee turning bitter with age on the porch.

She slammed the car door and marched up to Lane. "You think a good deed will make up for what you did? What your brother did in your place?

"My property will be available to people who need it. I'm praying for a good outcome for them."

Macie tiptoed back to the porch as the voices carried in the morning's stillness. She should go inside and not eavesdrop, but the antagonism in Reagan's voice rooted her to a spot behind a post. From there, Macie could hear but not see them. And they couldn't see her.

"You should have prayed for that 'good outcome' the day Matt left Crooked Creek."

Who was Matt, and where had he gone?

"What do you want, Reagan?" Defeat drained Lane's voice.

"My sister won't help you."

"Is that her decision or yours?"

"It doesn't matter."

At the sound of a slamming car door, Macie peeked around the post. Reagan sat behind the wheel of her car. She and Lane stared at one another, then she drove off. He shook his head and entered the barn.

Macie's sympathy for Lane surged, as well as her curiosity over the argument with Reagan. Why would the woman drive out here to tell him about her sister when a phone call would work?

Macie's fists clenched. Had Reagan wanted to start an argument?

If Brianna had changed her mind, why hadn't she come herself? She'd seemed eager to volunteer. What was it with those Hartwell sisters?

And the biggest why?

Why were Reagan and Lane at odds?

Macie checked her watch. If she and Alex didn't move along, she would be late for her appointment.

She carried the coffeepot and cups inside. She had a job interview.

* * * *

As Macie drove away from Crooked Creek, her emotions churned. She tried to push aside the fact that her potential resignation would add to Lane's troubles. Macie shouldn't worry about it when she barely knew her boss, and her son's welfare topped her list of priorities. But she did.

Once she reached town, she parked in the lot behind the two-story buildings that housed the soda shop on one end and the antique shop on the other. The pharmacy sat in between.

When in town earlier this week, she'd dismissed the help wanted sign in the front window of Locke's Old-Fashioned Drug Store and Soda Fountain. After Wednesday night's incident at the barn, though, she'd made the phone call.

Macie steered Alex into the pharmacy through a back entrance. The farther into the store they went, the more the building's age and business inventory intermingled with the sweet smells of the 1950s-style soda fountain.

They walked through a wide, arched opening and crossed the black and white linoleum tiles. Six backless stools with red vinyl seats stood bolted to the floor in front of a shiny black Formica counter. A large mirror hung from the wall, reflecting a paunchy, balding man who looked to be at least fifty. White letters embellished the yoke of his black apron with "Locke's Old-Fashioned Drug Store and Soda Fountain."

Two ice cream tables and chairs occupied the narrow space near a plate-glass window overlooking Main Street. Several other tables sat scattered around the room. She led Alex to the one in the far corner. "Sit here, buddy. When I'm finished, we'll have a root beer float."

She really needed to stop feeding her son so many sweets. He'd probably consumed more sugar since their arrival in Hidden Veil than he had in the previous year.

Tugging the envelope containing her resume from the tote she carried, Macie approached the counter. She smoothed her best blouse and pasted on a smile. "Excuse me. Are you Mr. Locke?"

"Yes, ma'am." He glanced at the envelope. "You must be Mrs. Newman."

Gene Locke's colorful tattoos and colossal size gave him the look of a biker gang leader instead of an ice cream scooper. But his eyes sparkled with friendliness, putting Macie at ease. "I am. Thank you for seeing me."

Mr. Locke read through her work history—minus her job on Crooked Creek—and the two of them talked in between his attention to customers.

"As I told you on the phone, Mrs. Newman, I want to expand to include more offerings. My goal is to make this place a lunch counter for businesspeople downtown and visitors to Hidden Veil." He frowned as he reviewed her resume. "We're a growing but simple town, attracting people who want to live a laid-back, country lifestyle. You won't find golf courses, fancy condos, and five-star restaurants. Looking over your work history, I can't help thinking you're overqualified for making salads and sandwiches."

He didn't know her current job included cooking simple meals, plus housecleaning for two single men. "You mentioned on the phone that this is a management position. I have experience in that area, too."

He scanned the resume again. "I can't pay your Charlotte salary."

"I understand." What he was offering was more than Lane paid. Of course, she wouldn't have the use of the cabin. If she accepted this job, she'd need housing and someone to watch Alex during the day. In the end, it might dig a deeper hole in her savings, but she and her son would be out from under Lane's daily influence. "I noticed a stairway to the second floor of this building. Are there apartments up there? Do you know of any for rent?"

"A couple of apartments existed decades ago. Today, the upstairs is mostly storage space, and the rooms are in rough shape. To be honest, I wouldn't rent one to my dog."

That put an end to that idea.

Mr. Locke leaned a hip against the counter and crossed his arms. "So, why'd you leave your last job?"

"I wanted my son to grow up in a smaller town." It was the same answer she'd given Monte—the truth, if only a partial truth. "I assure you I left the restaurant on good terms."

He glanced again at the resume. "Is this a current address?"

Her employment at Crooked Creek was so recent, she'd chosen not to raise questions over her commitment to a job by listing it. She'd thought the position at the restaurant would be enough reference. Had she miscalculated this small-town druggist's desperation for an employee? "Actually, it isn't."

The door opened, and Mr. Locke straightened. "Excuse me, Mrs. Newman. Mornin', Lane. How's the plan for the center coming?"

Macie peered into the mirror behind the counter as Lane sauntered toward them. She reached out to sweep up the resume, but his reflection caught hers in the mirror before his attention dropped to the paper on the counter. Was he able to read it from where he stood?

"All's good, Gene. When you're finished helping Macie, I'd like to talk to you about it."

"Macie?" Mr. Locke eyed her. "I thought you said you were new in town, Mrs. Newman."

Her gaze shifted from the druggist to Lane and back again.

She probably looked like a cornered rat. She certainly felt like one. "I was about to explain. I've been here two weeks."

"I see." Mr. Locke studied her another moment, assessing her and the situation, then he turned back to Lane. "How's that new housekeeper working out for you?"

Macie froze as solid as the ice cream in the chest behind the counter. She had also miscalculated the power of the little town's grapevine and the intelligence of this businessman. Gene Locke knew of her relationship to the horseman as surely as Lane knew why she stood at the ice cream counter.

While pretending to read a list of shake flavors written on a board on the wall, Macie waited for Lane to set Mr. Locke straight. She waited for him to ruin her chance to find employment anywhere in the county.

"Uncle Monte couldn't have found anyone better. I'd give her a good recommendation . . . if she wanted one."

A silent groan deflated her lungs. Why must the horseman be such a nice guy? For two cents, she'd crawl over the counter and hide behind it.

"Lane!" Alex waved from his place at the ice cream table.

Lane pointed toward her son. "I'll talk to Alex while you finish your business."

"Won't be but a minute." Mr. Locke slid the resume into the envelope and across the counter to Macie, his decision clear. He lowered his voice. "It's still a small town, Mrs. Newman."

Macie's mouth opened, but nothing came out, so she closed it. Lane's presence had smacked the kiss of death on the interview.

She stuffed the envelope into the tote hanging off her

shoulder. She'd hired enough kitchen staff in the past to understand Mr. Locke's hesitation to feel he poached someone else's employee.

"Have you decided what you want?"

She had promised Alex. "Two root beer floats, please." Though she doubted she'd enjoy hers.

While she waited for her order, Lane flipped through the sketch pad to see the drawings Alex still hadn't shown her. The two of them talked in low tones, a conversation that left her out. Her son laughed at something Lane said. She longed to discover why Alex had drawn closer to her boss and was more distant with her lately.

Macie turned back to the biker lookalike. "Make my order three floats, please, Mr. Locke."

Ten

Lane leaned against the porch rail, coffee cup in hand, and gaze on Macie. The early morning sun illuminated strands in her blonde hair. *The sun rises and sets with her.* He scoffed at the ludicrous thought that flashed through his mind.

Her deep, indrawn breath signaled the awkwardness he'd sensed in her since his arrival. "Lane, I apologize for avoiding you. It was a childish thing to do."

More childish than not admitting she no longer wanted to work at Crooked Creek? Lane swigged the black coffee and swallowed, the heat burning his throat. He hadn't asked about her meeting with Gene, and for the past three days it sat, sandwiched between them like a big surly question mark.

He'd suspected he'd seen a resume sitting on the counter. Then, her I'm-up-to-something-you-won't-like expression had jammed his stomach into the toes of his boots. Most of the root beer and ice cream she'd bought him remained on the table, turning an unappetizing, chalky mocha color in the glass.

She must believe that the proverb about getting to a man's heart through his stomach worked every time. Only she had no interest in Lane's heart. She had no interest in the job he provided, either. How long before she applied to work somewhere else?

The wait was like sitting on Smoky during a roping event, when the barrier would break and the steer would dash into the arena. Would Lane pause and break out late, missing his opportunity?

"I'd planned to apologize Saturday morning, but—"

"I didn't stop." Instead, he'd waved and driven on with no time to dawdle before meeting Brianna. Maybe if he had stopped, she would have told him about the job interview. What a waste when his breakfast with Brianna never happened.

Macie turned her head and nodded toward the drive. "Company's coming."

Immersed in his thoughts, he hadn't heard the older model Chevy. The driver slowed, then stopped in front of the cabin. He might have laughed at the coincidence ... if he were in a better mood.

Brianna sat behind the wheel. What brought her here this early in the morning? What brought her at all after Reagan's visit?

The youngest Hartwell sister jumped from the car, slammed the door, and marched toward the porch. Her ponytail bounced back and forth like a hyped-up metronome, and a fire blazed in her eyes. "Lane, I heard Reagan came to see you Saturday." She nodded to Macie. "Good morning."

"Good morning." Macie stepped toward the door. "I should get ready for work."

"Don't bother leaving. I have a class soon, so I won't be long." Brianna's eyes flashed. "Besides, if you're going to live in Hidden Veil, you might as well learn what a bitter, rotten skunk my sister can be sometimes."

The Hartwell sisters had their spats, but Lane knew the three women were closer than many siblings—to Sutton's endless frustration.

Lane set his coffee cup on the rail. "Bri—"

"It's true, and you know it. I meant to show up Saturday morning as we'd planned, but a friend broke her foot and needed a ride to the hospital. I spent the weekend with her." Brianna sighed. "I should have suspected treachery when Reagan offered to stop by on her way to the clinic and tell you why I couldn't meet you, but I wasn't thinking straight. This morning she confessed without a shred of conscience." Brianna took a breath after the rush of words. "I'm here this morning to make my intention clear. I *am* volunteering, no matter what my sister told you."

Reagan didn't like him, true, but he never suspected she'd stoop to lying. "I appreciate your willingness, but I don't want to come between the two of you."

"You won't. If we're quarrelling, it's Reagan's fault." With the sudden quiver of her lower lip, the anger seeped away, and she shook her head. "I understand my sister's pain, but she's wrong, and it is far past the time she moved on. Matt made a choice, and blaming you won't change what happened."

Lane's grab at the rail knocked his cup into the grass. Coffee splashed onto Brianna's sneakers and the legs of her jeans. He stared at the wet brown spots, unable to move, unable to find the breath to say he was sorry.

The screen door slapped shut behind him. The sound repeated a moment later. Macie rushed down the porch stairs and handed Brianna a damp rag. "Here. Use this."

"Thanks." Brianna dabbed at the moisture and returned the rag. She glanced at her watch. "I'll be late for my first class if I don't go. We'll talk later, Lane."

Once Brianna turned the car around and drove away, he loosened his grip on the rail. He had worried Brianna would reveal the reason for her sister's hostility toward him. His failure wasn't something he was eager for Macie to discover. Not yet.

He studied the sullen pinch of Macie's brow and waited for her to ask what Reagan had against him. Instead, she seemed lost in her own thoughts.

"Lane, about Saturday, I should be honest and tell you that—"

"I'm pretty sure I know already." Since she brought up the matter, it was best they clear the air. "I suppose you talked to Gene about a job because of what I said to you about Alex."

She blinked as if he'd caught her by surprise. "When you first mentioned your goal for this place, I decided being here long-term wouldn't be in Alex's best interest."

"I wish I could say I'm surprised, but from the first day we met, you haven't hidden your opinion of my plan for the therapy center."

"It's not that I don't respect what you want to do."

Lane picked up the empty cup from the ground and handed it to her, glad to see it hadn't broken. "You don't think it holds any merit."

"Not for my son." She stared at the barn. "However, I think you should know—"

"I only want to know if you're still thinking about leaving." He should have let her finish speaking. But his emotions swirled over Reagan's deception on Saturday—over the depth of her continued hostility toward him.

Macie said nothing for agonizing seconds, like she had to think it over. Hadn't she done plenty of that over the past days? "I can't make any promises."

At least she was honest. "Then let's move forward from here and see what happens."

Those perfectly formed eyebrows arched. "All right."

Although he might want to, he couldn't encourage Macie to remain at Crooked Creek. Not when she considered him a detriment to Alex, and their views about the center were at odds. Not when each day she tempted him to seek for himself the same dream he'd ruined for Reagan.

No, he couldn't encourage her to stay, any more than he could bring himself to persuade her to leave.

When it came to Macie Newman, Lane balanced on a fence rail, dividing the lands of Hope and Hopelessness. On which side would he fall?

* * * *

Near the barn, the constant, headache-inducing sounds

of construction made up for the silence inside the cabin, a cabin Macie occupied alone. Her frustrated growl disrupted that silence.

After searching upstairs for Alex, she assumed he had sneaked out of the house ... again. She found her proof when seeing the open back door. Only the screen door kept out insects, squirrels, Gypsy, and who knew what else.

This abnormal and sneaky behavior from her son must stop. Why not ask her for permission rather than steal away? Why choose to hide things from her? Surely, he realized how it worried her.

There was no question where she'd find him. She shut the door behind her and scurried toward the barn, passing two unfamiliar pickups and an SUV. The racket at the arena muted the crunch of gravel under her Nikes.

Alex followed Lane around like a miniature shadow. For the past two weeks, he'd sung the horseman's praises as if Lane were a celebrity.

"He's great at twirling a rope and let me try it."

"Lane showed me how to groom Jasper. I got to lead him to the pasture today."

"Lane sure knows how to buy a horse. That App is terrific."
App? Already, her son spoke the language of a horseman.

"Did you know Lane has a four-wheeler and a kayak?"

That last announcement sent a massive tremor quaking through Macie. Working around horses was dodgy enough. Now Alex talked of four-wheelers and kayaks.

Lord, please don't let Lane encourage Alex to use either of them.

Attending church with the Beckers had brought back the tendency to talk to God in short bursts. She shied away from what she really needed—a long, in-depth talk with Him. Time spent pouring out her fears, her anger, her distrust. A time of soul-searching. Now was not that time.

Macie's pace quickened, and her head pounded with the rhythm of hammers on wood and the grinding of a power saw. Silence would sound like bliss right now.

She rounded the corner of the barn, then searched for Alex among the four men working at the arena. It hadn't surprised her to see Lane's friends respond to his request for help. His big heart drew others to him—people like Alex. Yes, she could admit, even her.

But not Reagan Hartwell.

One day, Macie might summon the nerve to ask him what the woman had against him. On Tuesday, she had tried to admit she'd overheard their conversation—but he shut her down. Since then, they had discussed nothing of a serious, personal nature.

On the far side of the arena, the tallest and brawniest of the men reached into a large cooler and pulled out a bottled water. From Alex's description, she'd guess his name was Sutton Vance. All Macie knew of him was that he was Lane's best friend and team roping partner.

She recognized the blond as Jo's boyfriend, Kyle Callahan. The last man was a stranger. While Sutton looked like a farmer or cattleman—a man fit and tanned and accustomed to outdoor labor, like Lane, Kyle and the stranger were fit but without skin bronzed by the summer sun.

Nearby, Alex picked up a board and carried it toward Lane, who worked a running power saw. Macie's stomach dropped. She bolted forward, then pulled up short when Lane held his hand up. "Whoa, Alex."

He shut down the saw and sauntered toward her frozen son with an easy gait. The handle of the hammer hanging from the tool belt around his waist cuffed his thigh with each step. He eased the board out of Alex's hands and crouched in front of him. Macie couldn't hear their conversation, but it ended with both of them smiling and the horseman roughing her son's hair.

When Lane spotted her, her stomach fluttered. She had tried to overlook this recent physical reaction as natural and meaningless. After all, most women would find him attractive. His humor, patience, and benevolent character were harder to overlook. She had a hunch he could be as homely as Jasper and still provoke these flutters.

But he wasn't.

Lane closed the gap between them. Alex trudged behind him, head down and with Gypsy at his side. No doubt her child suspected she planned to shoo him home.

"I came to take my son off your hands."

Alex frowned. "Not yet, Mom. They need me."

Lane squeezed Alex's shoulder. "It's okay. We're almost done for the day. We'll tackle the rest of the job another time."

Except for her father, Macie had never met a harder worker than Lane. Daily chores. Paperwork. Training the horses. In addition, he labored to get the barn area in shape before the early-September barbecue for the volunteers and sponsors. If she had any say in the matter, he'd work without Alex. Her say looked less and less likely with each passing day.

She eyed her son. "Go wash up for supper."

"Aw, Mom."

"Now. I'll be there in a few minutes." *And we'll have a talk.*

Alex dragged his feet toward the cabin. He tripped while peering over his shoulder.

"Watch where you're going, honey, or you'll fall."

He mumbled a response she couldn't quite catch, but thought it ended with "alone." Based on his attitude lately, she filled in the blanks with the words *leave* and *me.*

Once he disappeared around the barn, her attention returned to Lane, and her heart quickened. He'd worked outside for hours—dirt clinging to the sweat on his skin and the clothes she would wash later this week. Yet, he couldn't look more appealing to a chef used to seeing well-dressed men smelling of a spicy aftershave.

She folded her arms across her stomach. Anything to keep from reaching out and brushing away the bits of sawdust clinging to Lane's faded red T-shirt, like flurries of wooden snowflakes. No way would she touch the cotton material, not when the tips of her fingers already tingled with the imagined feel of those rock-solid muscles beneath it.

But what harm could come in brushing off his cap?

He bent to place the board against the fence, and she snatched the hat off his head. He jerked upright, his eyebrows pinched.

"You'll get sawdust in your eyes." She slapped the hat against her leg. Dust floated in the humid, still air. As it settled, she stood on her toes to place the hat back on his head, not meaning to give it a roguish slant. Her good intention earned her a heart-melting grin that tempted her to want to brush off every piece of sawdust she could find.

She turned sideways, teeth clenched against the exasperation clinging to her like that sawdust on his clothes. She needed to keep her hands to herself and her emotions appropriate to her employment.

Eleven

Laughter carried across the arena as the other men packed up their tools and prepared to leave for the day. It reminded Macie that she and Lane weren't alone. She took a few steps in the other direction, and Lane followed. Stopping in front of the barn took them out of sight of his friends, allowing for more privacy.

She turned to Lane. "You've accomplished a lot today."

"I appreciate the guys giving of their time. It made it an easier day." He straightened the cap. "Don't be mad at Alex, Macie. He only wanted to help."

No, he wanted to be with you. "I'm not mad, but I could use your support."

"What kind of support?"

"Alex shouldn't run off without telling me, Lane. Next time, please send him home. You've seen what can happen under certain circumstances." Fortunately, there had been no repeat anxiety attacks. Yet.

"You're right. He should ask your permission first and not run off without telling you. But it's important to him to be treated like a normal boy."

"He is normal."

"That wasn't what I meant."

Lane glanced toward the arena, then strode into the shade of the barn. Macie followed him through the tack room doorway. It wasn't much cooler than standing in the sun. The room smelled of dust and leather, but it was private, away from his friends.

He pulled a string and turned on the light from a bare bulb hanging by a wire from the ceiling. Then he shut the door. "Alex feels smothered, Macie."

Smothered? "He never felt that way before we moved here." Before he met Lane. She sighed. "I look for him every day. Turns out, I don't need to look far, because I find him with you."

"I've never approved of Alex running off or encouraged him to spend time with me."

"Maybe you don't think you encourage him, but it's obvious to me that you do. And I believe you see it as a way for him to escape."

"Escape from what?"

"His mother's heavy-handed and controlling nature? It's clear you don't approve of the way I'm raising my son."

His eyes pressed shut, and he pinched the bridge of his nose. "I've never said you weren't raising him right."

"Not in so many words, but it's what you think." Macie waited for him to deny it. When he didn't, she sought to regain some self-control. Her shoulders heaved with remorse. Why blame him for her son's actions? "Loss changes a person, Lane, especially when that loss might have been prevented. Consider yourself fortunate not to have gone through the experience."

A muscle ticked at his eye. "What makes you think I haven't been through tragic loss?"

Macie flinched at his sharp tone—unexpected coming from him. She studied the lines of tension surrounding his tight lips. Deep indentions cut between blue eyes that were both troubled and incensed.

It was as if God lifted a curtain, allowing her to see through Lane's irritation right to the pain behind his question. Her anger dissolved at the memory of his discussion with Reagan. "Are you talking about Matt?"

A few silent seconds passed. "What do you know about him?"

She rested a hand on his bare arm, warm and clammy from the physical exertion and afternoon heat. "I tried to tell you last week. I overheard you and Reagan at the barn. Your voices carried."

The muscles under his skin bucked, but she hung on. "She isn't my biggest fan."

Macie waited for him to explain, but he only stared at the scuffed floorboards in silence. She was about to tell him it wasn't her business when he looked up. "Matt and Reagan were high school sweethearts. They were engaged when he enlisted in the Army . . . and died in Afghanistan."

Her heart clenched. A soldier with no opportunity to become a living veteran like those Lane planned to help. "I'm so sorry."

That didn't explain Reagan's bitterness or Lane's sorrow until Macie recalled Monte's comment on the first night she met Lane. "He was your brother."

Lane paused, then exhaled one clipped word. "Yeah."

Guilt nibbled at her like a minnow nipping at a swimmer's bare toes. "I am sorry for your loss and for what I said a minute ago. It was thoughtless of me. Now, I understand your purpose in turning your ranch into a place to help veterans. You're honoring your brother."

Lane's reasoning didn't change her concern over its effect on Alex, but it elevated her respect for her boss to an even greater height . . . if that were possible.

From their talks, Macie had learned of the financial burden Lane faced. He had cut back on a successful horse business to devote time to establishing the center. For him, it was a labor of love. Reagan should be pleased about the center, pleased that her fiancé had generated such loyalty and dedication in his brother.

"You are an extraordinary man, Lane Becker." Despite the desire to keep their relationship friendly, yet professional, her hand slid down his arm. A startling and uncomfortable awareness shot through her. While her brain shouted at her fingers to let go, they wove through his as if they'd searched for and found their way home.

He dipped his head and lowered his voice. "Don't put me on a pedestal. I don't deserve it."

"A pedestal? I don't believe any of us belong on a pedestal. But how many people would work so hard to pay homage to a lost loved one? You are extraordinary."

The ring on Macie's finger burned her skin. She let go of Lane's hand, then turned and walked away from the tack room before she proved how much she meant what she said.

* * * *

Lane let go of the breath he'd held when he thought, for a gut-pleasing second, Macie would kiss him. Then she was gone.

He stepped out of the barn, unable to take his eyes off her as she walked toward the cabin. How he wanted to be worthy of those warm words and the touch of her hand.

Sutton hung around after Kyle and Trey drove off. Lane expected his friend's question.

"Have you asked her out yet?"

Bingo. "No, and it isn't in the plan."

Sutton crossed his arms. "Why not?"

"She isn't ready. Right now, she has her hands full with seeing to Alex's well-being."

His friend choked on a laugh. "The way she looked at you when she came to get the boy . . . I'd say she's ready."

Heat rushed to Lane's face as he stretched his tight shoulders. "What's the real problem?"

"She asked about Matt."

The humor in Sutton's face vanished. "You and Monte are tight-lipped about him. What did she want to know?"

"She overheard a conversation I had with Reagan."

Sutton's grimace reiterated his aversion to anyone named Hartwell. "I'm guessing that wasn't pleasant."

"No."

Lane related Reagan's visit as he accompanied his friend to his truck. Sutton yanked open the door of his battered pickup. "How did you explain things to Macie?"

"Simple facts. Matt's engagement to Reagan, his enlistment, and death in Afghanistan. No details."

"And?"

Lane swallowed. "And she admires me for wanting to help vets because of Matt. She thinks it's out of a need to honor him and his service."

"You know it is." Sutton climbed into the Ford cab and leaned out the open window. "I grew up with Matt, too, remember? He was a good kid and smart. So what if you pressed him hard sometimes? You didn't bully him into enlisting. He was an adult. It was his decision, not yours."

"That's what Brianna said."

"It pains me to agree, but she's right. You weren't around when he enlisted, so stop beating yourself up." Sutton shifted the truck out of Park. As he backed up, he added, "And Matt was more competent than you ever gave him credit for."

That last statement almost echoed what Lane had told Macie about her son. Not that the two cases were the same. A boy struggling to cut loose of his momma's apron strings and a man becoming a soldier to prove his big brother wrong. Big difference. Wasn't it?

He couldn't stomach his old self before God got hold of him.

How could he ever discuss with Macie the details of his relationship with Matt? The things he'd said and done?

As he carried the extra fence boards to the workshop to store, his phone burst into song. He set the boards inside the building and yanked the phone from its holder on his hip. "Becker."

"Mr. Becker, my name is Sheila Kraus."

She'd said her name as though he should know her. He raked his memory for recognition, but came away blank. "Yes, ma'am. How can I help you?"

"I'm the one to help you."

"In what way?" Maybe she called to volunteer at Healing Springs. Or maybe she was a scammer.

"I'm with Blue Ribbon Equestrian Emporium."

"The western store?" Hopefully, Monte hadn't placed an order Lane knew nothing about, just as his uncle had hired Macie without consulting him.

"I think of our business as *the* place to shop for *every* equestrian's needs." The statement sounded like an advertising slogan. A low chuckle tickled his ear. "But yes, if you prefer, the western store."

"I wasn't making light of the business, ma'am. I've shopped there myself." The nearest store was in Raleigh, so he didn't get there often.

"I'm glad you like it, Mr. Becker." She paused, then said, "I understand you're opening a facility aimed at helping military vets with adjustment issues."

Adjustment issues? That was one way to define the problems they faced. "Yes, ma'am."

"Perhaps you'd allow us to help."

His heart raced. "In what way?"

"Our company proposes to supply the feed and care for up to three healthy therapy horses for the first six months. After that, we'll consider an extension."

The board had discussed individual horse sponsorships through donations. Three cared for by a well-respected organization was more than they had hoped to receive so early in the center's life. "That's very generous. We welcome and appreciate the support."

"In exchange, you would list the company's name as a sponsor on the center's website and promotional materials."

He had expected as much. "Not a problem."

"Before we commit, my attorney will go over your proposal for the center. I'll also tour your facility, and I want to see the horses. Afterward, if all goes well, we can meet to discuss a contract."

"I'll email everything to you. When you're satisfied, call me. I'll be happy to show you around the center." What existed so far.

"That sounds good."

Once he'd gotten her email address, they hung up. Lane pumped his fist in the air. Finally, the potential for a sponsor with clout and deep pockets. A well-respected company to back Healing Springs would provide both financial help and an endorsement for seeking funds from other corporations.

His gaze swept the area, trying to see it through the eyes of a successful businesswoman. A still half-repaired, outdoor arena. Nothing indoors for year-round use. No office for a therapist. One well-built but simple barn. There were fancier facilities for her to invest in. Why choose his?

Going through the mental list reminded him he still hadn't found an office for Ron.

Once he had stored the rest of the lumber in the shed, Lane paused in the center of the room. He studied the interior, stomped on the floorboards, and pounded various spots on the wood-slatted walls. A solid building, though about half the size of the cabin's main floor. His father had constructed it with windows for light and a small loft for additional storage.

Was it possible the answer to his office problem sat within sight the whole time?

A wood-burning stove on a side wall provided ample heat in the winter. He'd buy a window unit for air-conditioning and check into the expense of adding a bathroom. The budget might handle a reasonable outlay for renovation.

He rubbed the hand Macie had held as if he could rub off the feel of her dainty fingers. Now if God would only show him how to meet Alex's needs without increasing his emotional ties to the boy or the fear-filled Goldie.

No more early morning porch meetings. No more being alone with her. No more temptation to grab hold of the type of future his brother never lived to experience.

No more dreaming of a golden-haired widow.

Sandra Ardoin

Twelve

Gold, peach, orange, purple—topped by a cobalt blue—
surrounded the pale-yellow of the rising sun. A glorious day in
the country had begun.

Macie carried the coffeepot and two mugs to the porch, only
to see Lane's truck already at the barn. It was July Fourth and
her day off. Had he assumed she wouldn't rise early for their
morning visit?

He hadn't shown yesterday either. Later, he told her he'd
met Brianna at the Red Dog Diner for breakfast to discuss her
volunteer role at the center. What about today?

Macie settled into an Adirondack chair and poured herself a
cup of coffee. She watched the sun climb higher until the sky
showed signs of becoming that perfect Carolina blue. After half
an hour with no trace of Lane, other than his truck, she went
inside the cabin to get ready for her day.

The next time she looked outside, his truck was gone. Her shoulders drooped with a disappointment she had no business feeling.

So, what should she do with the rest of her day?

At nine, her phone rang. She dropped the dust rag on the side table, grabbed the phone, and swiped the screen. "Hello?"

"Hey, Macie. It's Jo."

"Oh, hi." The two women had texted a few times after her visit to the coffee shop a couple of weeks ago, and they had talked at church.

"Have you changed your mind about the picnic and fireworks tonight?"

Macie flipped through her mental book of excuses, looking for a firm but tactful way to bow out.

"The weather is supposed to be wonderful with clear skies and temps in the mid-eighties."

It was as though Jo knew one of her hang-ups. There was still the lake—the water. "I'm not sure fireworks would be—"

"Are we going to see the fireworks, Mom?" Alex stood at the bottom of the stairs, anticipation brightening his face.

"Excuse me a moment, Jo." Macie covered the phone. "I don't think so, Alex." Which in Mom-speak was "Absolutely not."

His little mouth fell flat and tight. "Why not?"

"It will be at the lake."

His brow crinkled, and he looked more like the scared child she'd known the past couple of years. She thought that settled the matter until he straightened, throwing his shoulders back with confidence. "I won't go near the water."

"Alex feels smothered, Macie." Of course, Lane's words would wind their way through her mind now. "You want to go?"

His head bobbed with a brisk nod. What was happening to her son?

"It's clear you don't approve of the way I'm raising my son."
"I've never said you weren't raising him right."
"Not in so many words, but it's what you think."
"Okay." She uncovered the phone. "We'll be there."

But she would keep an eagle eye on Alex and whisk him away at the first sign of trouble.

* * * *

Macie hadn't seen Lane all day, even when she took a light supper up to the main house. Being a holiday, she wasn't obligated to provide it, but she'd made enough sub sandwiches, potato salad, and apple pie for both the picnic and to leave for the Beckers.

Neither man was home, so she set the sandwiches and southern potato salad with its pickles, boiled egg, and mustard in the refrigerator. She left a note on the counter alongside the pie.

That evening, she followed the directions Jo had given her and drove to the lake. After a quick search, she found a parking space and opened the door for Alex. "Are you sure you want to do this, buddy?"

He jumped from the car. "You've asked me that five times,

Mom."

Probably. Although she hadn't counted, obviously, he had kept score.

Macie grabbed the picnic basket, handed the tablecloth to her son, and tried to keep up as she followed him through the grass toward the lake. Jo had texted her their location, and she quickly found the group. Macie breathed easier when she noticed they were still quite a distance from the water.

Within minutes, a dozen six-inch mini-meatball subs cut into thirds, the potato salad, and the pie joined the other dishes on a picnic table.

"Looks like we'll eat well tonight." Jo approached Macie. "I'm so glad you came."

"I'm glad you invited me." She glanced at Alex. "Us."

"Have you met everyone?"

Macie eyed the men and women talking in groups a few feet away. Kyle. Brianna. Reagan. She shook her head. "Not everyone."

Jo introduced her to the others, one by one. Shaina Weber. Reagan's date—Mason something. Brianna's date, Lee Culver. Kyle's friend, Mitch Hernandez, his wife, Stacy, and their two children. Macie officially met the stranger she'd seen the day of the arena repair. Alex had said his name was Trey, and he was a veterinarian. He was the only other one there without a date or a spouse.

No Sutton. No Lane.

Alex looked up at her. "Can I go play with Elijah and Jackson?"

Macie glanced at the Hernandez boys, then at the crowd in

the park. Her body grew taut at the idea of letting her son out of her sight, especially when she didn't know many of the people here.

"Please?"

"*Alex feels smothered, Macie.*"

Giving a child room to breathe was fine, but sometimes a parent needed to use common sense.

A small playground sat about fifteen yards away. "Stay on the playground where I can see you."

"Okay." He dashed off with the other boys.

Jo handed Macie a Solo cup filled with peach iced tea. "He's such a sweetheart."

"Thanks. I think so, too." Macie grinned. "But I could be a wee bit biased."

"You're entitled."

The heat of the day had eased, and the stillness of the air left the lake's surface placid. It sparkled with rays of sunshine. Reflections of trees hanging over the water in the distance added to the restful setting. They couldn't have asked for nicer weather or a more beautiful spot for a picnic.

Macie did her best to relax and enjoy the evening, but every couple of minutes, her gaze drifted to Alex and the Hernandez boys. It filled her with joy to see her son having fun with other children. But what if . . .?

"I'm surprised those boys haven't asked to swim," said Stacy. "Mine are like dolphins."

Macie forced a smile. "Alex isn't comfortable around water."

"Neither am I. I can't swim." Shaina drew in a breath. "And I grew up around the beach."

Jo tilted her head. "You've never mentioned that before."

Shaina's jaw tensed. "Didn't I?"

By the guarded look on her face, Macie sensed Shaina's hesitation to talk about that time in her life. "How long have you lived in Hidden Veil?"

"Almost two years. I share a house with my aunt." She laughed. "It's always strange to call her that. We're more like sisters, and she's about your age."

Which, Macie judged, was four or five years older than Shaina.

"Maybe you've met her. Harmoni Basinger? She owns In Harmoni, the soap and candle shop downtown."

"I've passed the place and mean to check it out one day. I have a weakness for candles."

She glanced at the playground again. Alex and the other boys had moved to the grass to kick a large ball back and forth. Since they stayed nearby and within sight, she said nothing to interrupt their play.

Macie shut down her worry and concentrated on the conversation of the other women sitting on the large quilt spread out on the grass. Thanks to Jo's friendliness, they had embraced her presence and welcomed her into their group. All but Reagan Hartwell. The woman wasn't unfriendly, just aloof, with Macie, anyway, not the others. Macie guessed it had more to do with her association with Lane than the fact she was a stranger.

Kyle walked up behind Jo, bent over, and laid his hands on her shoulders. "Has she told you yet?"

Jo twisted to look up at him. "I was waiting for us to do it together."

"Then let's do it."

Brianna Hartwell's eyes grew large. "Do what?"

Kyle helped Jo to her feet. She snuggled against him. "Consider this a personal invitation." Jo's glance bounced from one to the other of them. "Everyone, get out your phones and make a note on your calendars for January 6."

Beside Macie, Shaina sucked in a breath. "Is this what I think it is?"

"If you think it's a wedding announcement," Jo winked, "then you're right."

Shaina and Brianna squealed and jumped up to hug the engaged couple. Reagan rose slowly, a look on her face somewhere between "How nice" and "You've got to be kidding me." What was wrong with that woman?

Macie congratulated the engaged couple, not sure whether she was included in the invitation. After all, she hadn't lived in Hidden Veil a month. Besides, she might be gone by January.

She spun around to check on Alex, and her heart galloped. All the boys were gone. "Alex?" She jogged to the playground and searched behind the tube slide.

Child-like laughter coming from near the lake sent her dashing through the grass, the long blades stinging as they whipped against her bare legs. She jolted to a stop a few feet behind her son. He stood at the edge of the water, watching the other boys wade up to their calves in the lake. They called for him to join them.

She froze, her eyes on Alex's stiff back. Her heart begged her to rush to him, to protect him from another attack of anxiety.

But something else urged her to hold back, to see what happened.

"Nah, I don't want to get wet. I'm going back to the picnic table for some of my mom's pie."

The response from Alex was so calm, Macie's jaw dropped.

"Yeah."

"That sounds good."

The boys splashed back to shore and ran up the hill to Alex. When her son turned and saw her, he flashed a quick smile and ran past her to the picnic table for his pie.

Macie released a breath. Alex had dealt with his fear on his own, and he'd done it in a way that kept him from being ridiculed by the other boys.

Pride in her son lifted her feet as she strode through the grass behind him.

✳   ✳   ✳   ✳

"You're doing great, Alex." Macie stood outside the arena with her hands clutching the top rail until they turned as white as the board. Trickles of moisture having nothing to do with the July heat rolled down her back. Why had she agreed to this?

Lane stood inside the fencing and instructed Alex in lunging Jasper. Gypsy sat in the dirt alongside her son as the horse plodded in a circle at the end of the lunge line. "Don't turn, Alex. You'll get dizzy. Keep walking with him at his hip and let the line out a little. Give him more space."

More space. It's what Lane had preached to her about Alex.

The horseman turned and pried Macie's fingers from the

board. "Relax, Goldie."

She was getting too comfortable with that "Goldie" moniker and the man who used it.

"Jasper realizes Alex is a beginner, and the horse is well-mannered. Give the boy a chance to trust him."

"I guess I'm just . . ." She crossed her arms and refused to say she continued to be afraid to let Alex try new things. Lane already believed her fears smothered her son's courage.

How had she gotten to this point? Why do this to herself and Alex?

Although they had discussed seeking her permission before he ran off, she hadn't forbidden Alex from spending time with Lane, because . . . well, maybe because a boy needed a man in his life. Her son had missed a male influence over the past two years. Alex chose Lane as someone to admire and, other than the horseman's alarming interests, he had chosen well.

Then too, maybe she allowed his relationship with Lane simply to prove she could let her child out of her sight . . . within reason.

If she wanted to be honest with herself, she would add a third explanation. These moments gave her a chance to talk to Lane, to build on their friendship. Since the day of the fence repair, he had maintained a guarded distance and, spouting one excuse or another, stopped visiting her in the mornings. She missed their talks and the sudden change in their relationship. What had she done wrong? Was it because of their argument and her tendency to "smother" Alex? Or was it because she'd questioned him about his brother?

It probably had nothing to do with either issue. He probably believed she'd overstepped her bounds when she held his hand in the tack room. Ever since, he'd made a point of not being alone with her. Strange, when she had begun to think he felt something for her.

Macie shook off the self-examination. "I'll admit, I never believed Alex would develop a fascination with horses."

"He's a natural." Lane's steady gaze remained on her son. "I think you made the right choice. He enjoys working with Jasper."

The right choice? Or would surrendering to her son's relentless appeals lead to disaster? "It's been ages since he begged me to do something so . . ."

"Risky?" He baited her, but in a teasing manner.

"Different."

Positioned to keep half his attention on her son and the other half on her, Lane asked, "You and your husband never took Alex riding?"

"Derek's allergies made it difficult for any of us to be around animals. Besides, my husband gave horses a wide berth."

Jasper snorted. Alex laughed and gave the horse a verbal command to stop. Lately, he had made surprising strides in his self-confidence and bravado. Ironic that the beautiful animal was the only thing her husband feared, yet his fearful son delighted in a horse's company.

Macie's breath hitched when Alex walked up to the gelding and patted his shoulder in a firm manner. He resumed his place and ordered the horse to walk in circles again, this time in the opposite direction.

The anxiety hightailed it to the hills and her chest expanded with a lungful of pride.

A few minutes later, Alex shouted, "I'm getting tired."

Lane strolled toward the center. "Okay, reel him in the way I showed you, and remember to tell him what a good job he did."

Alex tugged on the rope, coiled it in imperfect loops, and handed the lunge line to Lane. "Good job, Jasper." Then he ran up to Macie. "That was fun! Mom, Lane's planning to rope cows in a contest. Can we go?"

The question came out of the blue. Surely, he wasn't serious. "You're asking to attend a roping event?"

Alex nodded, his head bobbing with enthusiasm.

"Why?"

He shrugged. "I watched him rope the dummy. Now I want to see him rope a real cow." With a quick look at Lane, he corrected himself. "I mean, steer. They're steers, because they're guys."

She whirled on Lane with a glower that asked, "This was your bright idea?" The next thing she knew, Alex would demand that Lane teach him to rope steers—guys with horns.

Her boss hiked his eyebrows and raised the hands of the innocent.

She turned back to her son. "I'm sure Lane will be busy, Alex. We shouldn't get in his way. It takes concentration to do well in those events."

Lane's grimace said she shouldn't put her dirty work off on him.

Alex turned to his mentor. "Can we go?"

"Your mom has the final say, Alex."

"See, Mom, he doesn't care. Does that mean we'll go?"

Lane cocked his head and awaited her answer with the same expectation animating Alex's face.

To do well in those events took concentration. That concentration helped to keep a competitor from getting hurt. What if she and her son were present to see Lane injured? How would it affect Alex? She placed a hand against the coiling of her stomach. What would it do to her?

But, clearly, saying no placed her in the role of a villain.

"When is this event?"

"Saturday."

Macie dug into the back pocket of her jeans and pulled out her phone. Turning it away from Alex's view, she typed in a request for the weather forecast, then studied the screen and frowned at the result.

"Well?"

She poked a button, and the screen vanished. It was still several days out. The forecast could change. "We'll see, honey."

Alex's frustrated breath ruffled the tawny hair hanging over his forehead. "That means no."

"It means I'll wait until closer to Saturday to decide."

She stuffed the phone in her pocket, unsure if she should pray for rain on Saturday or accept the opportunity to prove Lane wrong about her.

Thirteen

Lane escorted the Newmans along the pipe fencing toward the end of the arena. The team roping event was underway, and a line of horned steers stood head to tail in the alley, each awaiting his turn to enter the chute.

Working with Jasper proved another example of Alex's desire to be a fun-loving, active boy. If he reacted positively today, Macie might loosen her apron strings even more than in the past two weeks.

Alex had disliked his mother's indecision the first time he asked to attend this afternoon. Unlike Lane, he hadn't seen that she'd checked the weather forecast on her phone and saw a prediction of rain for tonight. Under those circumstances, Lane still couldn't fathom why she'd agreed to the outing. Because the weatherman didn't expect rain until late this evening? Most likely Alex had worn her down. Whatever the reason, she was making progress in letting go. Hopefully.

Lane glanced up and said a silent prayer for clear skies until they returned to Crooked Creek.

Alex peeked through the bars, knocking the western hat Lane had given him cockeyed, and pointed to the steers. "What's on their heads?"

Lane knelt in the dirt. He raised his voice to cover the bellows from the animals and cheers from those watching a team already working in the arena. "It's called a horn wrap. Think of it like a helmet. It protects the animal's head from rope burns." He pointed to the two men who stood near the chute. "See those cowboys? Once the header nods that he's ready, one of them pulls the lever that opens the doors to the chute. The steer runs into the arena, breaks the electronic barrier, and the time starts. Then the ropers go to work."

"And the other man?" Macie's enthusiasm had kicked in the moment they arrived at the arena. It softened her face and lit her eyes.

Lane would bring her here every day just to see that smile that set the broncs kicking inside his chest. Man, he was a glutton for punishment.

"After the release of a steer, he prods another animal forward along the alley and through a back gate of the chute, getting it ready for the next team." He'd already filled them in on what would happen once the steer broke free, and Alex had watched a few practice sessions with Lane and Sutton.

Sutton tapped him on the arm. "Hey, bro, it's close."

Lane forced his attention back to business. Though he had agreed to bring them, Macie had been right when she'd said he shouldn't let them distract him. The entry fee for the small-time event cost each participant little more than a casual dinner-for-two. There were also transportation expenses and time away from work. Allowing Macie and Alex to throw off his concentration wasn't fair to Sutton. His friend scrimped to pay to take part in these events.

"I'll catch up to you in a minute." He turned to Macie. "You and Alex will see better if you're in the stands." Where it wouldn't be so easy for him to spot them.

With her hands resting on Alex's shoulders, Macie rotated him away from the fencing, urging him to leave the chutes. Two steps later, she stopped and glanced over her shoulder. The lines between her eyes vanquished the earlier enthusiasm she'd expressed. "Be careful."

He should be grateful to know she cared about his safety, but nothing beat seeing her as stress free as she'd looked a minute ago. "Don't worry."

With their turn in the arena, Lane backed Smoky into the corner of the header's box and tugged his Stetson until assured it would stay on throughout the ride. One hand held the reins and the end of the lariat. He gripped the loop end in his other hand.

As he waited for his partner, seconds passed like minutes. The sudden mental image of himself as a teenager writhing in the dirt with a broken shoulder sped up his breathing. His pulse raced. What was happening? He had never let that high school crash affect him in the box. The incident was in the past and had no relation to right here, right now.

Don't let Macie's fear get in your head, Becker. Nope. Not gonna do it.

Lane twirled the loop a few times to loosen up, and his breathing calmed. Sutton sat on Rocket in the heeler's box to his right, looking at him as if he'd partnered with a stranger. The episode gave Lane personal insight into the power of Macie's influence on her son.

After a silent count to three, Lane bobbed his head. The chute opened with a metallic *clank* and the steer broke the barrier that began the clock. Smoky and Rocket lunged forward, keeping the steer moving straight as it bolted for the opposite end of the arena. The wind cooled Lane's face and his body floated as the hooves of the horses dug into the dirt to keep pace with the steer.

Lane leaned forward in the saddle, feeding the nylon rope into the loop and spinning it overhead, wide and flat. His gaze shifted slightly toward the stands, and Smoky veered off-track. Lane used his leg to edge him back in line with the steer.

Concentrate.

In his mind, he ticked off the seconds, but he waited until experience told him to let the loop fly. With its release, it dropped over the horns. *Perfect.* He yanked the loop and reined Smoky left, turning the thrashing steer to give his partner a chance to capture the back legs. With quick movements, he wound the end of the rope around the saddle horn several times. When he'd explained to Alex that it was called dallying, the boy laughed at the term.

Once Sutton's loop trapped both of the steer's legs, Lane spun Smoky around, keeping the rope taut. Rocket slid to a stop, stretching the steer out. The two men waited for the flagman on horseback to lower the red flag, signaling there were no fouls. Afterward, they loosened their loops, freeing the steer as the announcer broadcast the time. Lane shook his head. He'd blown it by letting Smoky get out of position.

He coiled his rope and reined Smoky to join up with Sutton. "That was on me. I got out of position and cost us time."

"What happened in the chute? You looked a hundred miles away."

"I got sidetracked for a minute." He couldn't even tell his best friend about the crazy fear that seized him.

"The way things are going, we might manage third or fourth. Not bad for two guys who haven't competed in months." Sutton grinned. "We caught him. That's what counts."

"We did." Lane might have missed, or if Sutton had hooked only one leg, the additional five-second penalty would have cost them a decent finish.

As they trotted toward the gate, he looked for Macie and Alex in the stands, but didn't see them.

Sutton laughed. "Man, you've got it bad."

As they rode toward the horse trailer, Lane ran a hand down Smoky's warm, damp neck, not willing to confirm or deny his friend's claim. At the least, he was "smitten," as Uncle Monte would say. Not that it did Lane any good. Not when he must keep his feelings for Macie from exploding and raining down sunshine and roses over the two of them.

Sutton gestured toward the trailer with his chin. "Your buckle bunny awaits."

"Watch your mouth." His friend used the term for a woman who followed the cowboys on the rodeo circuit to tease, but it gnawed at Lane to hear anyone, even his best friend, mock her.

"Macie is no buckle bunny."

Sutton simply laughed and shook his head. "I said it once already. You've got it bad."

Macie and Alex stood at the trailer, smiles on their faces. Alex's glance bounced between them. "That steer didn't have a chance, did he? Did you win?"

Lane dismounted and laid a hand on the boy's shoulder. "Not this time, buddy."

"I couldn't keep him still." Macie rubbed her ear. "His cheers wore out my eardrum."

"Aw, you cheered, too, Mom."

"Come on, Alex. Let's get these horses unsaddled and ready to go home." Sutton grabbed Smoky's reins and shot Lane a smug grin before leading the animals away. Often a grouch around children, Sutton's clumsy matchmaking attempt spoke volumes about his friendship.

Shouts from the arena filled the air with the loudspeaker announcement of the latest competitors's time. Afterward, the seconds ground on like a millstone. At least he and Macie weren't alone. Plenty of people wandered the area. If only she didn't stand there wearing that look of anticipation. Was she waiting for him to say something inspired? Something like, "I can't imagine wanting anyone else here tonight. You look like the answer to a prayer I haven't dared to pray."

He couldn't say that. Not out loud.

Finally, his mouth moved. "So, you cheered for us?"

"Who else would I cheer for?"

"I don't know. You could have found a tall, good-looking cowboy to focus on."

Oh, fine, Becker. Nothing like spouting a provocative statement.

"I did. That Sutton is a real lady killer."

She'd spoken with enthusiasm and a straight face. Lane's eyebrows shot up before he could stop them.

Macie gently jabbed an elbow in his side and laughed. "I'm kidding."

"I guess I deserved that."

"I'll admit, I enjoyed watching the two of you. I don't understand the timing of tossing that loop, but your skill impressed me." She glanced around the parking area. "That doesn't mean I don't think what you're doing isn't chancy. I saw your horse veer off. What if he'd gone one way, while you went the other? You could have landed on that steer's horns."

The cautious Macie had returned. Rather than argue "what ifs," Lane moved closer and lowered his voice. "You know, as far as chances that could leave a rider separated from his horse, you don't have a leg to stand on, Goldie."

Macie drew back. "What are you talking about?"

"You never mentioned you used to barrel race." His index finger sliced the air in the cloverleaf pattern of a horse running the barrels.

Her eyes grew as round as the wheels on his trailer. "Who told you that?"

Lane couldn't stop the cocky grin. "Alex said you have the ribbons to prove it."

"I never showed . . ." She shrugged. "He must have seen them packed away in a box when we moved. I should have tossed them years ago."

"But you didn't."

"No." She toed the gravel. "I competed in local, amateur shows. For fun."

"I understand that's not all you did . . . for fun."

"It sounds like my son is spreading tall tales about me. Okay, I also played softball in school and never missed the church's youth ski trip."

"What about the dirt bikes?"

She crossed her arms. "Only certain people are privy to that information. I wonder which one of Alex's uncles ratted me out."

He'd had his doubts about Alex's story. "Then he was right in saying you competed in motocross."

"No racing." She tucked her chin and mumbled, "Not officially."

Lane laughed. "You're trying a little too hard to play down your involvement in adventurous activities."

She huffed, but playfully. "Fine. I was strong-willed and ready to do whatever my three brothers did. As a tomboy and the youngest of four, I needed little persuasion to get on the bike. Afterward, my competitive streak took over."

"You know, if Monte were hearing this, he would call you a daredevil."

"He refers to you that way." A frown signaled a shift in her mood. "We are nothing alike in that area, Lane, not anymore. I'm a recovered daredevil."

Since her husband's death?

Funny the difference in their reactions to tragedy. He continued to take on challenges. The only difference being he no longer pushed others to follow in his footsteps, thinking he knew best. Macie backed away from anything with a hint of risk.

He rubbed the scar on his hand. "Our interests should be a choice, not based on what others talk us into."

She watched Alex help Sutton at the back of the trailer. "You're right. Trying to change someone never works out."

Her words hit too close to home.

Lane's phone played the newest country song he'd downloaded. He pulled it from the holder on his hip and eyed the caller's ID, grateful for the interruption to what had become an uncomfortable conversation. "Excuse me, Macie. This can't wait."

"I'll check on Alex."

He moved to a quieter place and hit the talk button. "Becker."

"This is Sheila Kraus."

"Yes, ma'am. I assume you've received the information I sent." Lane prepared himself for her response. He hadn't let himself presume his center would gain the businesswoman's support.

"Your plans for Healing Springs impressed me, Lane. It's obvious you're undertaking a worthwhile mission."

He released a pent-up breath. One hurdle jumped.

They agreed on a time to meet Tuesday for a tour, then Lane returned to the trailer, finding the efficient Sutton had everything nearly ready to go. Good thing, too, based on the clouds building on the horizon.

Fourteen

On the drive home from the arena, Macie sat next to Alex in the back seat of Lane's truck, leaving the more spacious area up front for Sutton to stretch out. Through the window, she studied the clouds building toward the northwest. They ran the gradient from dove gray to gunmetal.

Focused on drawing in his sketchbook, Alex paid no attention to the weather. Macie tilted toward him, angled to view various scenes from the team roping event—the steers, the horses, the cowboys. Alex even drew himself helping Sutton brush Smoky and Rocket. His talent amazed her.

Ever since she'd agreed to let him attend today's event, he had been more open with her. He showed her his drawings and talked nonstop about his "work" around the ranch. He told her about learning to identify animal tracks and the wilderness survival tidbits Lane provided. Seeing his excitement sparked her

143

own. Maybe the move here hadn't been a terrible decision on her part.

With another peek out the window, she silently willed Lane to drive a little faster. Her son had enjoyed today's outing. Even though she'd worried over the men's safety, she had enjoyed the time too. What a shame if the memory were ruined by a storm.

As the afternoon darkened, thunder rumbled over the sound of the vehicle's wheels and Macie's pulse sprinted. Once they reached the barn, she hopped from the truck. "Come on, Alex, let's get home."

"I can't go until I feed Jasper. Lane says the care of the horses comes before anything else. Jasper is my responsibility." He entered the barn without seeming to smell the approaching rain or see the lightning streak through the western sky.

Alex tended the therapy horse as if he owned him. Along with the work, her son had gained more confidence and ease around people. Wasn't that what she had hoped for in coming to Hidden Veil?

Busy unloading the horses, Lane and Sutton probably hadn't heard Alex over the clamor of opening the trailer's rear door, and the horseshoes that clanked on the metal ramp as the animals backed onto the gravel drive.

The ground shook with another roll of thunder. Alex's steps faltered in the aisle as he left the feed room. After a slight pause, he continued to Jasper's stall, carrying a plastic bucket. Macie observed his posture, the fingers wrapped around the bucket's handle—anything that revealed a sign of anxiety. He appeared calm . . . on the outside, anyway.

While Sutton led his horse to his own trailer, Lane backed his horse trailer under the open lean-to at the other side of the barn. A raindrop hit the top of Macie's head and another plopped into the dirt at her feet. She stood at the edge of the building as if able to guard the area against the coming storm.

Too soon, the clouds dumped their moisture, and she hurried into the building. Rain drummed the metal roof as she marched down the aisle. Trapped until the weather moved on, she needed to be at her child's side.

Alex stood in Jasper's stall. He rose on his tiptoes, his hands on the stall door as he peered through the wide-open sliding doors at the back of the barn. A curtain of rain obscured the landscape. Hopefully, Lane and Sutton had taken shelter.

"It's all right, honey. It's only rain."

He looked at her as though her voice reminded him she was there. A tentative grin couldn't dispel the shadow of fear in his eyes. "I know. I'm okay."

"Sutton, wait!"

At Lane's shout, Macie turned to the front of the barn. Sutton slid to a stop on the concrete aisle, wearing sopped clothing. A puddle formed under his muddy boots.

Alex's gasp produced a familiar croak.

Macie stepped into the line of sight between Sutton and her son. It was too late. "Alex."

The men whispered behind her before their voices disappeared. She assumed Lane had urged Sutton out of sight, probably dragged him into either the feed or tack rooms. Poor Alex. How long would it be before everyone in Hidden Veil knew of his problem?

Her son inched closer to Jasper, so close that they looked

fused together. The gelding remained calm and motionless as her son intertwined his fingers into the Appaloosa's mane and held tight. Alex remained still, his eyes closed. At least he inhaled deep breaths.

Macie grabbed the bolt on the stall door, but kept her feet planted on the concrete when Lane's words rushed back to her: *Give Alex a chance to trust him.* She pressed her lips into a tight seam to hold back words of guidance.

Within seconds, Alex's chest expanded and his shoulders relaxed. He released the horse's mane and leaned his forehead against the animal's withers.

"Honey?"

"I'm okay, Mom." He twisted to look over his shoulder. His timid smile provided her with a smidgen of reassurance. In the past, it had taken hours for him to smile again. "It was only Mr. Sutton."

She nodded. "Yes."

"I wasn't too scared."

"You did great, buddy." Macie curbed the urge to rush into the stall and pull him into a hug. She feared it would interrupt his desire to speak of the anxiety attack.

"I wanted to be brave, like the soldiers who'll come here pretty soon."

"You were." Even as he spoke of bravery, she spotted the quiver in his bottom lip, which enhanced the quiver of her own.

Macie once flippantly stated that God had a bizarre sense of humor. Now, with the help of the Beckers—and Jasper—she saw this stay on Crooked Creek as part of His brilliant plan. His love in action for her and for Alex.

Her precious child ran his hand over Jasper's side. "He's been laying down in the stall. I'd better brush these shavings off of him."

While her son worked, she walked toward the front of the barn and peeked into the feed room.

"We're in here." At Lane's words, she turned to find the men standing in the tack room.

Sutton stood against a side wall with his hand fisted so tight around a sealed can of soda she expected it to burst. His nostrils flared, and she imagined the damage done with the grinding of his teeth. "Sorry, Macie."

"It's not your fault. You didn't know."

He glared at Lane. "Think I can get out of here now?"

Lane glanced at her. She nodded.

Sutton stopped in the doorway and peered down the aisle before his long-legged, purposeful strides carried him into the evening. He slopped through the puddles. A door slammed, and in no time, his truck rolled down the drive to the road, spitting gravel in the air.

As Macie shook her head, Lane said, "Don't worry about Sutton. He has his own issues. I'm sorry I didn't catch him in time to warn him."

"I can't believe what happened. You introduced Alex to Jasper, and he used his relationship with the horse to calm his fear."

Lane's grin lit the room. "That's great, Goldie." He stepped forward, his arms wide and welcoming.

Macie stepped into them, cuddling against his wet clothes. "Thank you."

He rested his chin on the top of her head. "It was all on Alex and Jasper."

She could have stayed in Lane's embrace forever, feeling the warmth of his body and the beating of his heart. When he moved, she raised her face to find him staring down at her, his gaze revealing the same longing that thrummed through her.

His large hands enveloped the sides of her face. Then he dipped his head, his lips meeting hers—gentle and relaxed, then bold and possessive. The kiss fried her mind and body with emotions and reactions she hadn't experienced in so long. She never wanted this moment to end.

Selena's new foal released a high-pitched whinny from a nearby stall, and his mother echoed the cry. Lane jerked and pulled back. He ran his hands through his hair as if that were the only reason he had originally raised his arms. "Sorry, Macie. That was uncalled for. I got caught up in the celebration."

Before she could protest his apology, he slid past her, walked out the door, across the aisle, and into the feed room. She stood alone in the small tack room with the smell of leather and horse sweat surrounding her. Heat raced up her neck and into her face.

Macie wadded her disappointment into a little ball and tossed it in the nearby trash can, then walked out of the room to escort Alex home. Halfway down the aisle, her phone buzzed. She pulled it from her pocket. "Hello?"

"Mrs. Newman, this is Gene Locke."

The druggist from the disastrous interview? She shot a glance at the feed room where Lane rattled around, filling buckets with horse feed. "Yes?"

"I've been thinking about our meeting a couple of weeks ago. I was a little hasty that day, what with Lane coming in the place and all."

"We both know that was my fault." Her stomach sank like a torpedoed battleship as the most logical reason for Mr. Locke's call entered her mind.

"If you're still interested in managing the soda fountain, I'd like to talk again. Maybe Monday morning at nine?"

Macie eyed Jasper's stall when Alex opened the door and said goodnight to the horse. Getting her son away from Lane's influence had been her plan for the past month. But changing jobs now meant leaving Crooked Creek and the gentle persuasion that had won over her opposition to everything the place stood for. Her son's attempted management of the latest attack caused her to see merit in the compassionate horseman's vision for his ranch. She had brought Alex here, hoping for the result she had witnessed tonight. How could she take him away now?

"Mrs. Newman?"

What should she do?

She watched as Lane went from one stall to another, dumping feed into buckets and whispering sweet nothings to the horses. Whether for good or bad, the words tumbled out. "I appreciate your offer, but I'm staying at Crooked Creek." For now.

"Well, let me know if you change your mind."

"I will. Thank you, Mr. Locke."

A few minutes later, once they had returned to the cabin, Macie sent Alex upstairs to take a bath. She sank onto the sofa and leaned her head against the back with her eyes closed. What an emotional day!

Despite his pulling away earlier, Lane cared what happened to her and to Alex. He'd made it clear he wanted them both to find healing. Tonight, they each took a step in the right direction. Alex still had a long road ahead of him. Yet, for the first time in a long time, it felt as if she had turned a corner in her own life.

Macie tugged at the wedding band, moving it back and forth on her finger, not quite passing the knuckle. Despite a remnant of hesitation over the usefulness of prayer, she closed her eyes. *Lord, please let this decision to stay lead to an avenue of hope and not a dead-end alley.*

Lane paused after hammering a stud in place. He swiped his arm over his damp forehead and reached for the bottled water on the floor beside him.

The high temperature nearly baked him. No breeze in the shed—the new office—meant he and his buddies may as well have stuffed the wood stove full of burning tinder.

He swigged the water and scanned the skeleton walls that would enclose Ron's office and the new bathroom beside it. By the time they finished renovating the space, no one outside Hidden Veil would know it had been a storage and tool shed. His uncle griped about lugging many of the items to his cattle barn. Of course, Monte conveniently forgot that most of the possessions belonged to him, anyway.

During a break in the hammering, Lane turned to his friends. "I can't thank y'all enough for giving up your Sunday afternoon to help."

Sutton scoffed. "What am I giving up? To me, this is paradise."

"Yeah." Paul chuckled. "If I wasn't here helping you, I'd be working my way down a never-ending honey-do list."

Lane had no problem with a honey-do list if it came from the right honey. Preferably one with an oval face and sun-streaked golden hair that tumbled over her shoulders and down her back.

He blinked and blocked Macie's image from his mind. Last night was a close call, not only for Alex, but for him. How did wrapping her in his arms and kissing her like there was no tomorrow figure into keeping things between them professional?

Simple. It didn't.

If Reagan moved on and found someone new to love, Lane might feel free to do the same. However, every time he imagined a family life with marriage and kids, all he saw was Reagan's scowl and Matt's lifeless face.

He tapped his fingers on the plastic bottle, then screwed the cap back on and set it in a corner. Boots clomped across the wood floor. Lane recognized the *clump-clop* beat. His uncle limped toward the rear of the building.

"One of these days, you need to let a surgeon fix that knee."

"Not until it gives out. I come for my tool belt." Monte eyed the one around Lane's waist.

Lane passed the stove on his way to the new counter at the front corner of the building. He dug into a large cardboard box sitting on top of the Formica-covered counter, a slightly marred scrap piece donated by a home improvement store. He pulled out the tool belt, the leather darkened and worn in spots from dirt and years of use, and handed it to his uncle.

Monte hung the belt over his shoulder, pulled the box toward him, and peeked inside. "What else is in here?"

"I don't know. I haven't gone through it all yet."

His uncle removed the items one-by-one. A jar of old screws, a can of wood stain—the walnut color evidenced by the dried streaks running down the sides—and a half-dozen wood scraps. "Looks like a lot of junk."

Next, Monte pulled out a crinkled and yellowing sheet of paper folded into quarters. As he opened it and held it in his aged hand, the paper shook, creating a rustling sound. "How'd this get in here?"

"What is it?" Lane peered over his uncle's shoulder at the penciled words written in a childish hand. Monte handed him the paper. The title at the top read *My Hero.*

My hero is my Uncle Monte. He is the bravest man I know. He was a soldure . . .

Lane grinned at the misspelling. Spelling never made him *As* in school. In his defense, he was probably only seven or eight when he wrote this.

. . . and he fights our enemees so we can be free. Soldures are the best people.

"I don't remember writing this."

Monte's bushy mustache squirmed. He worked the buckle on the tool belt. *Open. Close. Open. Close.* "You didn't write it. Matt give it to me when he was a couple years younger than Alex. It was a school assignment."

Lane scanned the rest of the sentences that praised their uncle for his military service. He stared at the signature. Sure enough, it said Matt Becker. He hadn't realized his brother paid much attention to Monte's stories of his service during the Vietnam War. Matt rarely let his interest in them show.

His uncle shifted to take some of the weight off his bad leg. "I shoulda kept my big mouth shut."

"What do you mean?"

"All those stories about the war and the job me and my buddies did over there. I shoulda listened to your momma and daddy when they said I made it seem like a picnic to you boys."

Soldures are the best people.

"I'll tell you this, it wasn't no picnic, and if I'd been half as smart as I gave myself credit for, Matt would stand here today. I ain't sure your daddy's forgiven me yet for the boy's enlistment." Monte ripped the paper from Lane's hand and refolded it. He stuffed it in his shirt pocket and hung his head. "I ain't forgiven myself."

Lane's throat swelled. All this time, he'd thought Monte blamed him for Matt's death when he actually blamed himself. Did that mean Uncle Monte's feeling of guilt kept him from having anything to do with Healing Springs? "Is that why you're against the center?"

His uncle's one-shoulder shrug spoke for him.

In the silence, Lane realized the work on the addition had

stopped. He glanced at Sutton and Paul. They looked away.

He clasped Monte's arm and led him outside. "We were all surprised when Matt joined the Army. No one more than me. I tried to talk him out of it. He'd already enlisted. Listen to me. You didn't fail Matt, Uncle Monte. I did. I'm the one who failed to prepare him for that kind of life."

Lane was the big brother, the one who should have kept Matt safe rather than always taunting him into taking chances. He was the one his parents depended on to look out for his younger brother while Dad and Uncle Monte worked hard to keep Crooked Creek going. How many times had they warned him to let Matt be the person God created him to be, not the one Lane wanted to see?

"Why do you think I've worked so hard to start this center?"

Monte narrowed his eyes. "Boy, Matt didn't come to you the day he joined up to tell you he would do his best to be as good a soldier as me." Monte pointed to the building. "Now you honor him as he deserves, but don't do it out of guilt. That weight's on my back." His uncle limped away, the gravel crunching under his boots.

Lane thought about the implication of the childhood assignment. Had Matt joined the Army because of the stories he'd heard from Uncle Monte?

He shook his head to clear it of the temptation to absolve himself of his past destructive behavior. What difference did it make? It didn't take away from the fact that Lane drove his brother to be more like him. It didn't take away from the fact that Matt died trying to make Lane proud.

What a sorry waste.

"Come on, Alex." Macie grabbed her keys from the kitchen bar in the cabin. "We'll find some quiet at the main house."

Escape from the *whirr* and *buzz* of the power saw, as well as the brain-rattling bang of hammers, couldn't come too soon. She and Alex should have stayed in town once they finished eating at the Red Dog Diner after church.

"You go without me, Mom."

Macie stopped at the cabin door and rotated to stare at her son. Something was afoot. "Why?"

Alex stood near the bottom of the stairs. "I want to help Lane with the new office this afternoon."

"We talked about you seeking permission before going off on your own, remember?"

He wrinkled his nose. "That's what I'm doing. Can I?"

Macie shook her head. "Honey, Lane and his friends were

kind enough to let you help with the arena, but what they're doing today is different. A harder project. They don't have time to babysit a nine-year-old." As soon as the last words left her mouth, she wished she could inhale her mistake.

"I don't need a babysitter. Come on, Mom, I promise I won't get in their way, but I'm big enough to carry boards or help clean up."

"I know you are." A sigh escaped, and she prayed for the words to explain that, as grown men, Lane and his friends probably weren't used to having children dog their every step. "Sometimes, adults need time with adult friends. I think you should give Lane some breathing room. Anyway, you planned to read this afternoon, remember?"

Alex graced her with the now-familiar glower. "You don't want me around him. Why not? He's not like Daddy."

Her eyes widened. "What do you mean by that?"

He shuffled toward her. "Lane teaches me the safe way to act around Jasper and the other horses. He doesn't make me do things I don't want to like . . ."

Her pulse pounded in her ears. Like his father?

She forced one foot in front of the other. Leading her son to the sofa, she sat beside him. "Alex, your daddy never intended to harm you. He loved you."

"Then why didn't he listen to me? I told him I didn't want to get in a raft. I'm not good at swimming. He should have listened to me. Lane listens to me." His soft voice wobbled and his eyes glazed with tears. "I was messing around and fell out of the raft, Mom. It was my fault."

"Oh no, honey." Macie wrapped her son in a tight hug as if

she expected it to erase her baby's awful memories. "No."

"Daddy jumped in the water to save me." Alex pulled back and scrubbed at his tears with the heels of his hands. "The water carried me to the bank before he could grab me. He yelled at me to stay there. Then he disappeared under the water."

Macie scrambled for something to help ease her child's guilt. "People said your shouts brought others."

"It didn't save him."

"But you tried to help."

"I was afraid to go back into the water." Tears ran down his smooth cheeks. "I let Daddy drown."

Her throat ached with suppressed emotion. Had Alex's experience in the barn last night brought on these thoughts? "It was an accident, Alex. It had nothing to do with your fear of entering the water again."

An accident. People suffered through accidents every day. It didn't mean God caused them.

Although Derek had hoped to instill a sense of adventure in Alex, she and her husband had argued that week over the fact that he expected their son to enjoy rafting without ever giving thought to his fear of the fast-moving water. Added to the storm that day, it was a recipe for disaster.

She swiped at the tears on her cheeks, then thumbed away his. "You were a little boy. Even if you could swim like a dolphin, your daddy understood that you going after him risked your safety. He knew you couldn't save someone his size, and he never expected it of you."

"But why was I so s-scared of going rafting, Mom?"

Macie rubbed her son's back as she considered her answer.

"We all have something we fear, honey, and it's natural for us to protect ourselves from hurt. It's why we don't stick our hands in fire or jump off a high cliff." Or encourage our children to do something dangerous.

For the first time it occurred to her that perhaps Derek pushed Alex to join him in his adventures because she no longer would.

After Alex was born, Macie justified her decision to not share in anything she deemed unsafe with the example of a couple who chose separate planes when traveling. If one crashed, a parent remained to raise the children. She could easily allow herself to be swept along by a tidal wave of regret, but to her, it made sense, even when Derek objected. Was she wrong?

"What was Daddy afraid of?"

Her smile spread with the irony. "Horses. He wouldn't come near one."

Alex's eyes grew large. "I'm not scared of the horses. I like being around them."

"I know."

"Horses don't scare Lane, either."

Alex's comment prompted Macie to add, "Remember, I said everyone fears something. Lane is no exception. For him, it isn't horses, but it's something else, something we don't know about."

She had witnessed Lane's vulnerability regarding his brother's death. In a perverse way, it was nice to realize he was no superhero. He was simply a man who felt a deep sense of grief after a tragedy he had no control over. Like her. Like her son.

"What are you afraid of, Mom?"

His question broke into her thoughts and the words *losing you* popped into her mind. They remained there with her unwillingness to frighten him more.

Pounding hammers broke into her thoughts. Did she trust Lane to be sensible when it came to Alex's wellbeing?

"We'll tackle my fears another time." Macie rose from the sofa. "Now go change clothes. I'll give you an hour to help Lane."

Seeing even a tentative grin from him was worth giving in to his request.

She had always assumed Alex's attacks stemmed from his experience with water and the storm, not guilt. During the past two years, she had avoided discussing Derek's death with him, not wanting to upset him. It was possible her silence postponed his healing. And hers?

Derek had been wrong to push Alex into activities he wasn't ready to experience. However, her husband had a point when he accused her of encouraging their son's fear through an overprotective nature, a sentiment echoed by Lane.

That didn't change the fact that neither man had been around to pick up the pieces of a troubled little boy's life. Maybe that was part of the problem. For so long, she had convinced herself only she understood how to deal with Alex.

Macie Newman knew best.

Her time at Crooked Creek had proved that she might be the one who hadn't understood. After Derek's death and Alex's first panic attack, she turned her back on God, on the therapist, her family, friends, and Eva. She had tried to turn Alex's back on the things that interested him if they might lead to any kind of physical injury.

Macie still couldn't understand why some people survived tragic circumstances and others didn't. Maybe she never would, but she had blamed God for what she lost and hadn't thanked Him for what she still had.

She closed her eyes. *I was so wrong, Lord. Forgive me. Heal us. Take this fear from me.* She paused. *And grant Lane grace and healing regarding his brother.*

Once Alex rushed out the door, Macie grabbed her phone from the kitchen counter and sifted through her contacts until she found the number she sought. She stared at it and drummed her fingers on the granite surface, then made the call.

Not only did she need the love and presence in her life of her heavenly Father, she needed the love and presence of others.

"Hello."

"Eva, it's Macie."

After a brief pause, her mother-in-law said, "It's been a while."

"I know, and I'm sorry."

* * * *

With one arm resting on the window frame and the other on the steering wheel, Lane drove his truck across the bridge leading to the barn. The smell of mud and moss and foliage along the creek bank drifted through the open window and the morning sun warmed the skin exposed by his shirt's upturned sleeves. He approached the cabin, and his foot let up on the gas pedal.

Macie sat in a chair on the porch, coffee pot on the little table next to her. She looked up from the book propped on her lap. After a brief wave, she returned to reading before he could lift his arm to wave back.

It had been over three weeks since their last shared coffee date, eight days since that breath-stealing kiss. Every weekday morning Macie sat on the porch, the sight of her tempting him to stop.

What if he hit the brakes, skipped up the steps, and plopped into the other chair? Would she tell him to get lost, or would she offer him a cup of coffee? Should he even take the chance?

The truck's tires skidded on the stones as he slammed his foot on the brake. The truck lurched at the sudden stop, and he jerked forward over the wheel. By the time he straightened and glanced toward the porch, Macie had set her book on the table and pushed out of her seat.

She leaned over the rail. "What happened? Do you have a flat tire?"

He hoped not, but it wouldn't surprise him to find he'd worn a hole in the tread with that maniac move. "No. Tires are good." *Just testing the brakes?*

How was he supposed to approach the fact that he'd changed his mind about meeting in these early hours—for today, anyway—without her thinking he was a jerk? Probably too late for that when he'd kissed her like a starving man, then ran like a scared rabbit.

He slipped the gearshift into Park and set the emergency brake. "Coffee still hot?"

She looked at him as if he'd asked her to ride in a barrel down

Morrow Mountain. "I'll get another cup."

That sounded promising.

Once Macie entered the house, Lane yanked off his ball cap, peered in the rearview mirror, and fluffed his hair to rid it of the perennial hat head. All that did was to emphasize the cowlick above his right eye. He resisted the urge to spit on his fingers and plaster it down.

He climbed out of the truck at the same time she walked back outside. They both took care not to slam the doors and wake Alex. He sauntered up the porch steps as if his legs were actually solid instead of feeling like a soft rubber and settled in the chair he'd used on previous occasions.

"Nice morning."

She poured the coffee and handed him a mug. "Yes, it is."

He sipped the caffeine, hoping to wake up his brain enough to say something worthwhile. "Not too hot today." *Scintillating conversation, Becker.*

"No. Not too hot. Not too cool. It's just right."

He choked and almost spit out the coffee. "Was that a joke, Goldie?"

"Oh, I never joke about the weather, cowboy." She added a cocky smile that had him chuckling with his mouth pressed to the rim of the cup.

Lane relaxed against the wood slats of the chair and they talked for several minutes about various topics, from the progress on the new office to the menu for the barbecue next month and Alex's latest drawings. He was glad the boy finally showed them to his mother.

"I saw the sign you installed by the road." Macie cut her hand through the air as she recited what it said. "'Healing Springs Equine Therapy Center at Crooked Creek Ranch.' I like the colors you chose, too—a soft blue and pale yellow. They're soothing to the eye."

"Thanks." He leaned forward, his hands wrapped around the mug. "It's beginning to seem real."

Lane scanned the area. Memories of Matt as a kid rolled through his mind like movie scenes—memories he hadn't thought of in years. The camo shirts his brother wore. The books he read. The American flag tacked to Matt's bedroom wall. The childish words Matt had written on that paper throbbed in his mind like a heartbeat. More and more over the past days, he had questioned the reason for Matt's decision. Even though it didn't lift his responsibility for the way he had treated his brother growing up, what if Matt joined the military because he wanted to join? What if he'd always wanted to enlist?

"What happened with your visitor yesterday morning?"

Lane cleared his thoughts and sipped his coffee. He had spent the past several days spit-shining the property for the visit by Sheila Krauss. "It went well. She left a contract that her attorney drew up. The woman is serious about sponsoring the therapy horses."

"That's wonderful, Lane. Caring for the horses must be a good chunk of your budget."

"True, but until I sign the contract, it's not a done deal. I sent it to our attorney yesterday afternoon. He'll sift through the fine print for any detrimental chaff."

"Do you think there's a problem?"

"Not really. She's a tough bird, though." And, he suspected, someone who would run roughshod over anyone who got in her way. She reminded him too much of himself in the old days—stubborn, arrogant, and intimidating. "I don't want any surprises."

"I'm sure it will work out."

At the sounds of Alex moving around inside, Lane broached a topic he had considered for several days. "Speaking of horses, Alex has formed quite a bond with Jasper."

"The horse has been good for him. I never imagined my son as a would-be horseman."

Like he had never imagined Matt as a soldier. "Would you object to me teaching Alex to ride?"

Her mood sobered as she ran a finger around the lip of her mug. "Is that why you stopped this morning? To ask me that?"

He had expected an immediate and violent shake of her head—the "not a chance" response he had seen often enough. He hadn't expected to see hurt in those blue eyes. "I stopped because I . . ." Had a moment? Realized he'd been an idiot? He went with honesty. "I've missed our morning talks."

"Me too." Macie dropped her gaze to her lap and played with a pulled string at the edge of her shorts. She twisted it around her finger. "I called my mother-in-law on Sunday."

Lane set his coffee on the table. He knew from previous conversations that the strained relationship between them bothered Macie. "How did it go?"

"Better than I hoped. I apologized for shutting her out and told her I would bring Alex for a visit one weekend." She chuckled. "We ended the call with both of us sniffling."

"That's a weight off your mind, Macie. I'm glad. What

prompted you to call her?"

"It was too long coming. Alex and I both need family who care about us." She finished her coffee and set the cup on the table and sighed. "About those riding lessons . . . Alex would like it, and I would like to teach him."

She surprised him with her agreement, but figured she wanted to handle the lessons to be sure someone carefully monitored Alex. Someone who didn't know her story might take offense. Not him. "Good."

Lane meant what he said about being glad she called Eva Newman. With that action, he recognized the growth in Macie, as he had seen it in Alex. They weren't the same people who arrived at Crooked Creek weeks ago.

In the back of his mind, Lane couldn't help but wonder if an upcoming reunion would lead Macie to a return to her old life in Charlotte.

Sixteen

Lane led Jasper from the barn, saddled and ready to ride. He handed Macie the reins. "You're sure you're all right with this?"

Was she? Macie eyed the Appaloosa. She couldn't imagine him being anything but laid-back. "Don't give me the chance to change my mind." She clicked her tongue, and the gelding moved forward with no further urging. She led him toward the arena where her son waited.

"I can do it, if you want me to." Lane walked with her, positioned on Jasper's other side.

Macie kept her gaze on the arena. "Thanks. It's something I need to do." She undertook this lesson to show her son she wouldn't always object to him experiencing life first-hand rather than through drawing pretty pictures.

She also needed to prove to herself she could control her own fear and loosen her grip on his daily activities. Within reason, of course. Always within reason. Shudders raged through her, declaring she had a long way to go.

When her hand tightened on the reins near his mouth, Jasper sidestepped. *Calm down, Macie.* She loosened her grip and rubbed her hand along his neck. "Sorry, boy."

Lane followed her into the arena. He stood at the rail near the gate and watched while she called Alex to her side. Years had passed since she had worked with horses. Even though she had told Lane this was something she needed to do herself, his presence provided reassurance, if not a bit of intimidation.

As she reviewed the preparatory steps to riding, the flutters inside subsided . . . somewhat. "Does your helmet fit?" She reached for the strap at the side of her son's face to test its tautness.

Alex jerked his head sideways. "I can do it, Mom."

Once she showed him how to check and tighten the cinch for the girth, she helped him slide his left foot into the stirrup. She tamed the impulse to boost him up.

His right leg whipped over the gelding's back, and he settled into the saddle with the ease of someone who had ridden for years. Unlike the horseman at the rail, her son's size and weight had little effect on the leather. It didn't groan and creak with the movement.

"I feel tall."

Lane laughed. "One day, you'll be ready for a horse the size of Smoky."

If possible, Alex grew even taller in the saddle.

Macie tapped his knee. "Heels down and relax your leg muscles. Don't grip with your knees."

"I know. Lane showed me what to do." He rested the balls of his feet on the stirrup and let the heels of the boots she'd bought him angle slightly downward.

After attaching the lead line to Jasper's bridle, she checked Alex's posture and showed him how to relax his hands on the reins. "I'll lead you around."

"Why can't I ride by myself?"

No way. "Because you're not ready for that."

Alex turned his attention to the man beside the gate—his mentor and supporter. "Lane."

"Nope. Your mom isn't doing anything I wouldn't do. One step at a time, Alex."

Macie shot him an appreciative grin. It was nice to have someone back her up. In fact, she might get used to it as long as ... Before her thoughts burst into thousands of paper hearts with Lane's name on them, she turned back to Alex. "Are you ready?"

"Ready."

She stood at Jasper's head and walked the horse around the arena fencing. He really was a sweet, gentle animal. No wonder her son had formed a bond with him. Being near the gelding was like a puff of air to a spark. It rekindled her own interest in riding.

Half an hour later, Macie halted the horse near the spot where they had begun the lesson. "That's it for today. Lane and I have work to do."

Alex groaned, but kicked free of the stirrups and slid to the ground without waiting for her to teach him the proper way to dismount. She'd save that for the next lesson, one she was looking forward to giving her son.

As they left the arena, an older-model Lexus pulled up to the barn. The driver exited the car wearing gray suit trousers and black dress shoes. He'd rolled the sleeves of his white button-down shirt to his elbows, and the smile on his middle-aged face exhibited an easy-going mood.

"I'll take Jasper, Mom." Alex grabbed the reins from her hand and disappeared inside the barn. The horse's shoes clacked with a slow and soothing rhythm on the concrete aisle.

"Glad you could make it, Ron." Lane strode to the visitor and shook his hand.

Ron? She had heard the name mentioned, but couldn't recall the circumstances.

"Macie Newman, this is Ron Gregory."

"It's nice to meet you." Her smile weakened. She knew that name.

"You, too."

Lane's steady gaze held hers. "Ron is the center's therapist."

Her feet shuffled backward. "Well," she jabbed her thumb over her shoulder, "I'd better help Alex with Jasper, then return to the house. We have things to do."

Attempting to repair her relationship with Eva and allowing Alex to experience a few new activities did not mean she was ready for, or in favor of, introducing her child to another mental-health counselor.

* * * *

Macie lost her carefree welcome the moment she realized Ron's identity, and Lane read her mind as if God had made her skull of glass. She was not about to allow a counselor anywhere near Alex.

Ron watched her scurry into the barn and lowered his voice. "Was it something I said?"

Although tempted to confide in the therapist, no matter how much Lane wanted to intervene, the responsibility of Alex's emotional welfare belonged to Macie. The kid proved to be stronger than his mother believed and seemed to have made progress with his anxiety, but Lane knew better than to push either of them. Macie might return to Charlotte—with or without a new job. "No, it's good."

Ron hadn't driven from the VA hospital to Hidden Veil since May. He turned full circle and his gaze skimmed the property. "Where is this new space you told me about?"

"Let me show you." Lane walked a step ahead of him and entered the renovated building. He pointed to the unpainted walls at the back. "Your office is the larger room on the left. Across from it is the bathroom. In a few days, we'll have the doors hung. Out here, we included a sitting area and kitchenette. We found an old, but decent, sofa and chair for break times or less formal meetings. I'll bring in the small refrigerator I keep in the tack room. It's left over from my college days, but still works."

Ron peered into the empty room in which he would operate and released a low whistle. "You've done a lot of work, Lane. It looks good."

"It's coming along. We'll finish in time for the barbecue in three weeks."

"I'll haul a desk up here before the opening and set up the office."

"Good. If you need help—" A large box truck rumbled down the drive, catching Lane in mid-sentence and stealing his attention. "I'd better see to this."

Ron headed toward the back of the building. "I'll look around some more."

The truck stopped at the barn, and the driver climbed out. Nothing on the side panel hinted at his business. "I'm looking for Lane Becker."

"Found him."

"I got sacks of horse feed in the back."

"I'm not expecting a feed delivery."

"Sign at the road says Healing Springs, same as on the form I'm holding." Lane followed the hulk of a driver as he strutted around the truck to the back and opened the doors. "Where do you want them?"

He read the brand name on the sacks. He had expected Sheila Krauss to provide funds for the feed, not the feed itself. He held up a finger. "Give me a minute."

Lane put some distance between himself and the driver and placed a call to Blue Ribbon Emporium's main office. Based on the noise coming from the tack room, Macie and Alex were still at the barn.

After several minutes on hold and an "It's important" to her admin, Sheila Krauss picked up the line. "What can I do for you, Lane?"

"I've received a feed delivery." The order must have been waiting for him to sign the contract. He hadn't even realized the store sold their own feed.

"Good. Recently, we branched out into providing our own brand, so I'm eager to promote it. Perhaps, after using what we sent, you'll provide a quote for our marketing materials."

"Please don't misunderstand my gratitude, but I assumed you planned to pay the bill, not provide the feed."

"That was your impression?"

"Yes, ma'am." Lane had never spent much time around corporate types, but he recognized the condescension in the woman's voice and her subsequent silence as intimidation. "For years, I've fed my horses a particular brand because I trust its nutritional value."

"And you don't trust our brand?"

He'd need to walk a fine line on this one. "That's not what I meant, Ms. Krauss. As you said, it's new and—"

"If brand loyalty is your only objection, Lane, I would suggest you become familiar with our product. The contract states that my company will—and let me quote—'provide for the care and upkeep of three therapy horses for six months, to include blacksmith, veterinary wellness calls, and quality feed.' I assure you, our product meets that description."

He'd taken the wording in the contract to mean the store would pay the bills for whatever feed he ordered. He had assumed wrong. For all he knew, she could have sent the cheapest line. He didn't like the idea of cutting corners on what his horses ate.

From the day she toured his property, it was clear Sheila Krauss was a formidable woman who enjoyed being in power. Years ago, she had proved her mettle on the Girls Rodeo

Association tour in the days before it became the Women's Professional Rodeo Association. She knew how to stand toe-to-toe with barrel-racing competitors, hotshot cowboys ... and clueless, rookie managers of non-profit therapy centers.

He had to admit that using her own feed made sense. Besides being added promotion, it would cost the company less than supporting a competitor by paying the bill for his brand choice. It wouldn't hurt him to have an open mind about using it.

"Was there anything else, Lane?"

"No, ma'am. Sorry I bothered you."

He ambled over to the driver, who remained at the rear of the truck. "Let me help you stack these in the feed room."

Once the man drove off, Ron stepped out of the office building. "Trouble?"

"Just a surprise from one of our sponsors."

Lane wasn't a specialist in legalese. That was the job of the center's attorney, who he would call shortly. Mr. Thornton had gone over the contract with the board. Lane would have the man go over the details with him, too. He wanted to prepare himself in the event there were more surprises.

"That'll do it, Alex." Lane leaned the stall fork against the wall outside the tack room. He removed his gloves and scrubbed an arm over his forehead, swiping at the sweat and dust from mucking out stalls.

"Finally."

Lane laughed. Alex had cleaned one stall—Jasper's—to Lane's five. The boy had been thorough. He even broke a sweat and managed to cover his clothes with shavings. "You did a good job."

Macie entered the barn. "A good job at what?"

Alex glanced at Lane, then at his mother. "I cleaned Jasper's stall all by myself. It was fun."

That attitude would die a quick death, but Lane kept his opinion to himself.

Macie stopped alongside her son, sniffed and, with an exaggerated scrunch of her face, waved a hand through the air. "I can smell how much fun you had."

Alex pulled on his t-shirt, took a whiff of the material, and wrinkled his nose. "Yeah, I don't smell as good as the new shavings."

Lane resisted the urge to copy Alex but hated to think how badly he needed a shower about now.

A shower reminded him of the rainstorm the night of the roping event. For the hundredth time, he wished he had caught Sutton before he entered the barn. His rain-soaked state had caused his friend the distress of knowing he had upset Macie and Alex. No matter how much Sutton groused against his siblings and vowed never to have his own kids, Sutton would never hurt anyone on purpose, especially a child.

Good had come from the incident. Alex had used Jasper to temper his fear, which led Macie to see potential in the therapy center. Maybe, in the future, she would consent to allowing Alex sessions with Ron.

He leaned the stall fork against the tack room wall. "We

deserve something cold to drink." He removed his work gloves and grabbed a water bottle from the dorm-sized refrigerator. He handed it to Alex, then pulled out two more, one for Macie and one for himself.

"Thanks." She grabbed the bottle by the top, avoiding his touch.

With a swig of the cold water, Lane washed down the dust coating his throat. He couldn't blame her for being cautious. Lately, he'd given off mixed signals. As though someone took an eraser to it, that professional line he'd determined not to cross vanished little by little each day as he argued whether it made sense to deny himself happiness because Reagan Hartwell refused to move past her loss.

Grief hadn't stopped Reagan from dating a string of losers, even if she dumped them after a few dates. If only she'd give Trey a chance. Lane shook his head. The veterinarian's close friends knew he suffered from an unrequited love for his vet tech. If Reagan stopped feeling sorry for herself long enough to discover Trey could be the right man for her, it might set Lane free to have a future with someone he loved. Maybe Macie.

At the sound of tires on the gravel, he crushed the empty bottle and tossed it in the small recycling bin. The place had become busier and busier the closer they came to opening the center, something he must learn to deal with if he planned to run the non-profit therapy center and the for-profit business as a horse breeder and trainer. He lumbered outside to find a bearded stranger standing beside the driver's door of a black SUV.

The man looked around. After spotting Lane, he stepped

closer. "Are you Lane Becker?"

"I am. What can I do for you?"

"My name is Pete Singer. I hear you're looking for people to help out when the center opens."

That was a new one—having a stranger drive up and volunteer. "Do you know anything about horses?"

Singer scratched the back of his head and grinned. "Enough to pick out the front from the rear."

Lane liked the man's unpretentious sense of humor. "That's a start, Pete."

"And I know what that's for."

When he pointed to the barn, Lane twisted. Alex stood in the opening, holding his stall fork and staring at their visitor with his mouth open. More than likely, the boy stared at the tattoos that snaked up and down the man's arms, among them an American flag and the head of an eagle. The images disappeared under the short sleeves of a sand-colored t-shirt, the same kind Lane's brother had worn. "Just lean it against the wall, Alex. I'll get it later."

Macie grasped the tool. "Go home and clean up. I'll put this away." She watched as Alex jogged to the cabin. Once he reached the porch, she took the fork into the tack room.

"Amazing how your kid did what your wife asked without arguing."

Pete's assumption that Macie and Alex were family tugged at Lane with that now familiar longing. He considered setting the man straight, but the creases jutting from the edges of Pete's eyes and the sadness in his expression stopped Lane. The tattoos, the faded Army tee . . . easy to guess the guy was former military.

"Volunteers are always welcome, especially when their military service helps them relate to the vets. How did you hear about this place?"

"From a friend." Pete's back hunched and his self-assurance appeared to shrivel. "You should know that I went through the same therapy at another place."

Macie passed by them on her way to the cabin. Lane motioned her to his side. She looked at him, brows drawn together, but she didn't protest. He wanted her to hear about Pete's experience—good or bad. "You found the program worthwhile?"

"Best thing I've done since getting out." Pete's attention shifted to the front pasture and the horses grazing there, then back to Lane. "It saved my marriage, too. My kids have been slower to come around, but I can't blame them. They're young and only now see me at my best. I'm not the man I was before my service. I never will be. But I landed a good job and am trying to put my life back together. With work, my time is limited, but I figured I could do my part and show my brothers and sisters there's hope, you know?"

While Pete might have lingering issues, Lane liked the confidence in his bearing, the steady gaze, and determination to help others. "Let me show you around."

They toured the barn and moved on to the arena.

Macie tagged along. "When did you get out, Pete?"

"Six years ago." He blew out a breath. "What I said about wanting to volunteer is true, but I gotta be honest with you. When I heard the name of the owner of this place, I came for another reason."

Lane halted at the arena gate. "What reason?"

"Ten years ago, I served in Afghanistan with a guy from around these parts named Becker."

Apprehension tied Lane's gut in a knot. How many hundreds of North Carolinians had served since 9-11? More than one man by the name of Becker must have seen service in Afghanistan.

"Did you have a brother?"

With his back to Pete, Lane choked the lever on the arena gate, hoping to conceal the tremble of his fingers. Somehow, he breathed Matt's name.

"Yeah, that was him. I came here because I figured you might be kin." Pete hung his head. "I'm sorry, man. He was a good guy."

Pete's words turned to ice in Lane's brain. *He was a good guy.*

Why had it taken death for Lane to realize Matt's genuine goodness and his own flaws?

Seventeen

Lane should have let Macie return to the cabin. Through this stranger—Pete Singer—chances were good she would discover the type of person Lane once was and how his actions had led to his brother's death.

"I thought you should know. If it hadn't been for Matt, some of us wouldn't have come home alive and whole."

Lane released his hold on the gate and spun to face his visitor. "What do you mean?"

Pete stared into space before answering Lane, as if taken back to Afghanistan ten years in the past. "About two months before Matt's death, six of us were on patrol. We hadn't seen a hostile all day. Late afternoon, we headed back to base . . . came near a village." He ducked his chin and shook his head. "I'm still not sure how Matt spotted it, but I'm thankful he did."

"Spotted what?"

Pete raised his head. "The buried IED."

Lane's stomach dropped to his boots at Pete's mention of the hidden explosive device. The deadly IEDs had caused the loss of lives and limbs over the years. Too many men and women had ended up disabled. Too many harbored horrific stories that affected their emotional health and led to a need for services like Healing Springs.

Pete tugged at one of the stud earrings he wore and said, "Most of us were green back then and tired after walking a day in the heat. One of us probably would have stepped on that IED and blown himself and others to bits if your brother hadn't noticed something odd about the ground ahead."

"Odd?" Lane stepped forward.

Macie moved with him, seemingly every bit as invested in the story.

"He shouted for us to stop." The eagle on Pete's arm bulged with the clench of his fist. "We asked him later how he recognized an IED in a ripple of sand. He told us you taught him to always pay attention, because a life could depend on it. Can't tell you how often he drummed into us that sloppy kills."

Sloppy kills, Matt! Didn't you learn that from my mistake? Lane rubbed the back of his scarred hand. How much had his brother revealed about that day on the ski slope? Lane's words and actions continued to haunt him.

"He said you taught him how to track, how to anticipate a quarry's move, to look ahead and not at his feet. He said to watch for what shouldn't be there. It was nothing we hadn't already learned, but the rest of us got careless that day. Your brother, he didn't take nothing for granted. I don't doubt, had he lived, he'd at least have the rank of captain today."

"Why weren't we told of this incident after . . .?"

"Matt refused to be singled out as some hero." Pete shrugged. "He was a team player."

Lane stood mute, his mind and body as wooden as the fence posts behind him.

"Your brother looked up to you."

Why, when Lane had caused Matt the worst day of his childhood?

A half-smile tipped one side of Pete's lips as he held out a hand. "I guess I owe you as much as him."

At Macie's touch to his arm, Lane blinked and broke free from the shock that held him frozen. He grasped Pete's hand. "Thanks for letting me know." The impassive note in his voice was all he could manage.

*   *   *   *

Macie's knuckles stung, but the pain was worth it to have heard Pete Singer's story. With his focus on the tattooed veteran, Lane never noticed that she banged her hand against the fence when he whipped around at Pete's news.

Was an IED how Matt Becker died? Even if Macie received no further details about Matt's death, she couldn't leave Lane's side when he clearly needed emotional support. Not after he'd faithfully supported her these past weeks.

She inched closer and laid a hand on his sun-warmed back. If he felt her touch, he didn't show it. The moment he learned Matt had served with Pete, his face blanched, giving the new

181

white paint on the arena fence a run for its money. Now, her fingers pulsed with the quiver of nervous muscles under his damp shirt. Or maybe it was her response to the story she heard.

Once the tour of the Healing Springs facilities ended, Pete filled out forms to volunteer, then sauntered to his car. At the door, he turned back. "I'm guessing you're as much a man as your brother, so you'll do fine work here."

Macie and Lane stood near the barn as Pete Singer drove away. Across the drive, the therapy horses grazed. Their ears waggled and tails swished at biting flies. For them, this afternoon was normal ... safe. But Pete had upended Lane's day.

Sloppy kills. Was Derek too inattentive to Alex and the river? Had it led to the rafting accident? Had her husband gotten sloppy?

"Your brother was a hero."

"He was fresh out of high school, an innocent kid who never should have enlisted or been stationed someplace dangerous like Afghanistan."

At the snap in his voice, Macie opened a small space between them. More than grief churned inside him. The distant stare, tight mouth, and stiff posture screamed of a rock-hard anger, one she instinctively knew he hadn't aimed at her but at himself. She recognized the expression after seeing it often when looking in the mirror. But why blame himself?

"You should check on Alex." Lane glared at his boots as if they pinched his feet, but something less physical caused him pain.

She really should return to the cabin but didn't want to leave

Lane after the shock he'd received. "He'll be fine for a few minutes. Do you want to—" She'd refused to let her son talk to a therapist about his father's death. Now she expected Lane to talk about his brother's death? *Hypocrite.* Yet an inner pull urged her on. "Do you want to talk about what happened to your brother?"

His biceps bunched with the curling and uncurling of his fingers. She braced herself, prepared for him to claim it was none of her business. Instead, his shoulders drooped, and he slid down the side of the metal barn to sit in the dirt, his arms encompassing the knees drawn to his chest.

Macie wanted to wrap her arms around him, coo soothing words, and comfort him as she would Alex. It hurt her to see such a powerful man on the verge of shattering.

But Lane wasn't a child. Besides, right now, he needed a listening ear more than he needed pacifying. In the background, a horse kicked its stall as Macie waited for Lane to say something.

He pressed the heels of his hands to his forehead. "I killed my brother, Macie."

The statement snatched her breath. She joined him in the dirt with her arm nestled against his. "Why would you say that? Matt died in Afghanistan." No response. "Lane?"

He stretched his legs across the ground and leaned his head against the barn wall, his gaze locked on the sky. "Of course, I didn't shoot him, but I might as well have." He pointed up, his intense gaze on the sky. "My brother and I had next to nothing in common. Our personalities and interests were as different as those clouds up there."

Macie glanced at the plump forms hovering over their heads. "It's common for siblings to have distinct personalities ... like the shapes of those clouds." She studied his face, his drawn mouth and downcast eyes. "What was he like?"

His brow creased, and moments passed as if he organized his thoughts. "Matt would spend hours on the computer playing video games or get lost in reading some adventure story. I told him he lived in his head instead of in the real world. I'd badger him until he shut down the game or closed his book and came outside with me."

"You wanted his company."

"No. Well, probably." Lane drew in a breath as deep as his memories. "You won't drop this until you get the whole disgusting story, will you?"

He believed she was being too nosy. It wasn't true, not really. With his brother's death, Lane's wounds were every bit as deep as those the Newmans suffered. "You've asked me to face my fears, cowboy. How can I allow you to hide from whatever bothers you?"

She thought he wouldn't answer until he said, "We went skiing a few years before Matt enlisted. He preferred the lodge and the easier slopes near it. I kept at him to try a harder run. Finally, I goaded him into following me to an intermediate course. I knew he was nervous, but I wouldn't let him take the easy way down. About halfway, he lost control and tumbled into my path. I swerved to avoid him and skimmed a tree. My body twisted and my glove caught on the sharp end of a broken limb, ripping it off." Lane ran his thumb back and forth over the scar she had noticed the day they met. "Sixteen stitches. I deserved each one."

She winced. After a moment, she bumped his arm. "Did you hurt the tree?"

He stared at her as if doubting he'd heard right. Then a brief, deep chuckle acknowledged her effort to lighten the mood. "It's nice to know you care, Goldie. No. The tree and my brother came away without a scratch."

So far, she'd heard nothing to warrant his bleak outlook.

As if reading her mind, he heaved a sigh. "I yelled at him and told him to pay more attention to what he was doing." Lane intertwined his fingers and poked his thumbs into the corners of his closed eyes. "I did more than yell. I knocked him to the ground and screamed that I was ashamed to have a weakling for a brother."

Macie's teeth clamped down on the insides of her mouth to restrain her reaction. Often during the past weeks, she had compared Lane to Derek. Her husband's courage, tenacity, and willingness to try new things first drew him to her. Lane possessed those same traits, but he also showed a conscientiousness and common sense that Derek sometimes lacked. His story exposed a different side of the horseman. It was hard to hear about, and one he deeply regretted.

Maybe he wasn't perfect, but neither was she. "You were injured—hurting—and lost your temper."

"I was a jerk and a bully." His throat shuddered with an audible swallow.

"All right. You handled the situation on the ski slope wrong, but maybe your brother learned a lesson he carried with him as a soldier." With her palm against his cheek, Macie turned his face toward her until they stared eye-to-eye. The beginning of his five o'clock shadow was like fine sandpaper on her palm. "Why can't you accept that? Why do you blame yourself?"

Lane turned away from her touch. "Because *I* should have been there, Macie. It should have been me in Afghanistan."

"I don't understand."

"Monte used to tell some whopper stories about his time in Vietnam, and I crowed for years about becoming an outstanding soldier like my uncle."

A sliver of understanding worked its way into her mind. "I suppose that means if you had enlisted and ... died," her head spun at the thought, "we should lay your death at Monte's feet."

His gaze jerked toward her. "What? No."

"Then why does the responsibility for Matt's death rest on you?"

"Because I made him feel incompetent. Joining the military was a way to prove himself."

"That's what he told you?"

"He didn't have to. Because of me, Matt went to Afghanistan and died at the hands of an enemy sniper."

She and Lane were not so different. She'd told Alex that what happened to his father was an accident and he wasn't responsible. Yet she still believed she should have stopped it.

"I let Derek talk me into taking Alex rafting instead of listening to what our son wanted, which was to stay home. Ever since that day, I've blamed myself for Alex's problems. I decided I could protect him from future harm by cocooning him in a no-risk lifestyle. Sounds like you tried to do much the same thing with Matt."

"At least Alex is alive."

She shook her head, stunned into silence, yet understanding the emotion behind his quiet words.

* * * *

Lane had said too much and ruined whatever good opinion Macie had of him. Her continued silence wore on his nerves. "Say something, Goldie."

His desperation seemed to get through to her. Her shoulders rose with a deep in-drawn breath and fell when she let it out. "You only wanted what you felt was best for Matt. It was your brother's choice to enlist."

He recalled his conversation with Monte and the questions it raised about the decision Matt made. "I didn't prepare my brother to handle the duties of a soldier."

A not-so-subtle *pfft* burst from Macie. "Listen to yourself. Didn't you hear what Pete said? Your brother saved his friends, and he credited you with teaching him to be observant and not complacent. You taught him to track the same way you've been teaching Alex. What he learned from you saved lives, Lane. It saved his life the day they approached that IED. I'd say he was more than prepared."

Despite the common sense in her argument, Lane couldn't get past the fact that if it wasn't for his bullying tactics, Matt would be alive. He would have married his high school sweetheart, Reagan . . . had kids. He wouldn't have needed to prove himself.

"Remember how God used the sale of Joseph by his brothers to save people from starvation during a famine? Later, He used Moses, a fugitive, to save the Israelites from Egyptian cruelty. Do you really think God couldn't use you, through Matt, to save others during a war? True, you could have chosen a better teaching method, but do you believe God can turn our flaws into His miracles?"

God could turn his flaws into miracles? "Just considering it makes me feel no taller than that dandelion growing at the corner of the barn."

"Good. I wouldn't want you getting a big head."

Her words coaxed a ghost of a smile from him. "Honestly, I never wanted you to discover the person I was back then."

"I'm glad I did." She grinned. "Now I know you're not perfect."

He scoffed. "Nowhere close." And he was not Joseph or Moses.

She sighed. "How could I see you as a bully when you've shown nothing but patience with Alex? Based on what you've told me, it's clear you're not the same person today as you were growing up."

He gazed at the area that soon would become a haven of restoration for veterans. "I'm not. At least, I try not to be."

"Instead of beating yourself up, focus on the things your brother accomplished and be proud of him."

"I am. I was proud of him before talking to Pete."

Lane stood, and Macie let him pull her to her feet. He held her hands, convinced they were all that kept him from collapsing as he thought back to that day on the ski slope. Pain and concern had caused him to lash out, but it was no excuse. "I should have recognized Matt's capability in an emergency during that skiing disaster. It's funny how looking back on an event without the self-loathing can clarify it.

"After helping me from the snow, Matt wound his scarf around my hand, over and over, to help staunch the bleeding. He told me to hold my arm in the air. I expected him to freak over the blood, but he acted calm and knew what to do." Laughter at the memory eased the weight on Lane's chest. "I took one look at the open gash on the back of my hand and felt lightheaded. Broken bones don't bother me. The sight of blood? Turns my stomach."

Macie squeezed his hands—a gesture of encouragement that emboldened him to continue. "Lately, I've been reliving memories of Matt and me as kids. Maybe my treatment of him stemmed more from my fear than his. Dad spent several years on the professional bull riders circuit. He was gone a lot when I was a kid. In my mind, as Matt's big brother, it was my job to protect him and see that he could protect himself."

"I understand."

He inhaled a lungful of the warm, still air. Of course she did.

As long as he was confessing, he'd go all the way. "One time, when I was nine, Dad put me in charge of watching Matt while he competed in a Texas rodeo. I talked him into going to the creek to find animal tracks. I hiked into the woods behind the cabin, then followed the creek partway up the ridge. I thought he was behind me, but when I looked back, Matt was gone. He was seven years old, and I'd lost him somewhere in the woods.

The sheriff and Uncle Monte found him four hours later. For a long time after that day, Matt stuck close to the house."

If it was possible for eyes to speak, Macie's eyes would have whispered words of compassion and sympathy. Words that wrapped around him like a hug. "I guess that was why I pushed him so hard. I was determined he would survive if he found himself in a position like that again. None of us could go through that fear a second time."

Since that awful day, Lane strived to see his brother capable of caring for himself in a world that tested a person's ability to survive. He'd failed in more ways than one.

Man, maybe he was the one who needed to talk to Ron.

"I've asked God to forgive me multiple times for the way I intimidated my brother, because I've never let myself believe once was enough."

"Once is all He asks of us. Any more and we diminish His grace."

Diminish God's grace? Was that what his guilt caused him to do?

Macie touched the side of his face. "Lane, you're helping me to see there's a difference between living a full life and living a fearful life. I wish I could say with confidence I was there, but I'm trying.

"I'm also trying to accept that God has a plan to bring each of us closer to Him. Sometimes that means going through some tough days. My heart tells me His plan for my life is perfect. My head, though, calls my heart a liar. I'm trying to trust that, one day, my head and heart will accept that plan—both the good and the bad. In return, I hope you'll try to see how God used your faults to make Matt into the man He meant him to be." She paused, then added, "Together, we can help each other."

"Iron sharpens iron?"

She nodded and held her hand out as if expecting him to shake on the deal.

The voice inside—the one Lane had ignored for years— agreed with her. From now on, he'd do his best to accept God's forgiveness and not slip back into self-condemnation. He wouldn't spit on God's grace. He'd celebrate Matt and see him for the man he was—a man of strength, intelligence, and courage.

Rather than seal their agreement with a handshake as she'd intended, Lane took hold of her fingers and pressed his lips to them, avoiding the ring she still wore. "It's a deal, Goldie."

Eighteen

Alex slapped his helmet on his head and fastened the strap. "Let's go, Mom."

Macie grinned as her son sprinted toward the cabin door like his pants were on fire. "I'm coming." She grabbed the backpack cooler with their lunch.

Alex reached the door just as Lane knocked. Her son yanked the screen door open, brushed past her boss, and skipped the porch steps, landing in the grass after a single bound. "Hey, Lane."

"Hey to you, too, Alex."

Jasper whinnied, and humor crinkles lined the edges of Lane's eyes. It cheered her to see the cowboy relaxed after their heavy discussion about Matt.

He held the door open for Macie. "He's in a hurry."

"I didn't think I'd ever get him to sleep last night. He's

excited about his first trail ride. It's all he wanted to talk about. Thanks for taking us."

He pointed to Alex, already mounted on Jasper. "We'd better move before he leaves without us."

The bay mare Coco stood between Jasper and Dandy, Lane's chestnut gelding. Macie held out her hand for Coco to sniff, then ran her fingertips over the snip on the mare's nose.

"I'll take this." Lane slipped the pack onto his back.

A few minutes later, the horses trotted through the rolling pasture behind the barn, headed toward the wooded hills at the rear of the property. Once they left the fenced pasture, Lane led the way down a single-horse path through the trees with Alex riding behind him. Macie brought up the rear.

The leafy canopy blocked much of the sunlight but failed to provide a cooler ride. Whatever sun broke through the branches dappled the ground of the hillside with dots of creamy spotlights.

Sweat from the humidity drew voracious mosquitos that left Macie glad she had worn a long-sleeved cotton shirt.

The trail wound through the trees at a manageable incline and descent. Sometimes, though, she leaned forward to take the pressure off Coco's back as they climbed or leaned back as they traveled downhill. Birds trilled and, unseen but nearby, a creek flowed with a quiet, comforting gurgle. The surrounding sounds threatened to lull her to sleep.

Lane half-twisted in the saddle to face her. "The trail widens near the creek up ahead. If you're okay with it, we'll stop there for a lunch break."

"Fine with me," said Alex.

Macie eyed her son. He seemed okay with the idea of being near the creek. Remembering her deal with Lane, she kept her fear at bay. "Sounds good."

She shifted in her seat and stretched her back. She enjoyed sitting on a horse again, though she'd pay for this excursion tomorrow.

Lane's brow furrowed. "Something wrong, Macie?"

"It's been a while since I've ridden. I hadn't realized how much I missed it."

"Which means we need to do this more often." Lane focused on Alex. "How are you doing?"

"I'm great." He leaned forward and patted his horse on the neck. "So's Jasper."

Once they reached a slight clearing, Lane pulled up and dismounted. Macie followed suit and spread out the small quilt Lane had tied behind his saddle like a bedroll. She opened the backpack while Alex helped Lane with the horses. "I brought ham and Swiss sandwiches, chips, pickles—"

"What? No gourmet menu?" Lane settled on the quilt next to her. "What kind of chef are you?"

She wrinkled her nose at his teasing. "For your information, cowboy, the chips are homemade, and I'm a superb chef."

Alex reached for a sandwich.

"Not so fast, buddy." She opened a box of wipes and handed Lane and Alex one each. "Wash your hands and faces."

"Aw, Mom. We're supposed to be roughing it."

"No wash, no food."

Lane feigned a gasp. "We'd better do as she says. I'm starving."

"Yeah. Me, too." Her son gazed at the creek. "I guess I should

194

wash my hands over there. Wouldn't a cowboy do that?"

"Absolutely not!" Macie covered her response with a nervous chuckle. "This is cleaner."

"Okay." Alex rubbed the moist cloth over his hands and scrubbed his face. He dropped the cloth. "Done."

Lane held out a paper bag. "Unless you're leaving a trail for someone to find you, trash goes in here."

"Yes, sir." Her son dropped the wipe into the bag.

Macie continued laying out the food, hoping she'd brought enough for the appetite that fresh air and an hour of riding had on a man and growing boy. She could eat Jasper's weight in potato chips herself. It was a good thing she'd also brought carrot sticks and a fruit salad.

After they ate, Alex sat on a large rock near the creek and drew in his sketch pad. Macie worked hard to give him some freedom and not watch every move he made.

Actually, she stood in awe of how far her son had come. Two months ago, Alex wouldn't have gone within twenty feet of the water. Then, they went to the lake on July Fourth. He refused to wade into the water like the other boys, but he didn't run from it. Tears pricked her eyes. She sniffed and blinked them away, too happy to give in to sappy emotion.

A few minutes later, he ran back to them. "Mom, guess what I found."

"What, buddy?"

"A cave."

"A cave?" She got up and walked with him to where he'd sat. "Where?"

Alex pointed to a spot in a gully several yards away. It was hardly more than a small black hole at the base of a rock outcropping. Low to the ground, anyone entering would need to crawl, especially an adult.

"I remember it." Lane stood on the other side of Alex. "Matt and I pretended men used it during the county's gold mining days. We imagined miners digging for a rich vein there."

The statement caught Macie by surprise. "Gold mining?"

"It's still found occasionally." A faraway look entered Lane's eyes. Then he laughed. "Matt and I used to come here with mom's pie pans, looking for placer gold in the creek. We even crawled inside that space when we were kids. There's little clearance for an adult to sit up without hitting their head."

"Sounds like a claustrophobic's nightmare." And a place Macie declined to explore.

Alex stared at the elongated black hole. "Can we check it out?"

"Not a chance."

Lane turned to Macie. "Maybe just a peek from the outside?"

"Please, mom?"

How could she say no to those two sets of pleading eyes? "A peek only."

"All right!"

"Great!"

Like adventurous boys, the two of them hiked through leaves and dead limbs into the gully. Lane kept his hand on Alex's shoulder as if to restrain her son from racing ahead and doing more than peeking inside.

Macie shut her eyes. *Oh, Lord, how do I handle this? How do I let into my life, my heart, another man who thrives on adventure and encourages Alex . . . and me . . . to do the same?*

It was too late for God's answer, because the question was not "How do I?" but "Why have I?"

A few minutes later, Alex jabbered to her about snakes and spider webs and darkness. "I don't want to go inside. It's too scary. But Lane said he'll show me the old pan he used for finding gold and how to do it." He grabbed his sketch pad and climbed back up on the rock to draw while she and Lane returned to the quilt.

"I never thought I would see my son restored to the boy he was before his father died. Thank you for helping him, Lane."

"You've changed, too, Macie. You've loosened your hold on him."

Lane's keen gaze locked onto hers. Her head swirled with all the things she would like to say but couldn't—wouldn't—say out loud. Not until she was certain of her feelings and the possibilities for the future.

Macie broke eye contact and began loading the leftovers into the backpack. "I've been looking at therapy center websites. Most show images and videos."

Lane added the trash bag to the backpack. "Yeah, I began working on ours a few months ago, but didn't get far. There's too much else calling for my attention, and there isn't room in the budget to pay anyone to keep it up."

"But it is important, and updating the photos is necessary. At the least, include the new therapy horses and information about the upcoming barbecue. By the way, someone needs to act as a photographer that day. Photos should go on the social media sites."

"What social media sites?"

Her jaw slipped. Was he serious? "You have no social media accounts for the therapy center?"

"I haven't taken the time to set any up."

She shook her head. Another idea hit her as she eyed the path they had traveled. "What about special trail rides for the vets and their families on holidays?"

"Those are great ideas, Macie, and I appreciate brainstorming with you. But right now, my focus is getting the center up and running in time for the first session in September. If I don't, there'll be no use for a website. Once things settle down, we'll discuss your ideas in depth." He picked up the second half of his sandwich. "Or maybe I can find a volunteer to handle the website and social media for us."

Was that a hint? He was normally direct about what he wanted, so it didn't seem so.

Macie's brow crinkled. *Ignore it and talk about something else.*

But the compulsion remained as the idea brewed. Did she have the time or desire to help the center? Her college classes had provided some experience in web design, and she had updated the restaurant website. She didn't need to volunteer to take the whole project on, just update the site for the opening. "I suppose I could look at it for you."

In the process of lifting the sandwich to his mouth, Lane stilled, his eyes wide. "Really?"

She laughed. "Don't get too excited, cowboy. I said I'd look at it."

"I'll take anything you do to make that job disappear from

my plate." With his Cheshire grin, she braced herself. "How would you like a seat on the board as our fundraising chairwoman?"

After the initial burst, her laughter withered. He wasn't joking. "Don't press your luck."

* * * *

Lane pulled into the feed store parking lot and backed into a space near the front door. "Let's go."

Alex hopped out of the cab and slammed the passenger door. Lane winced at the violence against his truck, but he appreciated the kid's eagerness and self-confidence, something he hadn't shown two months ago.

The boy led the way into the store as though he knew every inch of the building. It was much more impressive than the old location—the metal Quonset hut that now housed Lane's church.

Alex spotted the western saddles on racks. "Is it all right if I go over there to look at them?"

Lane paused with his hands on his hips. Macie had agreed to let him bring Alex, but if anything happened to her son, he'd be toast. Over the various sounds of an active business, young male voices rose from the opposite side of the store—bold, noisy, and, he suspected, unsupervised boys.

He glanced toward the back of the store where they kept the sacks of feed. Trey had recommended a special blend for the five mares and their foals in his pastures. The saddles would be in his line of sight. He could watch Alex while finding what he needed. "Okay, but don't move from this area."

"I won't." Alex made a beeline for a saddle with a purple snake skin-patterned seat and a jeweler's shop worth of silver—flashy, and more than likely, one of the most expensive saddles in the shop.

Lane looked around but couldn't locate the feed he'd come here to buy or any employees to help him. About every ten seconds, he glanced toward the area where Alex moved from saddle-to-saddle, running his hand over the leather and the suede seats.

"Whatcha need, Lane?"

He whirled around. "Hey, Bryce." The high schooler sauntered up to him, dressed in a t-shirt advertising some band Lane didn't recognize. Man, he was getting old. He told him which mare and foal feed he wanted. "Will you haul the sacks out front and load them in my truck while I pay?"

"Sure thing." Skinny as a sapling, the kid tossed the nearest fifty-pound bag over his shoulder and carried it to the front door as if it weighed less than a king-sized pillow.

Lane chuckled and turned toward the saddles. The surrounding air grew thick. Where was Alex? His gaze darted from one corner of the area to another. No nine-year-old boy. He tried to stay cool and force himself to walk, but his feet hurtled him to the front of the store. "Alex?"

Hoping to find him crouched and inspecting the underside of a saddle, he wove through the merchandise with a better appreciation for Macie's feelings whenever the kid pulled a disappearing act on her. "Alex!"

With each aisle Lane passed, the voices of the boys he'd heard earlier drew closer, but no sign of Alex. He passed shelves of grooming supplies and feed supplements, along with panels where halters and bridles hung off hooks.

He paused in the middle of the store in front of the gardening supplies and fought to calm his racing heart. Ever-increasing horrors entered his mind. What if Alex felt sick and rushed to the restroom? Or what if someone snatched him?

Visions of Matt as a seven-year-old, lost and terrified, swam through Lane's mind, and the panic rose to new heights.

"Y-you'd better put it back."

Alex.

"Make me."

"Stealing is wrong."

"Only if you get caught."

The other boys laughed. Something metallic hit the floor with a clatter as if it fell off a shelf. The second troublemaker said, "Pick it up, geek."

Geek? Lane's jaw set with his drive to save Alex from a couple of bullies. He marched toward the voices coming from the next aisle and rounded the end of the shelving unit.

"I'm not the one who knocked it off."

At the strength in Alex's voice, Lane lurched to a stop. He waited to see what would happen next.

"I have my phone. If I press this button, the cops'll be here before you can run outside."

The statement shut down the boys' laughter. Lane peeked around the corner. Maybe around the age of twelve, the boys stared at the phone Alex held with his finger poised over the display. He expected them to snatch it or respond with something threatening. Instead, they looked at each other.

Little by little, Alex lowered his index finger until it almost touched the keypad of the phone. "Put back the tape measure."

The taller one scowled at Alex, tossed the tool in a bin, and said to his companion, "Let's get away from this loser."

With an undaunted strut, they left the aisle. A moment later, out of sight, their sneakers pounded the tile floor, heading for the store entrance at record speed.

Lane's pride in Macie's son swelled. "Good job, Alex."

Alex's glance shot his way, and his ears reddened. "You saw?"

"Some of it. Smart and impressive."

The boy's face crumpled with the look of impending tears. "I-I'm just glad they're gone."

Lane laid a hand on his shoulder. "You handled yourself well. Were you really set to call the police?"

He held up his phone and pointed to an icon. "No. Mom put a weather app on my phone, so I pulled it up. But they didn't know that."

Laughter burst from Lane. "Like I said, impressive."

"I didn't mean to leave the saddles, but those boys . . ."

They reached the cash register. Lane withdrew his credit card and handed it to the cashier to pay for the feed. "They led you astray?"

"I guess. They wanted to show me something. I didn't think it would be a big deal."

"You were wrong. It scared me when I couldn't find you, and I could see your mom serving my head on a silver platter for losing you."

With his toe, Alex poked at the corner of a stained tile with a chunk of linoleum missing. "Sorry."

"Apology accepted."

Alex's interaction with those boys today—and his growth over the past weeks—made Lane realize it was possible for someone to have an inner strength that wasn't always on full display.

Once more, the incident in the feed store reminded Lane of the day he lost his little brother in the woods. As he drove home, Macie's entreaty looped over and over in his mind. *"Instead of beating yourself up, focus on the things your brother accomplished and be proud of him."*

More and more lately, he'd taken her advice regarding Matt. His quick reaction the day of the skiing accident. Sutton's assurance that Matt was more competent than Lane gave him credit for. His bravery in combat. Everything pointed to a strength in his brother that guilt and fear had blocked Lane from seeing.

It was both humbling and liberating.

Nineteen

Macie propped her elbow on Lane's desk. With her fist resting against her cheek, she stared at the screen of his laptop and blew out another sigh. How had she let him talk her into this job? Not completely gullible, she had drawn the line at taking on the position of fundraiser.

She pulled up the photographs of each of the therapy horses. Because she had caught him in mid-yawn, Jasper looked as if he were laughing at her. Although not the image she wanted for the website, Alex would find it funny, so she texted it to him. Maybe, if his phone held a few photos of the horse, he'd keep the instrument handy instead of running off without it.

Macie shuddered. Alex told her about the encounter with the boys at the feed store. He was proud of himself, but if he hadn't remembered to take his phone that day . . .

She clicked on the next photo, the small Appaloosa stood

with his head high and ears perked—a royal portrait. She downloaded it to the page and typed a brief paragraph about the horse next to his image.

It took several minutes to format the page correctly. Then she spent the next hour doing the same for the other five horses. By the time she uploaded the photograph of Thorn, a copper-colored bay Warmblood, she fought the temptation to shake the laptop. She already knew her next task, find an easier-to-use page-building plugin for the website.

Soft footfalls on the stairs attracted her attention, but she kept her eye on the computer. "Hey, would you mind bringing me a glass of water, buddy?"

"Eight ounces or twelve?"

Macie jumped from her seat at the voice of the woman standing in the doorway of Lane's office, grinning at her.

"Based on the many good things Lane has told us about you, I'm sure I'd enjoy being your buddy."

Though they had never met, Macie recognized Lane's mother from the photo sitting on the fireplace mantel in the den. What stories had Lane told his mother? "I'm sorry, Mrs. Becker. I thought you were my son."

"I must let my hair grow out." Blue eyes twinkled as Fay Becker pushed her fingers through the salt-and-pepper strands that hung in spiky lengths of an inch or two. Despite having different facial features, the woman's hairstyle and tall, thin build reminded Macie of Jamie Lee Curtis.

Mrs. Becker walked into the room. "Call me Fay."

Macie met her halfway. "I'm Macie ... Newman. It's a pleasure to meet you, ma'am."

Why hadn't Lane mentioned his mother's arrival today? Was his dad here, too? She mentally pictured each room, hoping her housekeeping met with Fay's approval.

Did she have enough pork chops for supper?

Lane should have told her of their impending visit.

"Lane wasn't expecting us, and I know it isn't fair for my husband and me to drop in on you."

Macie's thoughts must have shown on her face. "It's no problem."

"We were on our way to visit friends in the mountains. If you're all right with it, we'll stay here overnight, then come back on Saturday for the barbecue."

This wasn't Macie's house. She had no say. Even if it was hers, she would never turn the Beckers away. "The guest room is ready for company. Where is your husband?"

"Cliff and Monte took the four-wheeler to check the cattle." The momentary concern that darkened Fay's expression disappeared as she rolled her eyes. "To quote my husband, 'You might haul the cattleman to the city, but you gotta bring him back to the country once in a while.'"

Macie laughed, enjoying Fay's sense of humor and down-to-earth friendliness. So much like Lane's. "Would you like some iced tea?"

A few minutes later, Fay Becker slipped into a chair at the breakfast table, and Macie grabbed a glass from a cabinet. She looked down. Oh, no. She'd left the breakfast dishes in the sink, figuring she'd take care of them after working on the website. How could she subtly slide them into the dishwasher without attracting attention? Macie sighed. Lane's mother had probably

A Horseman's Mission

already seen the dirty dishes.

Macie poured a glass of sweet mint tea for Fay, then set the cold pitcher on the table. "I'll be upstairs if you need me."

Lane's mom caught her wrist. "Oh, no, honey. Pour yourself a glass, then sit a spell and let's get acquainted."

When the boss's mom said sit, Macie would sit.

Fay studied her. "If you don't mind me saying, you looked a bit ragged up there, so I'm thinking you could use a break."

"Just technologically frustrated." Macie brought a glass to the table, filled it with the tea, and glanced at the sink. "I'm also embarrassed that I didn't get the kitchen cleaned this morning. I wanted to upload some photos to the website."

Fay waved a hand through the air. "I understand busy. My son sang your praises for all your help with the website and the gathering on Saturday."

Not wanting to read more than warranted into Lane's talking about her to his parents, she said, "Your son … and Monte … have been good to us. It's the least I can do. Alex has learned a lot from both of them." So had she.

"I think Lane is learning from you, too."

"Me? What could he learn from me?"

"He told us about the man who served with Matt." The humor that had given Fay a youthful appearance earlier twisted into deep lines between her eyes and along her forehead. "We never realized he blamed himself for Matt's decision to become a soldier. Thank you for helping him see that God's forgiveness and relief from guilt can't be bought by good deeds, even deeds as admirable as helping hurting veterans."

"It's something he knew already. He only needed a

reminder."

His mother released a sigh. "Growing up, Lane was relentless in his effort to teach Matt to be more like him."

"Even though his goal was to protect Matt, he regrets the way he went about it."

"I know."

Macie wasn't sure how to approach the question on her mind, or whether she should, but she plunged ahead. "Fay, as a mother, how did you handle the riskier side of Lane's interests and Matt's service? What kept you from going out of your mind with worry about their safety?"

"It wasn't easy to see any of my guys take part in activities that could—and often did—land them in the doctor's office. It still isn't easy to accept. Ranching and rodeoing are not safe occupations. Getting up in the morning is a risk." She grinned. "No matter how hard I tried to protect my husband and Lane, they did what inspired them.

"Eventually, I came to realize I'd make myself sick worrying about the men I loved—and drive them crazy in the process. Or I could lay my husband's and sons' safety in God's hands."

Macie hesitated to ask. However, she sensed, through the understanding in the woman's eyes, that Lane's mother wouldn't mind. "What about Matt? God didn't . . ." Would Fay think of her as too inquisitive or tactless, maybe too weak in her faith? "I buried a husband, but I can't imagine the pain of burying a child. Don't you sometimes doubt His protection?"

Fay drew in a deep breath, and her fingers played with the edge of a rattan placemat Macie had found in the dining room sideboard a few weeks ago. "I thought Matt would always be the safe one. Then he went off to Afghanistan. I prayed every day that he would come back alive and whole. Seeing him carried off the plane in a flag-draped casket … that was the hardest thing I'd ever experienced. My consolation came in knowing my boy had a strong faith. He was ready for the day God called him home."

She flashed a sad smile at Macie. "Do I doubt? No. Do I question why? Absolutely. And that's okay, because God knows it comes from that pain you mentioned."

Macie shook her head. "I don't understand the purpose of suffering like that, or of a father dying in front of his child."

Lane had talked about her to his parents, but how much had he told them about Alex? What was the point in hiding her troubles from this woman who had seen her own?

For the next few minutes, Macie talked about Derek, his death, and Alex's anxiety attacks. "Things are better, but sometimes I still feel like I'm drowning in the fear. How does something like that please God?"

Fay reached across the table and squeezed Macie's hand. "Sweetie, since that day in the garden, we've lived in a world filled with evil, fear, and loss, a world that didn't spare God's Son. He knows how tragedy affects you and me. It helps me to remember that He had a plan for Matt's life. Who am I to stand in the way of my sons fulfilling God's plan, no matter the cost?" She ran a finger through the condensation on her glass. "It's hard to describe the peace that came when I released both Matt and Lane to the One whose ways are higher than mine."

"I'm trying to trust Him."

"That's a good start. Acceptance and the lessening of grief

don't come overnight. Lane has matured in the past ten years. He isn't the same man, but I believe he's fulfilling God's role for him."

"He still takes part in risky activities."

Fay smiled. "Our boys are not our personal possessions, Macie. God gives them to us to care for temporarily and to teach them about Him. Of course, we should do our best to keep our children safe. It's our responsibility as parents. But holding on to them as though our lives would be over should something happen is idolatry, don't you think?"

Idolatry? Was Macie holding on to Alex as if she owned him ... worshiped him? It sounded ludicrous. Yet...

"Lane tells me Alex adores the horses."

"He adores Jasper. Lane has taught Alex to pan for gold in the creek." Macie still marveled at Alex's willingness to go anywhere near the water.

"Ah. I remember those days and losing my good pie tins. Did that rascal use them to teach your son?"

Macie laughed. "I'm afraid so."

"My boys always thought they'd get rich." Fay sipped her tea, then set the glass down. "What about you? Are you happy here?"

From the way Fay tilted her head and appeared to hold her breath, Macie suspected Lane's mother had more in mind than whether she enjoyed her job. "I am."

Anticipation turned to satisfaction with the woman's nod.

God had placed Macie and Alex at Crooked Creek with people whose faith had strengthened hers. She and Lane had agreed to move on without the guilt. Maybe she had moved past the time to let go of the paralyzing fear.

* * * *

Macie fished through her purse and drew out the list of items to buy for Saturday's barbecue. Lane had specified much of the menu, but left the method of preparation and the decorations to her. Good, because she would kick and scream at pouring bottled barbecue sauce over her delicious and tender meat.

She pushed her cart down a kitchen aisle after traveling the miles to the nearest Walmart. With the exception of some lovely votive candles from In Harmoni, she knew she'd never find what she wanted in little Hidden Veil.

Lane had rented a tent to protect guests from the heat and the possibility of rain, along with round tables to seat six and matching chairs. He'd received permission to borrow serving tables from the church.

At the restaurant where she previously worked, they set the dining tables with white covers, cloth napkins, heavy silverware, and red roses in crystal vases. Golden chandeliers, dripping with teardrop prisms, cast a soft glow on the patrons seated in upholstered chairs. None of those accessories coordinated with the outdoor, western-themed gathering Lane had planned.

Macie had searched hours on Pinterest to choose the type of table trimmings that best accented clear plastic plates loaded with pulled pork barbecue, baked chicken, potato salad, and baked beans. She searched for something simple, but tasteful. Country trimmings in line with Lane's budget—most of which went to purchasing food.

She chose to place two small canning jars stuffed with white lights and greenery on either side of a larger jar holding a bouquet of baby's breath and daisies. Lane promised to make the rustic wooden boxes they would sit in. She'd asked All That Blooms, Hidden Veil's florist, to arrange the flowers in the jars and deliver them on Saturday.

After gathering everything else on her decorating list and adding a few non-perishable groceries to her cart, she got in line at the checkout counter. Her phone rang. Drawing it from her purse, she gazed at the screen and sighed. "Hello, Eva."

"Good morning, Macie. I'm calling to ask to see Alex. I thought I'd drive there next Saturday and bring him back to Charlotte to stay with me for a few days. Maybe a week?"

"I'm sorry, Eva, we've made plans for that weekend. As happy as Alex would be to see you, he's looking forward to the event for the therapy center." She explained to her mother-in-law about the kick-off barbecue. "One of the therapy horses has already made quite an impact on Alex. You should see him ride. He's a natural."

"You're letting him ride a horse? By himself?"

"I am." Macie recognized the pride in her voice. "I'm learning to give him a little more freedom."

"That's good. Maybe I'll see him ride sometime." Eva paused. "I don't want to intrude, but is this event private, or can anyone attend?"

"Well, it's for the sponsors and volunteers, so—"

"Perfect. I checked the center's website and researched other such organizations. What your employer has planned sounds worthwhile. It's possible I can help."

Eva wanted to support Lane's endeavor? A couple of months ago, Macie would have bristled at her mother-in-law's take-charge, presumptuous attitude. But this wasn't about Macie or Eva. This was about Lane's attempt to help others.

"I'm sure he would welcome you."

"Good. I'll look forward to talking with him then."

"I'll let him know you'll be there. In the meantime, I'll talk to Alex. I know he'll want to spend time with you." If he could pry himself away from Jasper for a week. "I'll suggest he go home with you after the barbecue. Does that sound all right?"

"That sounds wonderful. Thank you, Macie."

Macie teared up at her mother-in-law's gratitude. She'd been wrong to keep Alex and his grandmother apart. "Then I'll see you next Saturday."

She slid the phone back in her bag and stood rooted to the tile floor. Had she really agreed to a separation from her son? For an entire week? What if he suffered another attack, and she wasn't there? What if Eva sicced her shrink on him? The old fears built like steam in a boiler. Should she call her mother-in-law back and cancel?

Fay Becker's words penetrated her alarm. *It's hard to describe the peace that came when I released both Matt and Lane to the One whose ways are higher than mine.*

Now was a good time to seek that peace. She promised herself to call Alex every day. Okay, every other day.

There was one non-negotiable. Macie would make sure Eva knew she hadn't changed her mind about Alex talking to a psychologist.

With more errands to run and the clock ticking to noon, she

pulled into a fast-food restaurant for a quick lunch. Minutes later, she sat in a booth and pulled out her phone, scanning the list of all that remained to be done for the center's big event.

From the corner of her eye, she spotted someone standing beside the table and gazed up and into the face of Reagan Hartwell.

Carrying a tray that held a salad and a bottle of water, Reagan stared down at her, the faintest of smiles on her face. "I never imagined finding a culinary expert like you in a place like this."

"Their cheeseburgers are favorites of mine." Macie lowered her soft drink. *Great. She eats low-calorie, while I'm filling my face with a hamburger, French fries, and a soda.* "I didn't expect to meet someone I recognized from Hidden Veil."

"I'm running errands for my boss, Trey Abbott. He's a veterinarian."

"I've met him."

"That's right. At the lake." Reagan drew in a breath. "I apologize for my rudeness that first day you came to church."

And for lying about her sister's appointment with Lane? Of course, unless Brianna mentioned it, Reagan probably didn't know Macie was aware of that incident and would feel no need to apologize.

Macie motioned toward the bench seat on the other side of the table. "Join me?" She could see her momma's smile over her daughter's use of those manners she'd instilled.

Reagan scanned the busy dining room before sitting across from her. "Where is your son?"

Knowing the woman considered Lane a sore subject, Macie hesitated to answer. But why be tentative in mentioning a worthwhile endeavor or a good man? "He's helping Lane put the finishing touches on the new office."

Reagan stabbed a cherry tomato with the plastic tines of her fork as if the vegetable were the horseman. "You might reconsider letting Alex spend time with Lane. He isn't the best influence on a child. You could ask his brother . . . if he were still alive."

The hamburger soured in Macie's mouth. She studied the lines on Reagan's pretty face. If she weren't careful, the sullenness would age her before her time.

A sadness hovered over Reagan like a cloud. Not quite grief, yet more than anger, influenced the sagging mouth and hooded eyes. "I'm sorry about Matt. He was a hero."

"A hero?" The lines around her mouth tightened as she huffed. "Look what it cost him . . . what it cost us. All because Lane bullied him into enlisting in the Army."

It was possible Reagan hadn't known her fiancé as well as she thought.

Macie pushed aside her sandwich. As much as Reagan professed to dislike Lane, she hadn't heard the whole truth. Perhaps it was time she did. "When I called Matt a hero, it wasn't a platitude. I meant it. One of his Army teammates came to the ranch to volunteer for the center. He told us Matt spotted a buried IED before one of the men stepped on it. Because he learned from Lane to be alert to signs, Matt saved them all."

Reagan dropped her fork in the bowl and sank against the booth bench. "What are you talking about?"

After relating Pete Singer's visit to the ranch and the story he told, Macie added, "If Matt hadn't noticed the unusual look of the ground, who knows how many of his teammates would have died or lived the rest of the lives maimed. Lane taught him that skill."

"Why am I only hearing about this now? Why didn't Lane tell me?"

"He only recently learned of the incident himself." *And you probably wouldn't have believed him, anyway.* "He's not one to brag about his own deeds."

"Since when?"

"Since his brother died and left him feeling responsible."

Reagan bit her bottom lip. "You're a widow, Macie. You've experienced what it's like to lose someone, but did you lose your husband to someone else's expectations?"

"I lost him to his expectations for himself and our son." She explained the circumstances of Derek's death and his desire to expose Alex to exploits that teetered on the edge of danger. She stopped there, unwilling to relate Alex's problem to someone who was little more than a stranger. "Honestly, Reagan, you can't lay any greater blame for Matt's death on Lane than he's done himself."

Reagan shuffled the lettuce in her salad around the plastic bowl. "Matt's enlistment took me by surprise. Being a military wife wasn't how I saw my future."

Matt hadn't even discussed it with Reagan before enlisting? Had she transferred her anger at her fiancé, who was no longer around, to his brother, simply because he was handy?

"I've spent the past two years nurturing an anger with Derek over putting Alex in harm's way." Macie leaned forward. "Someone recently told me we shouldn't turn the ones we love

216

into idols by refusing to loosen our hold on them. Please, for your sake and Lane's, let go of the past and give yourself permission to heal."

"You think I've made Matt into an idol? You don't know what I really—" Reagan's lips sealed, and she swallowed hard but said nothing more.

Macie cocked her head. She didn't know what? Again, Macie wondered if there was more to the Matt and Reagan story than anyone knew. "Brianna plans to attend the barbecue. Why don't you come with her?"

Reagan picked up her tray and scooted out of the booth. "Thanks for the lunchtime company." She emptied the tray in a nearby trash can and set it on a shelf, then paused. Her shoulders slumped. "I'll consider the invitation."

Matt Becker must have been an incredible guy based on the fire of grief his memory sparked in Lane and Reagan, even after ten years.

Macie's heart broke for the woman, because in her spirit, Macie suspected, if she dug down deep enough, she'd find more to Reagan's heartache than the grief of loss.

Sandra Ardoin

Twenty

Standing bow-legged, with his hands on his hips and cream-colored paint splattered on an old shirt and worn jeans, Uncle Monte paused in the middle of what was now the Healing Springs office.

Lane breathed in the smell of fresh paint. It gave the building a greater sense of newness than the walls they had worked hard to build. "I'm glad it's done."

From the grunt and far-off look on Monte's face, Lane wondered whether the old man even saw what was in front of him. Nothing had surprised him more than his uncle volunteering to help finish the trim work on the walls.

"Is something wrong, Uncle Monte?"

That mustache worked back and forth. "Me and your daddy had a talk when they were here a couple of days ago."

Lane set the brushes in a jar of soapy water. "A talk about

what?"

"Seems someone blabbed about our conversation the last time I come in this building." Monte tilted his head and squinted at Lane, who said nothing. "Your daddy apologized to me. Can you imagine that? He apologized to *me*, the man who got his son killed."

"Uncle Monte—"

"He said Matt volunteered for the army the same way I did in the late '60s."

Lane scrubbed his hands on an old rag. "Lately, I've focused on memories of Matt as a kid ... things I'd forgotten or hadn't picked up on. I think Dad was right. It was Matt's decision to become a soldier."

"Maybe." Monte picked up his tool belt from the floor.

"Hey," Lane pointed to the wall. "Does this mean you'll attend the barbecue on Saturday? Macie has spent a lot of time preparing and shopping. I think it would please her to have you there."

"I reckon I could find the time. I mean, who else'll make them s'mores for the kids?"

Lane had no idea what Macie planned for the dessert, but if making the chocolate and marshmallow sandwich got his uncle to attend, s'mores they would serve.

"I just said I'd come to your shindig, Lane. Don't go thinking I changed my mind about working at the therapy center. I got no time for that."

"I understand." He winked. "But you'd be a great addition."

Monte's mustache worked harder as he peered around Lane. "Aw ... look at that there." He hobbled toward the back of the building while wrapping the belt around his waist. "Them boys got that baseboard all cattywampus. Reckon I better show them a thing or two about constructing a wall."

Nothing looked cattywampus to Lane. In fact, he had put Sutton in charge of the construction for a reason. It was his friend's second job, a way to supplement his farming income. The man knew how to build.

Laughing at his uncle's way of dodging a topic, Lane carried the jar into the bathroom to clean the water-based paint out of the brushes. A few minutes later, he entered the barn, ready to move the small refrigerator to the new office.

He strolled by the pasture and stopped. Jasper pawed the ground near the fence line. The gelding walked a few steps and pawed again before he rolled on the ground—not the pleasurable roll horses often indulged in, but the violent roll of an animal in distress.

Lane approached the fence and observed the Appaloosa. Jasper rose, bit at his side, and went down again. Dirt and grass clung to the horse's sweat-dampened coat.

No, no, no.

Lane rushed into the pasture. He couldn't let Jasper continue to roll. He tried urging him to his feet, but without a halter and lead rope, it did no good.

He yanked his phone from the holder and called Trey as he ran to the tack room. To his dismay, Reagan answered. "Abbott Veterinary Clinic."

"Reagan, this is Lane Becker. Is Trey available? I have a horse with signs of colic."

After a slight pause, she said, "Just a moment."

He jogged toward the pasture. Although Reagan had put him on hold, he didn't doubt she was hurrying to find her boss. She might dislike Lane for all she was worth, but she wouldn't risk her job or an animal's health over it.

"Lane?"

"Trey, one of the therapy horses is down." With his phone caught between his shoulder and ear, Lane slipped a halter over Jasper's head. Not eager to be kicked, he remained vigilant for more thrashing by the gelding.

Sounds of movement came over the phone. "I'll be there as soon as I can. In the meantime, you know what to do."

"See you soon."

Lane tugged on the lead, compelling Jasper to stand. They were both breathing hard by the time he succeeded. "Come on, boy, let's walk."

He led the horse back and forth in front of the barn. Thankfully, Jasper showed a willingness to move.

Trey arrived a few minutes later. He climbed out of his pickup and opened a compartment of the vet box in the truck's bed—his mobile clinic. "I see he's willing to walk. That's good."

"He doesn't have much choice. This guy is essential to the center, and it would devastate Alex if the worst happened to his favorite horse. The two of them have bonded."

"Then let's make sure that the worst doesn't happen."

A horse with colic suffered abdominal distress, so using the stethoscope, Trey listened to Jasper's stomach, then took his temperature. He treated the gelding with an analgesic and a laxative.

Monte rounded the corner. "What's going on?"

Lane shook his head. "Colic."

"He okay?"

Trey patted Jasper's neck. "I've seen worse cases. We'll monitor him, but I think he'll be all right."

Lane fed his horses properly, provided fresh water, and cared for the pastures. He did everything in his power to lessen the chance of colic in a horse. His stock was too valuable—on a personal and financial level—to choose short cuts.

It was one reason he hadn't given in to Sheila Krauss and opened the sacks of feed she sent. He'd read the ingredients on the label. While nothing detrimental stood out, it didn't have the nutritional elements he preferred.

So how had this happened?

"Alex'll cross the bridge any time now."

At Monte's words, Lane eyed the drive from the house. It was getting late in the afternoon. Macie would send Alex to fetch them for supper soon.

He turned back to his uncle. "Will you go to the house and ask Macie to keep Alex there? Jasper needs more time to recover."

His uncle ran a hand over his mustache and stared over Lane's shoulder at the bridge. "Too late."

Alex shouted, "What's the matter with Jasper?" He ran toward them, the usual smile missing.

Lane told Monte, "You'd better get Macie."

Before he left, his uncle tried to talk Alex into returning to the house, but the boy was having none of it.

"He can stay with me, Uncle Monte."

Once his uncle hobbled toward the bridge, Alex inspected

the horse. "Is Jasper sick?"

Lane flashed him a smile to relieve his worry. "Just a stomachache. You get those sometimes, don't you?"

Alex nodded, but approached Trey. "Will he be okay?"

Using the back of his hand, Trey nudged his glasses up the bridge of his nose. With a friendly grin, those tortoise-shell frames, and an ever-present optimism, Trey could waylay any animal lover's anxiety. "Give him some time, and he'll be running around like a colt."

For safety's sake, Lane guided Alex away from the Appaloosa's dancing hooves. "Why don't we let Dr. Abbott look after Jasper? I could use your help with the other horses."

Alex hesitated. After seeing Trey's encouraging grin, he followed Lane to the barn but kept looking back at the horse.

Lane entered the feed room, tugged on the cord for the light, and grabbed a bucket. He raised the lid on the plastic barrel and looked inside. Almost empty. He'd gotten busy and forgotten to fill it. He grabbed the knife on a shelf to slit open another bag.

"Why don't you use what's over there?" Alex pointed to the Blue Ribbon sacks against the wall. "I already opened one."

Lane glanced inside the bag through the jagged tear in the paper. His stomach sank. He struggled to control his voice and not frighten Alex. "You fed this to Jasper?"

"I couldn't reach what was in the barrel." The boy shrank back. "Did I do wrong?"

No, Alex, I did.

"Did you feed any of the other horses, Alex?"

"J-just Jasper."

Lane kept his voice quiet, yet his ears picked up the

underlying strain in the boy's answer.

Macie stepped into the room. Her son rushed to her and wrapped his arms around her waist. Her brow crinkled in confusion, and she gazed at Lane.

"I made Jasper sick, Mom."

Lane knelt at Alex's side. How could a boy so new to country life recognize moldy feed? "Hey, whatever made Jasper sick, don't go thinking you caused it."

"He won't die, will he?"

"He'll be fine. Dr. Abbott knows what he's doing."

"Lane is right." Macie smoothed a hand over Alex's head. "Alex, why don't you make sure Jasper has fresh water in his stall?"

"Okay." Dragging his feet, he left the feed room.

Macie turned to Lane. "What happened?"

"Colic." He walked to the open feed sack, peered inside, then reached in for a handful of the pellets and sifted them through his fingers. The smell hit his nose first, but the bits of cottony white growth explained Jasper's problem. "This is the chief suspect."

"Mold?"

He dusted off the bits of feed that clung to his hands. "Yep."

Macie examined the feed in the bag for herself. "You stacked these in this room right away. It's dry in here and you'd already put down a moisture barrier."

"Yeah."

"Do you think it came like this?"

"That would be my guess." But he had no proof.

Locking his fingers, Lane pressed his hands together on the

top of his head. "I should have checked these sacks the day they arrived. The ingredients didn't satisfy me, so I left them here while I decided how to approach the subject with Sheila Krauss. I hate Alex feels bad for something that was my fault."

"How was it your fault? It seems to me the fault lies with that store's product and, maybe, Ms. Krauss herself."

He lowered his hands. "Are you suggesting she knew she'd sent moldy feed?"

"I'm not accusing her of it, Lane, but it's something to consider."

He sliced open another bag and found the contents of that one in the same condition. To be certain, he opened one more. Same.

"I'd probably open them all and find mold." He stared at the eight bags piled on the cement floor. "Why would someone with her background endanger horses? She'd have to know I'd discover the problem."

"It makes little sense, doesn't it? Now, her company will pay a vet bill."

His face warmed at realizing his lack of business savvy. "No. The sponsorship only covers preventative care."

"Oh. What will you do?"

"The only thing I can do." He pulled out his phone, hit a number in his contacts, and asked for Sheila Krauss. As he waited to talk to the rodeo star-turned-businesswoman, Lane shut the feed room door to prevent Alex from hearing his conversation.

"I'll give you some privacy."

"Not necessary." While the woman kept him hanging, he hit

the speaker button and soft music played in the background.

The music ended. "Sorry to keep you waiting, Lane. What can I do for you?"

"I'm calling about the feed you sent to Healing Springs."

"We've already discussed this."

"No, ma'am. We didn't discuss this. I can't use your feed without endangering the center's therapy horses."

"Endangering them? What do you mean?"

"Ms. Kraus, the feed you sent is moldy."

"Moldy?" Disbelief colored her voice, raising his doubt that she'd sent bad feed on purpose. "Then why would you feed it to a horse?"

Lane couldn't place the blame on Alex when he was at fault. "I wasn't aware of its condition until it was too late. One horse is being treated for colic as we speak. You've been a horsewoman all your life, Ms. Krauss. I'm sure you have no desire to put an animal's life at stake."

Macie gave him a thumbs up.

"If there's a problem, I doubt it comes from this end. It's been three weeks since you received the delivery. How do we know whether you stored the feed properly during that time?"

"The first sack was opened this morning. I store all the feed properly. In fact, I showed you the feed room during your visit and told you of the precautions I take."

"I assure you, our feed is good, but things happen. We can't predict them."

Someone knocked on the door. Macie opened it to reveal Alex. She placed a finger at her lips, then shooed him away and shut the door, all ears to hear the rest of the conversation, his side of it, anyway.

"You can send someone to pick up the sacks or I'll destroy them, Ms. Krauss. I won't feed what they contain to my horses."

Macie mouthed her advice.

He nodded. "On the website and in our promotional materials, we list Blue Ribbon Emporium as a sponsor. In good conscience, I can't continue advertising the stores if I doubt the integrity of your products." He restrained the temptation to point out the possibility of bad press. "However, I'm sure we can come to a compromise."

Sheila Krauss let a moment pass. "And what would that be?"

He gave her the name of a different pelleted feed her company marketed, not the most expensive but better than the bottom of the line product she sent. "I've checked into its quality and believe it will work for the therapy horses. In exchange for the added expense, I'll enlarge your company's name and logo on the website." After he opened a bag and checked it out.

A sigh came over the line. "I do not believe we sent bad feed, but you've taken issue with our product since the day we sent it. Perhaps it's best for both of us if I have our attorney draw up paperwork to dissolve the contract."

His hope for her cooperation fell. But was she bluffing?

He understood her refusal to take responsibility for the bad feed. It could end up a PR problem for Blue Ribbon Equestrian, and since he hadn't opened a bag right away, he lacked proof the feed arrived at his place already moldy. "Do what you think is necessary, Ms. Kraus. Send the paperwork and I'll sign it."

A long silence answered him. Was she going to counter her own proposal? "Your venture is expensive, Lane. You'll need a company like ours to keep it going."

She said his name like the kid calling Alex a geek. Lane's patience wore thin. As it was, he'd pay an unnecessary vet bill. But he could do nothing about that. "Yes, ma'am, and I'm sure we'll work it out."

Lane waited for a response. Finally, she said, "It seems we don't see eye-to-eye. I'll advise my lawyer to draw up papers dissolving our contract."

Her inability to give an inch stoked the theory she had dumped ruined feed on a charitable organization.

"That's probably best." After repeating her words and hearing the tone that said she'd hung up, he slid the phone back into its holder. "She isn't one to compromise."

Macie attempted a smile of encouragement, but her eyes reflected the loss he felt. "No, but I'm proud of you, Lane. You were firm and spoke truth, but didn't respond to her intimidation with your own."

"Threats only bring me down to her level." And returned him to those days when he'd practiced his own type of bullying. "Although I meant what I said about not promoting dangerous products, it will cost thousands of dollars per year to maintain the therapy horses. We have small donations coming in, but I counted on that sponsorship."

"We'll look for new sponsors. If not a company, we'll find individuals to take on the responsibility."

Even amid the disappointment, a grin slid across his face. "We? Does that mean you're all in, Goldie?"

Macie's brows arched, and her gaze ran over his face. As her lips parted, she slipped a step closer.

Could his heart beat any harder without breaking through his chest? Man, he longed to kiss her more than anything.

The tenderness in her eyes burned through him like a firestorm, pulling him in and snatching the oxygen from the air between them. This sense of breathlessness was all he needed to slip his arms around her, to draw her close until the gap between them disappeared.

He cupped his palm against her cheek. "Macie ..." His hands glided upward to the back of her neck. His fingers tangled in the flow of hair that drifted over her shoulders. Drawing ever closer, the heat of her breath washed over him and—

"Lane!" Alex pounded on the feed room door.

Macie jumped back. She pressed a hand to her throat and whispered a quick, "Sorry."

Lane willed his breathing to return to normal. "Come on in, Alex."

The boy opened the door and peeked inside. He glanced from one to the other of them, head tilted and eyebrows scrunched. "Dr. Abbot said to tell you he's leaving for another emergency. He says Jasper's gonna be okay."

For a minute Lane had let himself forget he had a sick horse. For a minute, there was nothing on his mind but kissing Macie Newman.

And it felt good.

Twenty-one

From her spot next to the trunk of her car, Macie watched Lane amble from the tent after setting up the borrowed tables and chairs. They wouldn't need the covering for rain today, but the summer sun was a different matter. It already had her swiping her damp forehead.

On second thought, it may not be due to the ninety-plus temperature. The dampness might have resulted from seeing the horseman and recalling that near-kiss in the feed room two days ago. She had wanted it more than she would have imagined.

Out of habit, she attempted to twist the wedding band, then remembered it no longer encircled her finger. She'd removed it this morning and set it back in the jewelry box. Even if nothing came of a relationship with Lane, she'd learned that a ring of gold couldn't shield her against the feelings she'd developed for him.

He approached the car. "I'll get the cooler."

"Thanks." She stepped away to give him room.

He grunted as he wrestled the three-foot cooler from the trunk, his arms bulging with muscles built over years of ranch work. "What's in here?"

"Ice, sodas, bottled water, and pitchers of sweet tea." At the main house, she and Alex had struggled to get the giant cooler into the trunk until Monte noticed their difficulty. The older man might limp and look frail, but that thin frame was like his great nephew's—pure brawn. Nevertheless, she asked Lane if he needed help.

"No, I've got it."

Macie pulled out a grocery bag from the back seat of her car. It contained packages of disposable clear plastic plates and paper napkins in a soft blue to match the center's brand. Last night, she and Alex had wrapped the napkins around heavy plastic utensils and tied each place setting with jute twine.

As she followed Lane, Macie tried not to trip over her feet. She couldn't seem to focus on anything other than that physique that drew his freshly-pressed western shirt tight across his back.

He set the cooler on the ground near the rectangular table assigned to hold the drinks and glanced at his watch. "We have about forty-five minutes before people arrive. The drinks should stay cool under the shade of this tent. What about the food?"

"In the cabin. I'll bring everything outside closer to time to eat." Macie eyed the other barren tables. "There's a lot to do. Where's Alex?"

"He's in the office with Sutton and Monte."

Only weeks ago, the thought of Alex spending time with someone other than her had elicited a twinge of anxiety. More than a twinge. Now a warmth settled inside her to see how comfortable her son had become with other people in the past two months. How comfortable she had become seeing him with others.

While her loosened hold on Alex had some impact, she credited much of the change to his relationship with the horseman at her side.

During one of their recent morning conversations, Lane had spoken of Sutton's family situation. The poor guy lived with an alcoholic father and an overwhelmed, sickly stepmother. He'd taken on much of the responsibility for providing for the family, including his five younger half-siblings. The last thing Sutton needed was another child dogging his footsteps. "I'll get him. He can help me set up."

"What else do you need?"

Macie pointed to the car. "There's a plastic tub on the back seat. Inside are the tablecloths. You can spread them on the tables." She had countered the throwaway place settings with inexpensive, white and yellow-checked fabric tablecloths.

Lane raised a brow. "You realize spreading tablecloths will ruin my manly image."

"Not a chance." The words popped out before she could stop them. "I'll bring out the boxes with the centerpieces."

At the office, she stopped inside the door. Alex sat on the floor and peered over Sutton's shoulder as he screwed on an outlet cover over an electrical plug. The men had turned the space into an office and gathering spot in no time and done a wonderful job.

Macie apologized when she discovered Lane's original plan to use the cabin. He assured her the old shed would work better, but she suspected he was only being nice. He was like that.

She walked around the room. The new drywall was painted the same blue Lane chose to represent the center. It provided a sense of openness, calm, and cohesiveness.

Lately, she had wrestled with the thought of speaking with Ron Gregory about Alex's situation. No matter how attached her son had become to Jasper, she wasn't about to believe the horse had healed Alex of his problem. But was she prepared to re-visit the idea of counseling? If so, it would be on her terms, not Eva's. Not even Lane's.

"Hey, buddy. I need your help."

Alex jumped to his feet. "What do you think of our work, Mom?"

Our. Alex considered himself a comrade of the men and they—even Sutton—treated him as someone important.

"I think everyone has done an amazing job." She walked to the counter where she had stored the centerpieces. "Help me carry these outside."

Each round table held six people. Once she'd decorated the tables, Macie eyed the overall effect. Pleased by the cheerful simplicity, she returned to the cabin to ready the food. Before she reached the door, a vehicle pulled up the drive. She blocked the sun with her hand to identify who had come early.

The familiar Chevy ground to a halt in front of her house, and the driver's door opened. Brianna Hartwell bounced out.

She slammed the door shut and glanced at the tent erected between the cabin and barn. "It looks like I'm too late to help you set up for the party."

"Not at all. I was getting everything . . ." The rest of Macie's sentence faded when the passenger door opened and another woman stepped onto the gravel.

Reagan nodded to Macie, then searched the yard at the same moment Lane walked from the barn and spotted her.

Macie ran damp palms down her capris. What if she had made a mistake and ruined today's event by inviting Reagan?

She held her breath while Lane and Reagan eyed one another. If all went well, her boss wouldn't fire her.

* * * *

Great. What brought Reagan to Crooked Creek, today of all days?

It was too late for Lane to duck back into the barn. She stared straight at him.

His talk with Macie the day of Pete's visit had made some sense to him. But it didn't erase the fact he'd bullied Matt until his brother felt as if he needed to prove himself.

He knew it. Reagan knew it.

Still, her antagonism toward him had gotten old. If she wanted trouble, he would nip that in the bud.

Lane slipped his hands in his back pockets and started toward her, stopping when she met him on the gravel drive. "Reagan."

"Hello, Lane." She glanced at the empty tables. "It looks like you and Macie have gone all out."

"We're hoping for a good time for everyone." Chit-chat wasn't Reagan's strong point, so this was like waiting for the timer on a bomb to tick down to zero. "What can I do for you?"

She crossed her arms and, looking down, overturned a rock with the toe of the flats she wore. "I came to ask you to forgive me."

He'd hadn't heard most of the mumbled words, but the words "forgive me" stood out loud and clear. "For what?"

She looked up and rolled her eyes. "Please. You know what an idiot I've been. Don't make me grovel."

"You're the last person I would ever expect to grovel." It should be him.

Her arms fell to her sides. "I'm sorry. I've laid the blame for Matt's death on you."

Even if Lane found the words to respond, he couldn't speak past the shock and awe that shredded his emotions. Those chocolate eyes that once glared at him with contempt melted with watery tears.

Casting aside any leftover resentment, he drew her into his arms, hugging her as if she were the prodigal returned.

"I-I've missed him so much, Lane."

"I know. I tried to make up for the day I lost him in the woods by pushing him to learn how to take care of himself."

She pulled back and sniffed. "Matt talked about that incident once. He was mad at you for a long time. But he got over it."

"I'm sorry you never got the chance to marry my brother.

We all looked forward to you being part of the family, especially Mom." He chuckled. "She couldn't wait to have another female to talk to."

"Your mom's sweet." She shrugged. "As much as he loved me, Matt wanted to do something meaningful with his life. He'd prepared for years to make the Army a career."

Lane pressed his fingers to his forehead. "I don't understand why he kept it from us. Why didn't you say something? I could have stopped him."

"As hard as it might be for you to believe, Mr. Becker, you were not the sun Matt revolved around." A slight grin creased her trembling lips and softened the statement. "Turns out, I wasn't either, and that hurt."

"It hurt us all."

"Sometimes, he mentioned joining the Army." She wrapped her arms around herself. "I brushed it off, thinking he wasn't serious. I never dreamed he would enlist. When he did, I remained in shock for a long time."

"If I hadn't—"

"It wasn't you, not completely. Even though he often resented your methods, once Matt started his training, he appreciated the way you pushed him. He claimed you were no harder on him than the military, and that if he wanted to accomplish his goal of being a good soldier, he needed to toughen up. You helped him become the man he wanted to be, Lane."

A large lump of humility and gratitude—to Matt, to Reagan, to God—clogged Lane's throat. "I wish he'd told me of his plan."

"You wouldn't have stopped him." She pulled a tissue from the pocket of her jeans and swiped it across her eyes. "Do you know why your brother played so many video games?"

"I always assumed it was because he liked them."

She chuckled. "True, but he also said they improved his cognitive skills. He learned to make quicker decisions and increased his reaction times. He believed those abilities would help to make him a better soldier."

Laughter erupted in Lane—a sound he hadn't associated with his brother in too long. "He fooled me."

"Me, too."

At the sorrow in her voice, Lane's mood sobered. "I'm sorry."

She shrugged it off with a bob of her shoulder. "You made an easy target for my anger. Blaming you took the heat of guilt off me. It's what I talked myself into believing." Before Lane could ask why she blamed herself, Reagan glanced over her shoulder toward the tent. "I like her."

His gaze followed hers to Macie, who stood near the drink table. She gave him a wary smile. Yeah, he liked her, too. "Something tells me Macie played a role in this visit."

"She invited me. Would you mind if I stayed for the barbecue?" A derisive chuckle escaped. "Who knows, you might talk me into volunteering."

The sudden change in her attitude left Lane dizzy. "You'd be welcome as a volunteer. But are you sure?"

She shrugged. "It depends on the quality of the party."

What a relief to see the old Reagan, a strong-minded woman with a quick wit. This was the woman his brother had hoped to marry. For too long, Lane had only seen the miserable and embittered one she turned into after Matt's death. "I'll sign you up now, because Macie is an amazing cook and party planner."

"I think she's just plain amazing." Reagan pummeled him with a playful punch to his arm. "And you should do something about it."

Amazing, yes, but after receiving Reagan's blessing, was Macie ready for more than friendship? If Alex hadn't interrupted them the other day, he was sure she would have welcomed another kiss from him, so . . . maybe.

Laughter drifted out the open door of the new office, and he winced. Sutton knew to expect Brianna, but she had been a young teen when her oldest sister, Paige, left town, so he often held back his rancor toward her. Reagan had been older and, along with her parents, kept Paige's location a secret from him.

"You should know that Sutton is here."

A frown marred Reagan's face. "He's Paige's problem, not mine. My sister left town without talking to him, so I understand his anger."

Yeah, she would. "It would have helped if your family had provided him with a way to contact her."

"It wasn't up to us to tell him what he wanted to hear. We followed Paige's wishes. That won't change unless she grants us permission to tell him."

Lane well knew the strength of the Hartwell family ties. "Fair enough."

Still, he had just regained one friendship and better run interference before he lost another.

* * * *

Macie added more ice to the cooler to keep the drinks cold. The longer Lane and Reagan had spoken without raising their voices, the greater the ease Macie felt over her decision. She had taken a chance inviting the woman today, but by the hug she'd witnessed twenty minutes ago, it seemed she'd made the right decision.

"Nana Eva's here!" Alex dropped a stack of plastic plates onto the end of the food table, where the guests would line up for the buffet-style meal. He ran out from under the tent to meet his grandmother.

Macie released a sigh. Although they'd hashed out their issues by phone, she forced herself to follow her son to the Lexus parked in the grass alongside the drive. Her steps faltered at seeing her mother-in-law here, where Macie had met a man with the potential to take Derek's place in her life and Alex's.

Theirs was an awkward embrace. "It's good to see you again."

Eva studied her with a tawny gaze that rarely missed the smallest details. "You look wonderful, Macie. Peaceful. Happy."

"It's been a worthwhile move for both of us." Without thinking, Macie's gaze drifted toward the gravel drive as Lane's truck passed the cabin on his way from the main house. She turned to Alex. "Why don't you show Grandma Eva the cabin while I finish getting things ready?"

He tugged on his grandmother's hand. "I'll show her Jasper first." He ignored his grandmother's expensive dress pants and the sandals that cost five times what Macie paid for hers.

Eva glanced over her shoulder as Alex tugged her toward the barn. She grinned. "First things first, you know."

Lane parked near the tent. He climbed out, pulled out the trays of meats Macie had prepared, and set them on the food table. She inhaled the aroma. Even through the foil covering, the pork she had rubbed with various spices smelled delicious. Alongside the meat, she arranged bowls of her special barbecue sauce.

"I drove from the house with the windows down. Otherwise, I might have stopped the truck and swiped a sample."

"Hmm . . . I remember your tendency to do that with cinnamon rolls." Macie inspected the foil for signs of tampering. "You didn't touch."

His gaze engulfed her in an emotional heat. "No, Goldie, but I'm tempted. So tempted." He walked away laughing.

Twenty-two

The volunteers and sponsors trickled in. Soon, the trickle became a traffic jam of cars and people. From her spot behind the food table, Macie scanned the crowd clustered around the heart of Lane's property.

Country music played in the background through speakers Kyle had set up under the tent's canopy. Beverages in hand, people gathered in small groups in the grass or sat around tables under the canvas shade. They conversed and laughed as if they had known one another for years. As far as Macie knew, for many, they had.

Even Sutton seemed at ease, although he avoided the Hartwell sisters as if they carried something contagious. Reagan appeared to keep Lane's friend at arm's length. Whenever Brianna—always the peacemaker—drew near him, Sutton thwarted her efforts with a subtle move.

Maybe one day Lane might tell Macie the full story involving Paige and Sutton.

Reagan approached the table. "Things are going well."

"They are, aren't they? People are enjoying themselves."

"Particularly Lane." Reagan glanced at the horseman, who laughed with Jo at something Kyle said.

"He's worked hard to get Healing Springs up and running."

Lane claimed to be one-hundred percent country, but he handled himself well enough in the business world. His interaction with Sheila Krauss earlier in the week proved that. While it had caused him concern to lose a large sponsor, Macie was certain he had done the right thing.

She settled her gaze back on Reagan. "I'm glad you came. You've made him happy."

Reagan's mouth formed a sad smile. "You're persuasive, but it was time for me to stop blaming Lane for Matt's decision to join the military. If only Matt had discussed it with me beforehand." She shook her head.

"I am sorry. I know what it feels like to be angry over a loss. Then there's the guilt when we aim that anger at the person who died."

Reagan opened her mouth, then shut it. After a moment, her expression changed. "Have you moved past it?"

Macie focused her gaze on the woman she hoped would become a good friend in the future. She suspected Reagan hadn't asked what originally came to mind. Even as she grieved, Macie had held onto her anger at Derek for dying and for exposing Alex to the trauma of his death. Her son's recent ability to control his fear and her growing return to her faith had eased some of that anger. "I'm getting closer."

Lane's mother flitted from one old friend to another. His father, an older version of Lane, remained at a corner table sharing cattle-raising stories with Monte, Sutton, and Trey Abbott. As the other men talked, the veterinarian sneaked glances their way . . . Reagan's way, Macie guessed. She seemed unaware of her boss's interest.

Jo stopped alongside the food table, the diamond in her engagement ring sparkling as it hit a shaft of sunlight peeking under the tent. "Is there anything I can do?"

"Yes. You can enjoy yourself."

"Oh, I am."

"Any progress on the wedding plans?"

Jo made a face. "Gran insists on being my wedding planner."

"You don't think she'll do things as you want them?"

"I'm sure she'll do a great job. I just worry about her."

Reagan poured herself a glass of iced tea. "Mrs. Bevins had a heart attack about three months ago."

Jo was quick to add, "She's doing fine, but I'm not sure she needs the stress. Fortunately, she realizes Kyle and I want a small, simple ceremony." She looked around. "Something like this would be perfect. Not outdoors, of course. Not in January."

"You can always wait until spring."

Reagan's teasing statement earned her a frown from Jo. "No way."

The children, including Pete Singer's three, ran around the yard, playing games. Macie had urged Alex to join them. He balked until she suggested he show them the therapy horses in the barn. His face lit and he raced to the other kids.

She caught Lane's eye and nodded her head, signaling her readiness to serve the meal.

He stepped onto a platform he'd built and placed at the opposite end of the tent. "Can I have your attention?" Everyone quieted down and settled into seats at the tables. "Thank you for coming, and I hope you're having a good time as we prepare to help men and women who have given so much to help us." He paused while his guests clapped.

Lane began by speaking of his appreciation for the volunteers. He announced they would each receive a calendar with their work schedules, along with Healing Springs t-shirts and caps. He thanked those who had pledged financial assistance, calling out names and urging each to stand for appreciative applause. "After the meal, Kyle Callahan will provide a short concert." More applause, then Lane introduced Ron Gregory, who gave a brief speech. The psychologist's enthusiasm for equine therapy bubbled under a gentle voice and an empathetic manner.

It prodded Macie to consider again whether she could trust him to help Alex.

* * * *

Lane couldn't believe it. People filled the tables, excited about their mission. Almost everyone invited had shown up. "If you don't mind, I'd like to say a short blessing over the food and the center."

He thanked God for His provisions and for those in attendance—their interest in the therapy center, their help and encouragement. His voice cracked when he thanked Him for men like Matt who gave so much of themselves—sometimes, their all—to defend and protect the country. When he was done, he cleared his throat. "Now, are y'all ready for barbecue?"

As the line formed and people helped themselves to the food, Lane hung back. He couldn't help it. The sight of Macie talking and laughing with their guests occupied his attention.

"Need a napkin, son?"

Lane turned to his dad. "What?"

Dad grinned. "You were drooling."

He quelled the instinctive reflex to wipe his mouth, knowing his dad teased him. "I'm that obvious, huh?"

"You're that obvious." His dad laughed. "Does she feel the same way about you?"

"I think so." He hoped so.

Dad's expression grew serious. "Monte mentioned what happened to her husband and son. Looks like things are going better for them."

"They've both made progress. Alex has grown attached to one of the therapy horses. He'll be a fine rider."

"He looks at you the way Matt used to do. A little awe. A little hero-worship."

The words caused an inward cringe that shuddered through Lane. "I'm not pushing Alex, Dad."

"And I'm not blaming you, Lane ... for anything." His father clapped a hand on Lane's shoulder. "I spoke with Pete Singer."

"He has quite a story."

"It's a story to make me realize how proud I am of both my

sons." His father swallowed hard. "I wish I could have been around more when you boys were growing up. It was my job to teach you to be men able to function and thrive in life. Instead, I left most of that to you and your mother. It's something I'll regret for the rest of my life."

"Dad, don't you think the Beckers have waded around in the guilt pool long enough? Someone with a good head on her shoulders told me to stop beating myself up and focus on the things Matt accomplished."

"She sounds like a wise woman. Now, got any ideas about how to show her your appreciation for her wisdom?"

Eva would take Alex home with her for a week. An entire week of having Macie to himself. "Stop drooling and ask her out?"

"Sounds like a plan."

✳   ✳   ✳   ✳

After the last guest left, Eva decided it was time to return to Charlotte. Macie prepared herself to say goodbye to Alex. She enfolded her son in tight hug, not sure she could let him go. "I'm going to miss you, buddy."

He squeezed her waist. "I'm going to miss you, too, Mom. I'm really going to miss Jasper. Don't let him get sick again."

He would miss the horse more than her? Maybe she had less to worry about than she'd thought. "We'll take good care of him."

Lane shook Alex's hand as he would any other man's. "I got rid of the bad feed, Alex. He'll be fine while you're gone."

A few minutes later, Macie stood in the center of the gravel drive as Eva's Lexus turned onto the road and disappeared from sight. She trudged back to the tent to pack up the non-perishable food. The meats and coleslaw were already in her refrigerator.

As Lane folded a chair and added it to a stack of others, Macie grabbed an ice-cold bottle of water from the cooler under the table. She twisted the top and handed him the drink. "I can't decide if I want to cry or congratulate myself for letting him go."

"A week will pass in a hurry." He didn't sound any happier about Alex's leaving than her.

She sipped from her own bottle of water. "It has been a nice day for reunions, hasn't it?"

"Yep. How did you talk Reagan into coming?"

"I invited her."

"An invitation alone didn't bring her here today, Macie. What did you say to change her mind about me?"

She hesitated. Would her answer anger him? "I told her about Pete's visit."

He frowned at his bottle. "I see."

"Do you mind?"

"No, I guess not. She had a right to know."

"I also told her it did no good to turn our loved ones into idols—advice your mother stressed to me."

"Sounds like I'm blessed with a wise momma." Lane set the water bottle on the table. "So is Alex. Speaking of mothers . . . I liked your mother-in-law."

In the few minutes Macie had time to talk with her, Eva had showed an interest in helping the center. Until she committed, though, Macie would keep that information to herself.

"I'm glad the two of you set your relationship back on the right path." He ran his hand down the plastic water bottle, then wiped the moisture on his jeans. "She gave me a check."

Macie stared at him. "She did?"

He nodded. "A generous one."

She hadn't expected Eva to work so quickly. "I'm glad."

They worked together to carry the food to the cabin where Macie planned to pack up the leftovers to be stored in the Becker freezer. Frankly, not much remained.

"People wolfed down the barbecue and trimmings as if they hadn't eaten all day." Lane eased up next to her and set a tray of partially eaten baked beans on the counter. "You turned a simple meal into something that tasted like it came from a first-class restaurant. Have you thought of opening your own place?"

She had enhanced Lane's simple menu by serving an eclair cake with a chocolate ganache, as well as a white chocolate truffle cheesecake. Desserts were her specialty, and she couldn't help but show off a little. "Maybe one day. Monte's s'mores were a hit."

Lane chuckled. "It's a toss-up who ate the most, the kids or Uncle Monte."

"My vote goes to Monte." Macie placed an aluminum foil cover over a tray of leftover chicken. "Everyone seemed to enjoy the afternoon. I'm glad it went well."

"Thanks to you." He clasped the left hand she had raised, his brow lined with a question. "Did you lose your wedding ring?"

She eyed her bare finger. "It's in my jewelry box where it belongs."

Lane's mouth tilted in a grin that spread warmth through her. Or it could have been the sudden intensity of that blue-eyed stare. "Macie, maybe I'm reading everything wrong, but I've been thinking . . ." He huffed and gazed at the ceiling while her pulse stampeded and impatience roared. "I'm trying to say I want more than anything to—"

Macie wrapped her arms around Lane's neck and weaved her fingers through his hair, drawing his head closer to her lips. A whisper away from him. "Then do it."

His embrace. The gentle brush of his mouth against hers. Then a kiss—a deep connection to the man she loved. It all left her begging for more.

Twenty-three

"This is a gorgeous spot, Lane." The picnic basket with yesterday's leftovers dangled from Macie's hands as she surveyed the area surrounding them.

To Lane, the beauty of the countryside couldn't compare to the beauty of her, especially when she looked relaxed and—dare he say it?—happy.

He spread a clean tablecloth used for the barbecue over the grass and joined her in scanning the area. "It's one of my favorite places on the property. When I was a kid, we had family picnics here. The oaks and hickories lining the creek offer shade on hot days, and the sound of the water flowing over the rocky bottom lulls a person to sleep after a good meal."

Today marked the first time in over a decade Lane saw this spot and felt nothing more than a pleasurable nostalgia.

"Oh, so you plan to eat your fill and fall asleep?" Macie set the basket on the tablecloth and straightened to gaze at him, her eyebrows arched.

The teasing glint in her eyes brought him closer until he stood boot to sandal with her and rested a hand over each of her hips. "What I intend to do, Goldie, is to keep my eyes open and on you."

She draped her arms over his shoulders. "That sounds more like it."

Man, he'd fallen fast for this woman and had no desire to stop the descent.

Lane drew her closer for a kiss that lingered, igniting a heat the shade trees couldn't alleviate. As his lips moved from her mouth to her neck, his mind registered a hint of gardenia, a scent that matched her personality—sweet and feminine.

He drew back before things grew out of hand. With a deep gulp of the sultry summer air, he attempted to ease his labored breathing. "We should probably—"

"I think so, too." Macie settled on the cloth and pulled out a container of barbecue sandwiches and side dishes from the basket—food left from yesterday's event.

The sun shining on the back of her head brought to his mind the image of an angel. He glanced away before he did something rash, like say so. "Have you heard from Alex?"

"He texted me goodnight last night, probably at Eva's suggestion." Macie's expression grew pensive as she handed Lane a plastic plate.

"Hey, he'll have a great time with his grandmother."

"I know. It's just . . ."

"You miss him."

She nodded. "We haven't been apart since Derek died. I'm also worried about . . . you know."

"He'll be fine. He's done great lately, and Eva will watch over him." He pulled a sandwich onto his plate, the tangy smell of her special barbecue sauce reminding him how hungry he was. "You've done great, too, you know."

Macie attempted a smile that fell flat. "Then why do I still find it hard to trust God for my son's safety? Why can't I put Alex in His hands and realize He loves my son as much as I do? Why is my faith so shallow, Lane?"

Tough questions. *Lord, help me out here.* "Your faith took a beating, honey. It's been tested in ways none of us want to experience. That you question yourself tells me you haven't given up on God. You want a strong faith."

"I do. And I'm trying."

"I know you are. I also know God is aware of what motivates your concern for Alex." Lane grasped her hand and gave it an encouraging squeeze. "You and Pete helped me to see I could waste time and emotional energy beating myself up over my mistakes, or I could ask God's forgiveness, hand Him the reins, and trust He'll deal with the problem according to His grace, judgement, and wisdom."

Macie wrapped her fingers around his and gave her own squeeze in return. "Thank you for your patience with me and with Alex. He enjoys spending time with you. I had my doubts, but I will admit, it's been good for him."

"Then I can file away in my brain that Macie Newman said I was right about something?" He winked, unable to stop himself from teasing her.

She grinned. "Don't get carried away, mister."

"No, ma'am." Lane handed her a Cheerwine soda, then opened a can of what tasted like a Dr. Pepper and cherry cola mix for himself. "Alex is a great kid, and I'll miss him, but I'm looking forward to this week. Just us."

"Me, too."

She said it with an eagerness he had hoped to hear. He wanted much more of these days in the coming weeks and months. Mostly, he wanted to know that this sweet, caring, smart lady—this devoted mother—loved him.

He wouldn't rush her by announcing his love for her. Not yet. And not without Alex's blessing.

* * * *

Macie backed Lane's horse out of the trailer. Once the gelding was on firm ground, he rubbed his face against her arm as if to say thanks for rescuing him from the cramped mobile space.

"Smoky likes you."

She handed Lane the lead rope. "I like him, too."

Sutton, who led his own gelding out of the trailer, rolled his eyes at them.

As the men prepared the horses, trucks pulled in and out of the field that served as a parking lot, towing loaded horse trailers behind them. Men and women walked by dressed in full western gear—some leading horses, some talking and laughing with companions.

This rodeo site had four bleachers on one side of the arena, about seventy-five percent filled with people watching a steer-wrestling competition. A tiny announcer's box sat in the center, rising above the bleachers.

Maybe one day she would get used to the idea that she'd once more become someone who enjoyed the rural life and its adventures—like accompanying Lane and Sutton to these roping events and watching as they galloped across a wood-fenced arena in pursuit of a steer.

Over the past week, she and Lane had kayaked on the lake, hiked the trails that looped it, and taken the four-wheeler up and down the hills surrounding the ranch. At first, she'd balked at the kayaking and four-wheeler rides, but she put the past behind her, choosing to trust Lane and not waste time or emotional energy on a what-if scenario.

In the early mornings, they talked while sitting in the Adirondack chairs on the porch of her cabin, cups of coffee warming the surface of the small table between them. In the evenings, they walked hand-in-hand through the pastures, stopping once in a while to share a kiss.

This was not how she had envisioned her employment on Crooked Creek Ranch. She hadn't seen herself falling in love with her boss. But she had. Bold. Adventurous. A man's man. Yet Lane was kind, sensitive, intelligent. He had helped her through this week, keeping her busy so she didn't dwell on Alex's absence.

She thought his emotions might run as strong for her, but he had said nothing about loving her. Besides, she had Alex to consider. How would her son feel about someone taking his father's place? He adored Lane, yes, but did that translate to wanting Lane as a parent?

Macie cringed inside. She was getting ahead of herself. Maybe one day Lane would speak of something permanent. There was no need to rush.

"You look lost in thought, Goldie. Anything I can do to help?"

While she had stood with her shoulder propped against the trailer, woolgathering, Lane and Sutton had saddled their horses for the team roping event in half an hour. "No. Have fun and take care of yourselves."

"Will do." Lane leaned over and kissed her cheek. "Sutton and I need to check in and warm up the horses."

"I'll head to the stands."

Macie found a seat high enough to give her a good view of the action in the arena. Alex would grouse at missing this, but he was having fun at Carowinds today. She hoped.

Eva had called, asking permission to take him to the amusement park with another family. While she appreciated that her mother-in-law asked, Macie almost blurted an automatic no. The high and speedy rollercoasters were a worry, but a portion of the property was a water park. What if Alex experienced an anxiety attack at seeing so many drenched people?

In the end, in an effort to regrow the faith she had let wither, she said a silent prayer and left it up to Eva and Alex to decide. Amazingly, her decision had not interfered with her sleep last night.

Tomorrow, her mother-in-law would return Alex to the ranch. Life would challenge her fear again in the future, but she felt herself standing on firmer ground.

As she watched the steer wrestling event and listened to the cheers and conversations around her, Macie nearly missed the ding of her phone. She pulled it from her pocket, opened the text, and her heart soared. Eva had sent a photo of Alex wearing a bathing suit, his body and hair as wet as a fish, and his smile as wide as the state of North Carolina. With the photo, Eva had included a message that they had returned to her house, safe and sound.

A collection of gasps surrounded her. Then silence. Macie craned her neck to see over the man in front of her and released her own wispy gasp.

All attention centered on the man curled in the soft dirt of the arena floor, still and with his hat upside down near his prone body. A woman dressed in jeans and a western shirt bolted from the stands with two children following her. They ran toward the west end of the arena.

At the other end, a rider had roped the wayward steer. Another one caught the reins of the injured cowboy's horse. Three men on foot rushed across the arena and knelt beside the downed man.

The announcer's voice blared over the loudspeaker. "Ladies and gentlemen, please say a prayer for our intrepid cowboy, Rich Booker, as the doc tends to him." He rattled on about the man, including rodeo statistics and a little personal history, then changed subjects, probably hoping to take everyone's mind off whatever had happened to the steer wrestler.

Not a person in the stands moved, including Macie, whose heart clogged her throat. Her imagination replaced the face of the cowboy with Lane's. She saw him lying in the dirt, unconscious and possibly with broken bones.

As though trying to convince herself she'd concocted a lie—created a mirage of sorts—her gaze whipped around the fence line of the arena. She looked for him among the competitors leaning over the top rail of the fencing, watching their incapacitated comrade.

With Lane nowhere in sight, she shut her eyes and inhaled deep and calming breaths. *Please heal the injured man, Lord, for his sake and that of his family. I know he isn't Lane. I also know that, even if it were Lane lying down there, he'd be in Your hands.*

The words were brave. The courage behind them . . . not so much.

Cheers and applause interrupted Macie's prayer, and her eyes opened to see the now-conscious steer wrestler struggle to his feet. He wrapped his arms around the shoulders of the men who flanked him on each side and limped toward the closest end of the arena, where the family who had rushed from the stands waited for him.

"Well, folks, aren't we glad to see Rich leave under his own power?"

The cowboy gave a feeble wave, acknowledging the relieved applause. No doubt, he was headed straight for the nearest hospital. Fortunately, he'd take the ride in a conscious state.

As soon as the arena was clear, the voice over the loudspeaker announced another competitor. The event went on as planned, but Macie's enjoyment of the afternoon had worn off. Her heart rate settled into a normal rhythm, but she paid little attention to the remaining contestants.

Lane and Sutton's turn in the chutes for the team roping event came up. She vanquished the fear to a far corner of her mind and cheered them on to a second-place finish.

Still, she couldn't forget imagining Lane's face on the body of the injured cowboy.

Twenty-four

Lane added another riding helmet to the row of six on the new shelf he'd built in the tack room.

"I'm back!"

At Alex's call, he rambled to the doorway, staggered by how much he had missed the kid. He had accomplished a lot in the past week, but his work lacked the enjoyment of having Alex around to dog his steps.

Of course, there was the flip side. He'd shared seven astounding days and dates with Macie. Sutton had spoken the truth when he claimed Lane had it bad.

"Welcome back. Did you have fun?"

"Lots." Alex stretched to look down the aisle. "Where is he?"

No point in asking what he meant. "In the back pasture. What did you do last week at your grandmother's?"

Alex pushed past him and entered the tack room. "We went

to different places like Discovery Place and Carowinds."

"I'd heard that she took you to Carowinds." Lane couldn't picture the older woman—at least in her sixties—or Alex riding the roller coasters.

"We went with some other people."

"Sounds like fun."

"Yeah. I've been there before, but not since I was a little kid. We also went to the zoo. It didn't have horses, but there were zebras."

"Zebras are like horses." *Sort of.*

"But they're too wild to ride."

"True."

"We went to a play at the children's theater. That was okay." Alex grabbed a plastic bucket and loaded it with grooming supplies, then left the room. "Did Jasper miss me?"

Not a "Did you miss me?" or "Did Mom miss me?" His only concern was being missed by a horse.

Lane laughed. "He said he did."

Alex paused in the aisle, his expression critical. "You made that up. Horses don't talk, not even Jasper. Not really."

Lane raised his hands. "Caught me." Where was the shy kid who'd barely looked at him when they first met?

"Can I ride him?"

He should check with Macie. After that spill Rich Booker took last night, he'd been sure she would retreat into her shell of fear. But she'd taken it well, showing no sign of it upsetting her, and she had let Alex ride before he left for his grandmother's.

Lane glanced at his watch. "Give me a few minutes to finish up here."

"I'll help."

Alex worked alongside him as they finished lining up the helmets on the shelf, straightened the tack room, and carried the orange cones Ron had ordered to use in the therapy sessions to the office.

With a halter and lead rope draped over Alex's shoulder, they hiked to the pasture gate. Lane prepared to whistle for the horse, but Alex laid a hand on his arm. "I can do it. I've been practicing." He let out a soft, shrill whistle—not piercing, but loud enough.

From the middle of the pasture, Jasper raised his head. Grass hung from both sides of the horse's mouth. He and nine other horses stared at them several seconds before they all lumbered toward the gate in no particular hurry.

Alex slipped the halter on Jasper as Lane had taught him and led the gelding through the gate. Smoky tried to push through. Lane shoved him back and shut the gate. "Not this time, Smoke."

At the barn, he helped Alex tack up the Appaloosa and walked alongside the boy as he led Jasper to the arena. Once she felt comfortable with his ability to handle Jasper, Macie had approved letting Alex ride the horse without her around, as long as he remained in the arena and someone else was there to watch him. Right now, that someone was Lane since she was working.

He stood inside the arena as Alex walked the horse along the inside fencing. "We have about forty-five minutes before your mom expects us for supper."

"Okay." Forbidden to ride at anything but a walk or trot, Alex urged Jasper into the jarring, faster gait. Not yet proficient in his seat, he bounced in the saddle.

"Heels down, back straight, and hands relaxed on the reins."

Alex readjusted his feet in the stirrups, loosened his tight grip on the reins, and continued around the arena at a trot. "Like this?"

"Looks good."

A few minutes later, Lane checked his watch again. He should shut this ride down. As it was, he would shuffle paperwork until late evening. "Come on, Alex. Time to go."

"Just one more round?"

"Nope. You need to brush him down before we head to the house."

Alex grumbled but turned Jasper toward the gate, his heels jabbing at the horse's sides. The gelding broke into a canter. It caught the boy off-guard and tilted him to the left. Too far away to prevent what he saw happening next, Lane helplessly watched as Alex lost his balance and tumbled off the horse.

Lane bolted across the arena to kneel alongside the boy sprawled in the dirt. "Are you hurt?"

Alex held his arm as tears welled in his eyes. He squirmed, trying to sit up, his attention focused on Jasper. The horse stood watching from several feet away. "Did I hurt him?"

"He's fine. Let me see." As gently as he knew how, Lane examined Alex's left forearm. "Can you move your fingers?" Alex wiggled his fingers. "Good. I don't think it's broken."

"My face hurts, and it stings here." He rubbed his elbow.

"You must have landed on your funny bone."

"It doesn't feel funny."

Lane fought a grin, relieved that Alex wasn't hurt worse.

"Nope. It never does, but it should feel better soon. Let me look at your face."

He eyed the cut on Alex's cheek. Blood seeped from the wound and drizzled down the boy's face. Not enough to be concerned about, but he didn't want to make matters worse by running his dirty thumb over the damaged skin. Alex would have a scab and a bright bruise on his cheek, but the cut didn't need stitches.

Yanking his phone from his pocket, he tapped Macie's number, then waited until she answered. "Hey, I'm at the arena with Alex. He's fine, but you should know he took a tumble off Jasper."

"What?"

When her voice screeched the word, he winced and pulled the phone from his ear. "He's okay, just a thump on his funny bone and a scratch on his cheek."

"I'm on my way."

Macie arrived in record time, her chest heaving and face red after crossing the distance from his house like an Olympic sprinter. She slid to her knees next to her son and ran a hand over his face as she examined the swelling lump. "Let's get you to the doctor, Alex." She pushed to her feet and grabbed her son's hand. "Where's the nearest urgent care facility?"

Lane ran a hand up and down her arm to soothe her. "Macie, he's fine."

Her eyes went wild. "He has a cut on his face that could require stitches. What if he has a concussion?"

"The helmet did its job. It's nothing more than a scrape and a bump."

"Look at him. He could have a broken cheekbone."

"Aw, for cryin' out loud, Macie. You can't run to the doctor every time he has a little accident. Boys play hard and get hurt. It's what they do." If Lane's mom had carted the Becker males to the doctor's office for every mishap or sniffle, she would have all but lived there.

"Please don't tell me how to care for *my* son."

Her son. Yeah, he got that, but where did it leave Lane should they form a family in the future? Would she allow him to treat Alex as *his* son, or make it clear it was hands off when it came to raising the boy? What about kids they might have as a couple? They would grow up on a horse ranch in the country with plenty of opportunity for injury. He ran his thumb over the scar on his hand. "These things happen and—"

"I'm okay, Mom." Defiance threaded through Alex's statement.

Macie turned her attention back to the boy and wrapped an arm around him as though she expected him to fall if she didn't hold him up. "That's great, but I'm having you seen by a doctor. As a precaution."

Lane opened his mouth to tell her once more she was overreacting, but shut it when she glared at him, waiting for directions to the urgent care office. "There's a small medical center in town. You're in no frame of mind to drive, so I'll take you."

"What about Jasper?" Alex pointed to the Appaloosa that had ventured close. The horse's head hung, as if in shame. "He needs me to brush him."

Lane removed the saddle and bridle and used the arena fence

to hold them. "I'll call Monte. He'll handle it." While Lane took care of the boy and the panic-stricken woman he loved.

* * * *

Macie tucked the covers around Alex. Her stomach somersaulted at the sight of the deep bruise and cut marring the smooth skin on his cheek. Would he have a scar?

Lane's lips had pinched when he'd opened the truck door for her at Hidden Veil's clinic. According to him, she'd blown the injury out of proportion. He probably would have told last night's unconscious steer wrestler to cowboy up and tough it out.

Although the doctor had assured her Alex was fine, she would rest better tonight after having had him examined.

"How do you feel, honey?"

Alex grimaced. "I'm okay. I'm no baby." The words were soft, but the tone stung.

She leaned over and kissed him on the forehead. "Get some sleep."

As she reached the door, he said, "I want to ride Jasper tomorrow, Mom."

"No." She hadn't meant for the answer to snap like a whip, but today had been trying. In her mind, all she saw was Alex lying unconscious in the dirt at the edge of the arena, similar to seeing Lane's image in the rodeo arena.

Maybe things had looked worse to her than they actually were today, but there was always that proverbial tomorrow.

"Then when can I?"

"I don't know."

Alex sat up in the bed. "Lane says a cowboy always gets back on his horse after it throws him off."

Lane says . . . Lane says . . .

Would neither of them listen to anything she said or take into consideration her feelings?

"Lane is a more experienced rider than you." When Alex scowled at her, she moderated her tone and shoved aside her frustration. "Get some sleep. We'll discuss it another time." Before he could argue further, she switched off the light and trudged downstairs.

She sank onto the sofa and scanned a few of the latest online articles from *Cook's Illustrated.* Unable to concentrate, she clicked out of the site and stared into the unlit fireplace.

Had she been too lax with Alex's safety lately, or was she reverting to the old Macie who saw danger around every corner? Wasn't there a center line she could walk?

What would she say when—not if—Alex brought up the subject of riding again? Her inclination was to restate the answer she gave him upstairs. But wasn't that placing her love and fear for her son over her love and trust in God?

She prayed for an answer, then settled on the couch with her laptop to work on the therapy center's website. Anything to take her mind off Alex's spill.

After a few fruitless minutes of staring at the screen, she shut off the computer and went to bed.

By the next morning, the swelling on Alex's face was gone, and the bruise looked less violent. He never mentioned riding, so she assumed he was too sore. Fine with her. She still hadn't come up with an answer that would please anyone.

* * * *

Macie parked the car behind the cabin and unloaded her personal groceries. Next, she called for Alex but received no answer.

Finding the upstairs empty, she peered out a side window at the ceiling of steel-gray clouds in the distance, then went back downstairs and turned on the TV, hoping to catch a local weather report.

The meteorologist pointed a well-manicured finger at splotches of bright reds and yellows splattered across the screen like an abstract painting. Macie studied the locations of the storms heading in the from the west and tried to judge their distance from Hidden Veil. Not far enough.

She peered out the window. Lane should have seen Alex home half an hour ago. She started for the door, then stopped. Shooing him away from the barn would lead to more accusations from Lane and Alex that she overreacted.

The blare of a sudden advisory sent her nerves jumping. Her heart hammered as the meteorologist stood in front of her screen and announced a tornado watch for neighboring counties to the west and the south. She pointed out in excruciating detail the precautions people should take to keep themselves safe during the dangerous weather. Fine for the weatherwoman. Her son probably wasn't overdue in returning home.

It didn't matter what Lane might say. The weather expert

backed up her concerns. Was he aware of the warnings?

Macie hurried out the door. As she hiked toward the barn, she searched the surrounding area for her son and the horseman. "Alex? Lane?"

She forced her steps to slow as she entered the barn, hoping to not spark a resemblance to a helicopter mom. Silence ruled the space. No one stood in the aisle and no sign of either of her guys.

Her guys? Since when had she thought of Lane as hers?

Since that amazing week when they shared time alone, and her imagination took flight to the land of Forevermore.

"Lane? Alex?"

A quick peek inside the feed room revealed its emptiness. Crossing the aisle, she stepped into the tack room, hoping to see the saddle Lane allowed Alex to use when riding Jasper. The stand was empty, the saddle gone. None of the others were missing, including Lane's, which was draped across the stand where it belonged.

Amazed by the steadiness of her fingers, she punched Alex's number on her phone. It rang both at her ear and nearby. She twirled in a circle, seeking the source. There, on the shelf holding the riding helmets. She grabbed his phone. He'd forgotten it . . . again. Or had he deliberately left it?

Macie backed out of the room and rushed down the aisle, peering into every stall. She shouted for her son and Lane. No answer. By the time she reached Jasper's empty stall, it was clear she'd wasted her time inside the building.

She trotted outside through the rear of the barn to scan the arena. Empty. Her gaze shifted to the back pasture. Smoky and

Dandy grazed with several other horses—none of them a freckled Appaloosa. Alex knew not to ride off on his own.

Anxiety thrust her into high gear. "Alex!"

Macie reached for her phone to call Lane. Her finger hovered over the icon. No. He'd think she was being overprotective again. She'd do a thorough search around the barn area, then she'd panic.

She combed each outbuilding and went through the cabin a second time. No sign of Alex or Lane. In the meantime, the ominous clouds blew closer. She pressed her fingers to her forehead. *Think. Think. Think.*

Alex hadn't liked her response last night to his wish to ride today. Okay, so her son probably defied her and was with Jasper. Maybe with Lane, too.

No, probably not with Lane. He wouldn't do that to her. Would he? Besides, his saddle remained in the tack room.

What if Alex rode off on his own and became lost? What if he fell off the horse somewhere in the woods?

What should she do? The thought of what might happen—what might have already happened—wrung the air from her lungs.

Macie fought the welling tears and tried to calm her breathing. Crying wouldn't find her son. Neither would unrestrained terror.

One hope remained. She prayed to find both Alex and Lane at the main house. *Please, God, before I break down and snap my last thread of self-control.*

Macie rushed down the road, crossed the bridge, and tore through the backyard to the deck behind the house. Her sandals slapped the wood. Turning the handle on the door to the den, she yanked. It didn't budge. She beat on the glass. Why had they locked her out?

Finally, Monte ambled across the den and let her inside. With one glance at her, the lines between his eyes deepened. "What's going on?"

"I can't find Alex. Have you seen him?"

He shook his head. "Not lately."

"He was at the barn with Lane when I left for the store. They aren't there now."

Monte's mustache twitched, a sign of concern. "Lane's in his office . . . went up there close to an hour ago."

"An hour? You're sure Alex isn't with him?"

"Saw Lane go up there by himself."

Red-hot anger overwhelmed her. She had entrusted her son to Lane's care, and he left Alex alone at the barn to return to the house.

Her feet pounded up the stairs to the office. She should have known better. Lane had no children. He didn't know what it was like to worry over one.

His composure during Alex's injury should have warned her against ever placing her son's wellbeing in the hands of another man who possessed a numbed sense of danger.

Twenty-five

Macie burst into his office, and Lane glanced up. His smile shrank when she leaned over his desk, her face red and breathing labored. Her hair stood up and out, like she'd survived a tornado. "What's wrong?"

She raked both hands through her hair, which explained why it was a mess. "Where is Alex?"

He leaned away from the anger that sharpened her voice. "He's at home. We finished at the barn. I walked with him to the cabin, then came here."

She pressed quivering fingers to her forehead and paced in front of the desk. "Did you watch him go inside?"

"Of course, I did. What's wrong?"

"Why didn't you wait for me to come back before leaving him?"

Lane felt like a suspect sitting in an interrogation room.

"Alex said you'd called and were on your way home. He told me you gave him some chores to do in the cabin and that you didn't mind him being by himself for a few minutes."

"And knowing me, you didn't think that last part was strange?"

Maybe, but Macie had come a long way in the past couple of months. Before Alex's injury, she had grown more relaxed regarding her son's activities.

In all honesty, Lane was behind on his paperwork and eager to spend time in his office. "What is this about?"

"He isn't there. He isn't anywhere."

Lane stared at her for a moment. Then the wild-eyed fear in her face registered the importance of those words. The desk chair wobbled when he vaulted from it and hustled around the desk. "He's gone? Gone where?"

Macie stopped pacing and whirled, a look of disbelief on her face. "If I knew, I wouldn't be here telling you. My son is missing and there's a dangerous storm coming. We need to find him."

Lane hadn't noticed any storm clouds. He restrained the urge to peek out the window. Doing so would only aggravate her fear . . . and his. He wrapped his arms around her. "Tell me what happened."

She dropped her forehead to his chest, her body stiff. "I've looked all over. He's nowhere near the barn or at the cabin, and Jasper is gone, along with the saddle Alex uses."

"Alex knows better than to ride the horse without one of us around."

"He also knows I'd never let him stay alone, not when a

storm is approaching."

Lane never imagined the kid had lied to him. Fighting his own bent toward alarm, he leaned back and tipped her chin up. "Did you call him?"

She pushed away and yanked Alex's phone from her pocket. "I found it in the tack room."

He tried not to let her terror infect him, or it would lead to rash actions. "Don't worry. We'll find him, Macie."

They had to find him.

"Don't worry? That's easy for you to say, isn't it, Lane Becker?" She shook her head. "This is your fault. You couldn't leave him alone. You insisted he be a guinea pig for your precious therapy center. You entertained him with your stories about the outdoors until he wanted to be like you. Well, he's not like you. He's a little boy—a frightened little b-boy." She covered her mouth to silence her sobs.

The tears that flowed down her cheeks acted like a wrench on his heart and a screwdriver to twist his guilt. Was she right? Had he encouraged Alex to take risks, just as he had his little brother? Had he led someone else into danger? Another child?

God, what have I done?

Lane glanced at the clock on the side wall. A little over forty-five minutes had passed since he'd left Alex at the cabin. Twenty minutes to sneak back to the barn and saddle Jasper. Where would Alex have ridden in twenty to thirty minutes?

"You checked the pastures?"

"What I could see of them. But the hills . . ."

"I'll check again. If I don't see him, I'll saddle Smoky." Maybe Alex wandered into the woods. Best not to mention that possibility to Macie right now. He grabbed his cell phone. "You wait at the cabin. He might come back while I'm gone. If so, call me."

Lane started for the hallway, but she grabbed the sleeve of his shirt and pulled past him. "No way. What if he has another attack, and I'm not there to help him? I'll leave a note at home, but I'm coming with you."

He opened his mouth to argue, but she rushed out the door and down the stairs before the first word passed his lips.

Fifteen minutes later, with Gypsy at his side, Lane found no trace of Alex in the pastures. He dug out his phone and called the house. "He's nowhere around. Uncle Monte, I think you should call the sheriff and report Alex missing."

"Will do. Then I'll head to the barn and wait."

By the time Lane returned to the barn, Macie had changed shoes and saddled the horses. Uncle Monte limped down the drive toward them. Lane grabbed three hooded raincoats and the emergency kit he kept in the tack room. They mounted the horses.

Lane eyed Macie. "The pan Alex used to search for gold is missing. It's possible he rode up the trail to the creek to do some panning. It's the place he's most familiar with, so we'll head that way."

Macie glanced at the sky. In the distance, lightning crackled through an army of clouds that varied in shades from cobalt to a smoky blue. They marched ever closer, an urgent reminder of the march of time. "Let's go."

She dug her heels into Coco's sides. The mare leapt into a canter with Lane's gelding on her tail and Gypsy running alongside them.

*   *   *   *

Once they reached the woods, Macie reined in Coco to follow Lane up a path too narrow to ride side-by-side. The dog trotted through the brush at the rim of the trail.

Even though Macie wished to urge her horse into a trot, she held back. Lane knew these woods and knew how to find any signs Alex left that would guide them to him. She had no choice but to let Lane lead.

They entered woods that once seemed welcoming but now reminded her of something from a horror movie. The scent of rain amplified the moldy smell of decayed leaves and earth. With the approaching storm, the full canopy of trees blocked what little sunlight remained. The branches above waved back and forth with the wind, rattling the leaves.

In a couple of months, those same leaves would turn color and fall to the ground. She and Alex would be gone.

Macie's hold tightened on the reins. "Alex!" Coco tossed her head at the sudden shout and pulled on the reins, begging for a loosened grip. Once Macie relaxed her hands and loosened her hold, the horse stopped tugging. "How far do you think he's gone?"

"Depends. He's had a good head start." Lane half-turned. "Why do you think he took off in the first place?"

Macie had dreaded that question. She had asked herself the same thing over and over since finding Alex gone. One answer kept coming to mind. "He wanted to ride Jasper today. I wouldn't let him. He said you told him real cowboys get back in the saddle after a fall, so I guess he's trying to prove something."

Lane eased back on the reins, stopping Smoky. He hung his head. "I'm sorry, Macie."

Blaming Lane for Alex's disappearance wasn't right, yet her brain hadn't stopped the accusation from tumbling from her mouth at the house. She longed to absolve him from guilt, but couldn't speak the words. "Let's keep looking."

Lane rode on, following the trail that wound through the towering oak, pine, and hickory trees, but she noted the slump of his body.

Gypsy trotted ahead, the dog's nose to the ground as though she knew their purpose was to search for and locate Alex.

They both called her son's name, to no avail. Lane's gaze darted from the ground to the surrounding branches and back to the ground. When they reached a wider area, she urged Coco into a trot to catch up and ride alongside him.

He waved her back. "Stay to my flank so I can see the trail."

Anything to help him track her son.

While riding through a slight break in the trees, a raindrop hit her nose. She wiped it away with her forearm as the *tap-tap* of more rain struck the leaves. It wasn't a downpour yet, but with the increasing wind, it would likely turn into one.

"What if he's l-lost?" Macie hated how her voice cracked. Why wasn't she a stronger person? Stronger in her faith? Stronger in trusting in her son's abilities? In trusting Lane?

"See that?" He pointed to an indention in the path. "Alex came this way."

Hope rose, but she tempered it. "Maybe it's from the last time we rode through here?"

Lane shook his head. "No, this is fresh."

She eyed the half of a hoofprint in the dirt. Dead leaves prevented the rest of the hoof from leaving a mark.

"At least he hasn't wandered off this trail. As long as he stays on it, we'll find him."

"And if he doesn't?"

He gazed at her, hope shining in his eyes. "Then we look for other signs."

They wended their way up and down the slope and along a ridge. The intensity of the rain and wind picked up. Macie slipped into the bright yellow raincoat Lane had tied to the back of her saddle before they left. She pulled the hood over her head.

Occasionally, a narrower, less traveled path veered off left or right. Lane would rein in Smoky, examine the ground, and move on. What he saw—or didn't see—convinced him they should remain on the main trail.

She flinched when his phone buzzed. He continued riding as he answered it. "Hey, Uncle Monte ... No, we haven't found him, but I've spotted tracks. He's on the main trail, heading for the creek ... Great. Thanks for letting us know."

He slid the phone back in his pocket, and Macie asked, "What did Monte say?"

"The sheriff's deputies are at the barn with a couple of four wheelers. He'll send them our way." He frowned, then reined Smoky toward a low-hanging branch and stopped to examine it. "Good job, Alex."

"What? What do you see?"

He grabbed the branch and held it out. The end of the twig-like broken branch hung down. Rainwater dripped off the still-green leaves and onto the ground. "It's a fresh break."

"You believe Alex did it?"

"I do."

"An accident? Do you think he hurt himself?"

He crossed his arms over the saddle horn and shook his head, sending water from his Stetson flying through the air. "Don't be negative, Goldie."

Macie knew he tried to calm her, but this time, the nickname irritated her. She wasn't the one lost in the woods. "We're dealing with a nine-year-old, Lane."

"And you treat him like he's four."

They stared at one another until she looked away. "You're right. I'm the reason Alex ran off."

∗ ∗ ∗ ∗

Lane shifted in the saddle and drew in a deep breath. The last thing he'd wanted was to add to Macie's distress. "I didn't mean to lose my temper. I just ... I know he broke the branch on purpose. I taught Alex ways to mark his trail when he went into unfamiliar territory. The approaching storm probably convinced him to leave the signs."

"Then why didn't he turn around?"

She asked a question he had no answer for.

The tops of the trees swayed even harder with the gusts of wind. Rain slanted through the branches, slid down leaves, and dripped off everything in its wake—including the saddles, the riders, and the horses. Thunder boomed. It was late in the season for tornadoes, but they weren't unheard of this time of year. And the temperatures had been erratic.

Thunder rumbled and Macie glanced up at the sky. "The storm . . ."

He reached over and squeezed her arm. "He's a smart kid. He'll lead us to him. Let's keep moving." It was their only option if they were to find Alex before the weather grew worse.

God, please keep us all safe.

No matter what Macie said about Alex running off because of her, Lane couldn't shake his own responsibility. He never bullied Alex into learning how to ride. However, he had encouraged him.

"There's another one."

Focused on his thoughts—on his culpability in Alex's disappearance—Lane had missed the branch Macie pointed out. He ran his fingers over the broken twig and wet leaves. "He's following the same trail we took the day of the picnic. Hopefully, we'll find him in the clearing."

"Hopefully."

The misery in that one word tugged at his heart. His conscience. His guilt. He couldn't even look at her. "I've worked around horses and ridden through these woods since well before I was Alex's age. I guess I wanted to share what I knew with him."

Why should he mention that everything he taught Alex came because the boy asked? And like Uncle Monte, Lane made it sound exciting. "Evidently, I learned nothing since my days with

Matt."

Several seconds passed without a word from Macie. Then, her voice rose above the rain. "I shouldn't have blamed you, Lane. Alex rode off on his own. It was his decision. It was also his decision to lie about being allowed to stay at the cabin alone. I never meant to suggest you treat my son in the same way as your brother. That's no longer you."

Sure, it was him.

A barrage of raindrops battered them. Smoky slid on an increasingly slippery trail as he picked his way around puddles and stones. It jarred Lane in the saddle. Jarred his mind, too. He was slipping into the old way of thinking. He never bullied Alex. He never pushed him to do more than he felt comfortable doing.

God had grown Lane's wisdom during the past ten years, and He had forgiven him for his bullying treatment of Matt. It was done. Lane had moved on. Macie was right. This problem was Alex's doing, just as Matt's decision to become a soldier rested with him.

Macie brushed the wetness from her face. "We've seen these signs because of what he learned from you. With the muddy trail, if he hadn't left them—if you hadn't taken the time to teach him—we couldn't know where to look."

Let us find him soon, Lord.

Lightning flashed, and a limb at the top of a tree to Lane's left cracked like a gunshot and crashed to the ground. Coco shied, almost unseating Macie.

"You okay?"

She patted Coco's neck and nodded. "We're fine."

Over the sounds of the storm, Lane heard a thrum and crunch of brush from up ahead. He drew back on Smoky's reins. Gypsy stopped and barked at whatever was ahead.

Macie asked, "What's that?"

"It sounds like—"

Jasper trotted around a bend in the trail, his hooves sliding on wet leaves and mud. The loop of the one-piece rein hung loose over his neck, the saddle empty.

Twenty-six

Macie gasped, and her hands shook. Seeing Jasper round the curve in the trail—riderless—every physical terror Macie could imagine ran through her head like scenes from a slasher film.

She pictured Alex lying in the woods, his body broken, bleeding internally, unconscious with a concussion, or—heaven forbid—a skull fracture. Had he worn a helmet? She hadn't noticed whether one was missing from the tack room shelf, but that was where she had found his phone.

"Whoa." Lane reached out and grabbed the rein. Jasper skidded to a stop between Smoky and Coco. The Appaloosa's head jerked and his sides caved in and out. His muscles trembled. Lane dismounted and examined Alex's frightened horse. "He doesn't look hurt."

"Where's Alex?"

Lane ran his hand over the saddle seat. "It's pretty wet, which means Alex didn't dismount—"

He fell off?

"—in the past few minutes."

So where was Alex? Macie eyed Jasper. As much as the horse liked to talk, he couldn't tell them.

"I don't see any mud on Jasper's coat or the saddle, so I don't think the horse slipped and fell." Lane gazed in the direction Jasper had come and called Alex's name. No response.

Macie did the same, but with the raspy emotion in her voice, her son wouldn't hear if he were more than a few feet away.

Lane mounted Smoky and reined the gelding closer to Coco. He laid a warm hand over hers. "Don't borrow trouble, Macie. Alex can't be far down the trail." His tense expression appeared less optimistic than his words.

She closed her eyes. *Please, God, I know I've failed to trust as I should, but protect Alex and let us find him safe.*

"Stay here, and I'll check on up ahead. The clearing isn't far."

Macie knew what he was doing. Lane hoped to shield her. If they weren't talking about her missing child, she would appreciate his sensitivity and consideration for what she might see. "I can handle it. You're not leaving me."

He studied her a moment, then led Jasper on, with Macie shadowing them. If she moved ahead, her impatience would lead to pressing Coco into a lope that would endanger them both on the slick trail. Staying behind was safer for everyone. But, oh, how her muscles and fear pressed her to move faster.

They rode through the rain, somewhat protected by the trees. The dog ran ahead and disappeared. Lane kept his focus on the ground. At the clearing, he swung out of the saddle, checked the mud, then called out, "Alex!"

Macie dismounted and hurried to his side. "What do you see?"

"He was here." He pointed to imprints in the mud left by a pair of small boots.

Nearby, Gypsy barked. Lane left the horses and Macie to follow the barking, stopping at the gully's edge where the three of them stood the day of their first trail ride.

"Do you think . . .?" Without finishing her question, she slid down the short incline and rushed through the gully to the rock ledge on the other side. "Alex!"

The crunch of stone on stone sounded from the blackness inside. Macie backed up, not sure what to expect, and bumped into Lane's chest. When she teetered, he caught her in his steady grip, his hands strong but gentle.

An arm poked outside the cavern, followed by the top of a head with a familiar mop of brown hair. Macie dropped to her knees, grabbed her son's hands, and pulled him outside the hole, into the rain and into her arms.

Alex squiggled in her hold. "I c-can't breathe, Mom."

She and Lane dripped rain, the perfect trigger to his anxiety attacks. She loosened her grip on him, held him at arm's length, and looked into his face. "Inhale. Exhale."

"I'm not scared. Not that way. You were crushing me."

"Oh. Sorry." She studied him head to toe, finding nothing but dirt on the seat of his jeans where he'd been sitting out the rain in the tiny space. In his hand, he carried a riding helmet. "Are you hurt?"

"No, ma'am."

She heard the timid "Yes, ma'am," and "No, ma'am," most often when he was in trouble. Smart boy. "What were you thinking to ride off alone like that, Alex? You scared Lane and me out of our wits."

"I wanted to show you I'm not a baby and could ride Jasper again after falling off. I wanted you to know that I'm as brave and able to do stuff as Lane and Daddy, Mom." His subdued voice sounded anything but brave.

"I know you are, buddy. You don't need to prove anything to me or Lane or anyone else. However, even bravery and talent aren't always enough to save us from foolish decisions or things outside our control." Like a severe storm or a capsized raft in a swift current.

"I kinda figured it wasn't too smart to do when lightning struck a tree and Jasper ran off."

"You put yourself and the horse in danger." Lane added his own scolding, using emphatic words, yet speaking with a mild voice. Did he realize he'd just proved how much he had changed?

Alex bowed his head. "I'm really sorry."

"We all make mistakes." Lane squeezed Alex's shoulder. "That's when we ask for forgiveness and move on. The key is to not repeat the mistake."

"Yes, sir."

As relieved as she was over his safety, Macie couldn't let the behavior slide. "That doesn't let you off the hook for lying to Lane and for taking Jasper without permission. Everything we do comes with a consequence, Alex. We'll discuss yours when we get home."

Dampness from the ground soaked through the lower legs of her jeans, and Alex's dirty hands had left mud on her pale-pink T-shirt. Gypsy sat beside her son and whined until Alex acknowledged her with gentle strokes along the dog's wet back.

Around them, small branches broke from the trees, sopping leaves blew off the top of the gully, and a rotten limb from a dead tree nearby crashed to the ground.

Lane tapped her shoulder. "The storm is picking up. We'd better wait it out here instead of heading back to the barn. Alex, I was a lot smaller the last time I was in that cave. Is there room inside for the three of us to ride out the storm?"

"It's too low to stand up, but it goes aways back." He glanced at Jasper. "What about the horses and Gypsy?"

"They'll be all right."

Macie glanced at the hole. "I don't know. It's creepy looking."

"I've been inside, Mom. It's dark, and it smells weird, but it's okay."

"Alex is right, Macie. You two get out of this wind before you're hit by a falling limb. I'll join you after I call Monte to let him know we found Alex. Hopefully, I'll have reception."

As Lane hiked toward the open area where the horses waited, Macie consoled herself by looking at sitting in the hole as an adventure too good to pass up. *Yeah, right.*

She prodded Alex back to the cave's entrance and crawled in after him. Little clearance existed between the top of her head and the rock above her. How would Lane do it? "Stay here in the center." Away from any clefts in the walls that could hide snakes or spiders. Her body shuddered at the thought.

Earth and mold tingled her nose. At least they'd found a dry spot to sit, though the stones that littered the cave floor were uncomfortable. She brushed aside as many as possible, hoping to prevent the feeling of sitting on a bed of nails.

Macie peered out the opening, keeping an eye on Lane. Through the wind and slashing rain, she saw him untie the third raincoat and first-aid kit from the back of his saddle. Then he removed the bridles so they wouldn't injure the horses should they bolt from the thunder and lightning.

As he trekked back to the cave, Macie scrambled farther into the darkness to give him room. She felt for her son and clung to his arm. "Are you sure you're not hurt, Alex?" Her voice echoed in the small space.

"No, but I feel stupid."

She wrapped her arm around her son's slim shoulder and drew him closer. "I've done plenty of things I've felt stupid over. But, Alex, we waste our mistakes if we don't learn from them and do our best to not repeat them."

"I'll try."

"I know you will."

With her prayer for his safety answered in such a positive way, she whispered a soft thank you to God.

Lane pushed into the cave as far as he would fit. Bent over, he blocked what little light they'd had. He turned on a small flashlight from the first aid kit and set it on a rock so it shone on the three of them. Lane wiped the moisture from his face. "The reception was spotty, but I think Monte heard me." He roughed Alex's hair. "It's a good thing you're not afraid of tight spaces."

"I'm not afraid of wet people anymore, either." Alex made a face. "Not much, anyway."

"That's good news, buddy. Sometimes we take baby steps. Sometimes, they're leaps. The goal is to take them and trust that God will be there to support us when we move our feet, or cushion us when we slip and fall." Macie rubbed her son's back. "I held tight to you to keep you safe, but it had the opposite effect. It made me more afraid. I'm learning to do better, so be patient with me, okay?"

"Sure, Mom."

She turned toward Lane, her heart softening at seeing the way the light from the flashlight played across the planes of his face. One day, she hoped to be worthy of the gift of Lane's love—if she hadn't ruined everything. "I'm so sorry, Lane. I shouldn't have lost it back at the house and taken my fear out on you. You've been nothing but kind, helpful, and supportive in the months we've lived at Crooked Creek. You've encouraged the best in Alex and myself and taught us to live again. In my panic, I forgot something. We can't move forward when we're tied to the past."

Lightning flashed outside the cave, then the ground rumbled with the thunder.

He touched her cheek, running his thumb over its curve, and wiping away dampness that had nothing to do with the rain dripping from her wet hair. "For years, I wanted to toughen Matt up so he could handle whatever trouble he met along his life's path. You wanted to keep Alex from meeting *any* trouble. I'd like to think we've both learned that God lays out a special trail—a special mission—for each of us, and that trail leads and ends where He deems fit."

Alex's gaze bounced between them. "Are you two getting married?"

"Alex!" Heat rose in Macie's face. Fortunately, the glow from the flashlight wasn't bright enough for Lane to see. She hoped.

The horseman's laughter echoed in the tiny cave. "You know how to put someone on the spot, Alex. That's a discussion your mom and I will have when the time is right."

Will have, not might have. Macie prayed the discussion would come sooner rather than later.

When the wind died, Lane twisted as best he could in the tight fit and peered outside. "Looks like the storm has passed."

They crawled out of the cave into shaded sunshine and sticky, humid air. The horses still waited at the edge of the gully—evidence of Lane's excellent training.

As he readied them to ride out, the deputies arrived on foot, muddy and winded. They had abandoned the four-wheelers when the trail became too muddy for safety.

The taller deputy pointed to Alex. "That the young man who got us out here in a storm?"

Alex stepped forward. "I didn't mean to cause trouble. Am I going to jail?"

The younger one narrowed his eyes. "No jail time for you, unless this becomes a habit."

"No, sir."

The deputy winked at Macie, proving he'd feigned his fierce expression. "I think he's learned a lesson. We won't need to do this again, will we, kid?"

"No, sir."

Macie placed her hands on Alex's shoulders. "I think we've all learned something from this experience. Thank you for your help."

Once they reached the ranch yard, Monte and a couple of reporters eager for a story involving a missing child greeted them. Macie wanted to escort her son to the cabin and shut the door on everything awful that had happened that afternoon, but that would mean taking a step backward.

She stepped forward and provided the reporters with a story of loss and fear and hope. A story of a horseman whose dream to help others find their emotional footing came true at a place called Healing Springs Equine Therapy Center.

Epilogue

"It seems Macie has become one of the center's staunchest allies and a valuable asset." Lane's mother sat bundled in a heavy sweater beside him at the picnic table in the grass outside the office. Her gaze centered on the woman who had charmed everyone from his parents to the sponsors, veterans, and volunteers.

Macie's charm worked overtime on Lane.

"You'll need to watch yourself, son."

At the sober warning, he turned on the bench. "I thought you liked Macie."

"I adore her." She pointed to the half-eaten food on his plate. "But I've seen how much of her cooking you put away. It won't be long before you'll have a hard time climbing into the saddle."

Lane glanced at his stomach. After eating Macie's fare for going on five months, it was still flat and firm. At her laughter, he shook his head. "Funny, Mom."

She bookended his face with her hands and kissed the top of his head as she'd often done when he was a kid. "There are worse things than carrying around a spare tire . . . like spending the future alone."

The hint was too strong to ignore, and an unnecessary one. But he wouldn't admit that to his mother. Not yet.

Macie carried the leftovers from the lunch she'd prepared for Ron and the four people helping at the center today.

For the past month, he had waited, wanting to give Macie and Alex time to work through more of their issues under Ron's guidance before asking her to share his life. The two Newmans had made tremendous strides in conquering their fears. While it remained an ongoing process, it seemed Goldie had found the right fit in therapists.

Returning from the cabin, Macie strolled toward him with purpose and a smile—a smile aimed straight at him. He had rehearsed a question over and over since the day they searched for Alex. It was time to ask it.

Unable to pull his attention from Macie, Lane rose from the picnic bench. "I left something at the house. I'll be back."

"Make it quick," his mother said.

In his room, he reached inside the top drawer of his dresser, pulled out a black velvet box, and opened it to reveal the marquis solitaire in a silver setting. He removed the ring and stuffed it in the front pocket of his jeans, then left to find Macie, his nerves as fidgety as Mexican jumping beans.

Lane had received Alex's permission before the boy left to spend a couple of days in Charlotte with his grandmother. Alex had *whooped*. While Lane loved the kid as much as if he was his biological son, he was pretty sure Alex saw their relationship resulting in his eventual ownership of Jasper. He was right, and Lane was already on the hunt for a new therapy horse.

After running his palms down his jeans to wipe away the nerve-induced moisture, Lane knocked on the outer door of the cabin. Through the screen, he spotted Macie washing dishes at the sink. She looked up. "Come on in."

He walked inside, certain she could hear his heart thumping like some lovesick cartoon character. He couldn't hear much of anything over the pulsing in his ears.

Macie dried her hands, met him halfway, and stepped into his arms, wrapping hers around his waist. He leaned down and touched his lips to hers. When she responded, he deepened the kiss until the world outside the cabin ceased to exist.

When they came up for air, Lane rested his forehead against hers. "Wow."

"Yeah."

It didn't matter if anyone had spotted them through the open door. By now, everyone knew they were not simply employer and employee.

Macie took his hand and led him to the sofa. "Don't you have another session coming up?"

"In an hour." What he had to say wouldn't take long, unless she continued to look at him with those doe eyes. Then, he might consider skipping the session.

"In the beginning, you know I had my doubts about your mission, but I'm so proud of what you and Ron are accomplishing. I've talked to a few of the veterans. You two, along with the horses, are working wonders, Lane." Macie shook her head. "I wish things had worked out with Sheila Kraus, though."

"I don't. We need people who believe in what we're doing, Macie, not someone who wants to use the center for advertising or to rid themselves of an unsaleable product. And we don't need Sheila when we have an anonymous donor."

"Who?" Red flushed her face. "Silly question. I mean, when did this happen?"

"I got an email about it this morning from a lawyer in Richmond, Virginia. Ten thousand dollars."

Her mouth dropped open. "You're kidding."

"The same thing happened last spring when the town held a fundraiser to help a family pay for their son's kidney transplant. Someone around here has money to spare." He shrugged. "If they want to remain anonymous, that's fine. Alongside the support of others like Eva Newman and her friends, we'll do all right this next year."

Macie grinned. "Eva is amazing."

"So are you. Your help with the website and publicity has saved me time and headaches. I can't tell you how much I appreciate it."

"You're doing good work here. I believe in it."

"Thanks." He sucked in a deep breath. Now or never. And never was not an option.

Sliding off the sofa, he rested one knee on the floor, took Macie's hand, and cleared his throat. Man, he had no doubts about what he was about to do, but he could sure use some of Matt's courage.

Macie's eyes widened.

"Macie Newman, I think I fell a little in love with you the day I ate your cinnamon roll, then saw you trying to take me on in the yard."

A puff of laughter slipped past the lips she'd covered with her hand, and a watery glaze formed in her eyes.

"After that, I kept falling ... and falling. You're all I think about and the one I want to see every minute of my day." He pulled the ring from his pocket and held it out. "Are you willing to risk a future with me, to be my partner in life and love? Will you do me the honor of wearing my ring for all time?"

She gulped, and her head bounced up and down. "Yes. Oh, yes."

Her excitement made his heart soar. Only one issue kept it tethered to the ground. "I can't promise to stop doing things that might lead to injury. I can promise I'll do my best to do them in a manner that's as safe as I can make it. So, I need to know. Are you all in, Goldie?"

"God never turned his back on Alex and me. But He provided blessings I failed to see, like leading us to Crooked Creek and to you."

She planted a soft kiss on his lips. "I want nothing more than to be your life partner, Lane. Through fun times and scary times. Through roping events and skiing and kayaking and four-wheeling—however we choose to live. I love you too much to let fear keep us apart." Macie held out her left hand, waiting for him to slide on the engagement ring. "So, yes. I am *all* in, Cowboy."

Her words untethered his heart, and it soared.

Get ready for Book 3, *A Hero's Nature*

Read a bonus scene exclusive to readers of *A Horseman's Mission.*

Get more insight into veterinarian Trey Abbott in this bonus scene exclusive to readers of *A Horseman's Mission.*

A Hero's Nature

Trey Abbott sipped the plain black coffee Macie had poured for him and sank into the back of the chair he occupied in Jo E's Java. Jo hosted today's early Thanksgiving potluck dinner for her friends. On this Sunday afternoon, he and a dozen other people sat in groups, talking and laughing.

His mom would have called them a baker's dozen.

It would have been an even fourteen if Harmoni Basinger had come. At least Trey would have had company in the "odd man out" category. But she'd stayed home with a cold. Too bad he couldn't have caught one, too.

He sighed. It wasn't an uncommon occurrence or his preference to be the only person at one of these gatherings without a partner, but since moving to Hidden Veil, he hadn't dated a woman more than twice. His work at the veterinary clinic kept him busy.

A rational excuse.

In reality, he only wanted one woman, and she saw him as

nothing more than her employer.

Trey listened as Sutton told of his argument with his youngest sister that morning. "She wanted to drive the tractor. What seven-year-old in her right mind would think I'd turn her loose in the fields on a 24,000-pound piece of machinery?" As much as Sutton groused about his siblings, no one cared for them better, certainly not their parents.

Over and over, Trey had conversed and laughed along with everyone else gathered at the string of tables Jo had pushed together. Honestly, he hadn't heard half of what the other couples said. As usual, every cell in his body was attuned to Reagan Hartwell.

Reagan had come with her latest safe date, a guy she could brush off when things got too complicated. A guy who couldn't come close to measuring up to her late hero fiancé.

A guy like Trey.

Being a hero wasn't in Trey's nature, something he'd heard from his father too often to count.

Why couldn't he receive an emergency call when he needed it? Like now.

He took that thought back. What kind of veterinarian and animal lover was he to hope for sickness or injury to any of God's creatures?

Why was he so down today? After a morning of worship and an afternoon spent with good friends, he should count his blessings. It was that time of year, after all.

"Hey, listen up, y'all." Lane stood near the counter in the coffee shop with his arm around Macie, who had tucked her hands behind her back. Conversation from the crowd of friends dwindled to silence.

A grin split Lane's face. It spoke of a secret, a secret most people in the room could guess. "During this pre-Thanksgiving celebration, we're thankful—first, to the Lord for all his blessings." Several "Amens" followed the statement. "And to Jo and Kyle for inviting us."

A round of clapping and vocal agreement.

Jo and Kyle. That wedding would take place in January. Maybe he should visit his parents that weekend.

He determined to shake off the private pity party and turned his attention back to Lane.

"As fun as this afternoon has been, with Jo's permission, Macie and I have an announcement."

Trey's stomach clenched. He knew, as everyone else did, what was coming.

"It's about time." Sutton hooted from a nearby chair, and the others laughed. "Did you get the answer you expected?"

"She said yes, you dolt." Lane reached out with a light cuff to the back of his best friend's head, bringing cheers and laughter from everyone, including Sutton.

"Of course, I said yes." Macie held out her left hand to reveal a diamond ring that hadn't decorated her finger earlier. "Someone has to supply him with a lifetime of cinnamon rolls and barbecue."

Trey cheered and applauded along with the others. They jumped from their seats in a rush to congratulate the couple. Though he didn't know Macie as well as he did the others, he figured she was a good match for the horseman. He was happy for Lane, for both of them. He was happy for all of his friends who had found that special someone to share their lives. Really. But Trey was honest enough to admit each holiday without the woman he loved at his side was harder than the last.

He pushed his glasses up his nose, a pretense that let him slide a discreet glance at Reagan as she hugged Macie. The two women had developed a friendship since Macie intervened in Reagan's hostility toward Lane. Thankfully, Reagan had resolved that part of her past.

Since hiring her as his vet tech three years ago, Trey had become good at discreet glances. With her green eyes and long, dark hair, she was gorgeous . . . and her love was unattainable.

He waited ten minutes after giving the joyful couple his good wishes, then said his goodbyes. He headed for his truck parked outside the coffee shop on Main Street.

"Where are you going, Trey? The celebration isn't over."

Trey turned to find Reagan standing behind him, her arms folded in front of her. He wasn't sure if she was cold or irritated. He could hope for the latter, but . . .

"I have things to do at the clinic."

"On Sunday?"

"I want to check on the Pierce's collie." He grinned to make light of his being the first to leave the dinner. "And there's always paperwork to do."

"Uh-huh."

The low response and the eyebrows drawn together said she didn't believe him. That was one thing he admired about her. He never had to guess where she stood. It was a two-edged sword.

Reagan cast a glance over her shoulder. Visible through the

large window of the coffee shop, Lane and Macie shared a kiss. "They make a great couple, don't they?"

"They do." He twirled his keyring around his finger as he studied Reagan's date, who sat at the table, staring at them through the window. "Blake—"

"Blaine."

"Sorry, Blaine." He couldn't keep them all straight. "He seems like a nice guy." A little too handsy, maybe.

"He is."

Her response was less than enthusiastic, and Trey saw another breakup in her future. He didn't get his hopes up after spending three years doing that. But he wanted to ask if this one would survive the holidays.

"Do you need help at the clinic?"

He could say yes. Reagan would ditch Blake or Blaine— whatever his name—and they would work at the closed clinic together on a Sunday afternoon with no one to interrupt them. They could talk while they worked. Maybe he'd finally tell her how he felt.

And he would lose her.

Trey smiled. "No, thanks. I don't plan to work long."

"Okay. Well . . ." She backed up to the door. "I guess I'll see you at the clinic tomorrow."

"Yeah." He pointed to the coffee shop. "Have fun."

She chuckled in that low, throaty way of hers. "More than you."

"Definitely." But her comment slit his chest like the slash of a scalpel.

Trey backed onto Main Street and turned onto the highway

that led to the clinic and the house alongside it where he lived. He left his friends as he'd arrived.

Alone.

Look for Trey's story in *A Hero's Nature*, Book Three in the Hidden Veil Hometown Series.

As an author of heartwarming and award-winning historical and contemporary romance, Sandra Ardoin engages readers with page-turning stories of love and faith. Rarely out of reach of a book, she's also an armchair sports enthusiast, country music listener, and seldom says no to eating out. Visit her at www.sandraardoin.com. Connect with her on BookBub, Facebook, Twitter, and Goodreads.